25/07/12.

Miriam Wakerly

Gypsies Stop tHere

A NOVEL

Strongman Publishing

First Published in Great Britain in 2008 by
Strongman Publishing
Woodland Edge, St Catherine's Road,
Frimley, Camberley, Surrey GU16 9NN

Reprinted in 2012 by Strongman Publishing

A CIP catalogue record for this book
is available from the British Library.

ISBN 978-0-9558432-0-4

Printed and bound by
The Atlas Print Group
a United Kingdom Company

Reviews

Kay Green. Full review on www.booksy.co.uk

"When issues are put into a personal story, they suddenly get a whole lot more complicated and endlessly intriguing. Author Miriam Wakerly knows the various sides of this situation very well, and has brought them vividly to life in the fictional setting of Appley Green... Cliché it may be to say it, but 'Gypsies Stop tHere' is a real page-turner - and for anyone who really gets the bug, there's even a glossary of Romany language and publications at the back of the book."

Scarlett de Courcier
http://bohemiacademia.blogspot.com

"Gypsies Stop tHere gripped me from the first page and carried me all the way through to the end on a wave of 'I don't want to put this down'. And then I picked up No Gypsies Served and had the same feeling all the way through that one.
Really, really important books. Really, really beautifully written. I think they should be on every school's curriculum."

Sue Cook, Broadcaster and Writer

"Few of us even try to understand gypsies and their way of life. Our knee-jerk reaction usually goes no further than 'not in my backyard', as I discovered first hand when a family of gypsies arrived in a village near where I live last year. The immediate reaction among the residents was a mixture of alarm and resentment.

In Miriam Wakerly's Gypsies Stop tHere and its sequel No Gypsies Served it's refreshing to see gypsies portrayed as individual people like the rest of us, making their way in life the best way they can. Reading this compelling story brings home the fact that it's perfectly possible for gypsies to be accepted successfully into our communities.

Wakerly's books do a wonderful job in helping to promote understanding where there is ignorance and tolerance where there is bigotry. I recommend them heartily."

1

"People threatened with eviction, due to no fault of their own, being unjustly hounded out. It's mediaeval the way they're treated, don't you think?"

It was no more than a minute since this young woman had arrived on the doorstep clutching a pile of A4 paper. She was wearing jeans, white shirt and, Kay particularly noticed, a bright eager expression that commanded attention.

"Hello, I'm Natalie," she announced, strands of long dark hair flying about in the late March breeze, catching on her lip gloss. "Mrs Brackenbridge, isn't it? You OK? Settling in?"

A mere two days had passed since the neighbours watched the furniture van leave. The way news flits around a village faster than e-mail was, Kay supposed, something she would just have to accept. It might make her wary of giving away too much about herself — the past, how Marcus had died. *All that.* The tragedy was something she battled to come to terms with, but as for the sense of loss, that was something else, still sharp, raw, the pain of it surfacing at least unexpected moments. His absence was like an empty space forever next to her. To share *all that* with strangers was not, she felt, going to be in any way helpful, so better to try and draw a line and move on. Would moving house help her do this? She had to acknowledge that only time would tell.

It was hard to imagine anyone in London knocking on a stranger's door making these solicitous enquiries. Kay found herself smiling at the voluble, precise enunciation that she, with her Zimmer, must apparently require in order to comprehend the spoken word. She guessed that the walking aid must age her by enough years to make her seem eligible for a bus pass. Had she stepped out of her MG convertible, she felt sure the tone of voice would have been something else. The well-spoken Natalie, whom she put at around twenty, had then politely extended a hand, seemingly willing to run the risk of Kay keeling over as a result of shaking it.

She nodded. "Getting there, thank you, Natalie. Neighbours friendly, but I've had no time to stop and chat! Something for me?" Kay replied, gently indicating the probable reason for this call, now wedged firmly in Natalie's left armpit.

Natalie had nodded. "I'm 'raising awareness'," the words accompanied by mimed quotation signs, "of the Parish Council meeting in the Village Hall tonight. If you could come that would be great! But," she added, awkwardly, " I could organise a lift if ... well, if transport is ... tricky ..."

Oh, not tonight, thought Kay, feeling dog-tired. Best to cut in quickly. "Really nice of you to include me, Natalie, but I'm just so busy ..." She would think of something – a book, a bath, a phone-call? Not strictly speaking a lie, just unspecified.

But Natalie had continued undaunted. "Many local people are up in arms again about the Travellers. Yes? You've heard about it?"

Kay had shaken her head. "Actually, no, I ..."

Once it had been spelled out for her, Kay raised her eyebrows, confused, unwilling to take sides, ready to disagree but becoming somewhat wary of the anger sparking in the pair of young eyes confronting her.

"Well, I ... I believe Gypsies can cause trouble with the mess they leave, litter, noise, petty crime. I mean it's what I've read or heard ..."

"*Exactly!* You see, the general public don't *really* have a clue ..." Natalie paused, trying to compose herself, perceptive enough, Kay noted, to see that, in her efforts to enlist potential supporters, antagonising them could be off-putting.

"Would you like to come in for a minute and convert me," she offered, feeling a wee bit guilty now.

Natalie frowned and raised her chin. "This is not like a … religious experience, or anything. I just want everyone to understand the facts." She thrust a sheet of paper at Kay. "Please, if you could find a minute to read this, even if you can't get along tonight. Thanks. I don't have time to stop and talk everyone through it today, but maybe another time, I could. If you're interested, that is. And, there is a petition. I'll just get it from my car …"

Kay silently reminded herself that she had retired to the countryside for a peaceful life, to mend her broken limb and heart, read biographies and travel books; maybe grow asparagus, apricots and olives; to gaze at stars and have some choice old friends to visit. A gentle existence was what she planned, to move on somehow without Marcus, achieving the right balance between happy solitude and controlled sociability, her game plan on course for a trouble-free life. No stress, no demons, nothing to sweat and fret over in the middle of the night. She'd had her fair share, after all.

The doorbell ringing had been a timely interruption, coming just at that moment when her hand clenched the mouse, index finger springing back involuntarily as if stung by a bee. She had spent thirty minutes giddily zooming around Google Earth, firstly alighting upon the lichen encrusted rooftop of her '50s childhood home in Gloucestershire, where she noted with some sadness that the vegetable garden her father once tended with such devotion was now supplanted by some devilish decking (probably blue and harbouring rats). Then playfully checking out the allegedly spectacular mansion owned by a former colleague, only to find, with some disappointment, that the Elizabethan manor house was even more picturesque (complete with knot garden) than he had boasted, she had proceeded, quite deliberately, to bring up an aerial view of Richmond Bridge and yes, there it all was. Corporation Island, the tennis courts on the other side of the

3

river, their road, indeed their house, as it must have looked a few years ago, maybe when Suzi was about ten years old, and the wine red maples Marcus planted in the back garden mere striplings. She gasped and held her breath for some moments, eyes unexpectedly filling up, a knot forming in her stomach ... just as she thought she was making real progress.

She smiled at Natalie as she reappeared shaking her head, trainers crunching on the gravel drive. "Sorry," she said, as she got closer. "Must've left it with someone, I'll have to backtrack ..."

"Well, as you said, come again when you have more time. Good idea. Then you can tell me how your meeting went."

After closing the door, Kay thought to herself, *what* am I doing? One minute shamelessly excusing myself from some local political *débâcle* and, in the next breath, offering interest, involvement and, above all, encouragement. Oh, yes, bring it on Natalie – I'm your woman. But this girl, Natalie, she seemed such a genuine, earnest young thing and, as a newcomer to this rural community, Kay thought it best to avoid being labelled as a toffee-nosed recluse before she'd even met the natives. This was her rationale underpinning a suspicion that she had simply had her arm twisted.

Well, she would at least read Natalie's flyer, she decided, lurching back towards the kitchen ... and then remembered Suzi.

Doorbell and phone had actually conspired to ring simultaneously and, *en route* to the front door, she had briefly lifted the sticky-to-the-touch, old-fashioned handset sitting on the hall table only to hear, "Hi, Mum, it's only me." A daughter, for sure, but did they not realise they both sounded much the same down the phone line, even though one was across the other side of the world and the other in Hampstead?

She guessed it was Suzi, although it was unusual to hear from her during working hours, especially as she would probably have only just reached the studio, but was less likely

4

to be Claudia, in another time zone. "Hello darling, hold on a mo," she had gabbled to her younger daughter. "Someone at the door. Can't rush. Still lolloping along like an ungainly giraffe … call you back soon, all right?"

"Make it between ten and eleven," replied her equally breathless daughter. "Bye."

But what could be important enough to interrupt work – her frenetic career as a 'fashion photographer'? Well, that was what she called herself to save time, and was her ultimate ambition, but in reality she was assistant to Eugene Simlico, a world-renowned photographer who was always setting impossible deadlines. She worked round the clock earning little money but full of dreams. Conversations with Suzi had to be quick, as she was always on the way to or from somewhere, or just finishing off something, or just starting a job she must finish.

As Kay warmed her *cafetière*, she couldn't help but be mildly puzzled as to how her hard-pressed daughter had found time to call her first thing on a Monday morning. Of course, she would be concerned about the house move and all the difficulties faced by her poor mother with a distinctly second-rate leg and under-performing hip, but she had done her bit, helping her unpack boxes all Saturday and they'd had a long phone-chat yesterday. It must be something new and specific.

Sipping coffee and in no rush herself, Kay sat in the conservatory adjoining the kitchen, her cane chair positioned wonderfully so that she could gaze out at her new substantial plot of land. It smelled musty, from being closed up, virtually untouched for some months after the former inhabitant had died. If only she could simply jump up to fling open the windows. Suddenly fresh air assumed a suffocating importance – because she was deprived of it. Maybe later she would try.

Forgetting the stack of framed pictures, the flotilla of cushions and curtains that had temporarily moored around her, she cast her eyes around the scene outside, taking in the bird table; nesting boxes lodged in a couple of silver birches; far over to the right under a rose-bower a mildewed swing-seat destined for a skip, herbaceous borders that, frankly, had gone to pot, and, straight down far beyond, the sizeable patch assigned for all things edible. Established bushes promised a good harvest of soft fruit. A wet early spring had produced a lush lawn, the glossy, untrodden grass half as tall as the daffodils shining through here and there in bright yellow clusters. The plans showed a public footpath running alongside her garden but she did not mind this, actually looking forward to chatting with ramblers and families over the hedge, which would need to be trimmed down to the optimum height. A territorial barrier, yes, but not a barricade. Nature seemed poised, ready to burst into blossom and leaf. She had dreamed of this for so long, not to be on her own, but to be surrounded by the blessings of the countryside. Already she could see two magpies, several fat wood pigeons and a flash of iridescent blue and brick red that could only belong to a jay. There was a movement over to the right, near a wooden bench-seat, which made her jump. What was that? More pigeons? A cat? An *intruder*? Her heart beat fast. A patch of weeds stirred again and a small rabbit scuttled across the lawn. Despite wistfully acknowledging that bunny and friends spelled disaster for any future cabbages and lettuces, she felt a warm rush of pleasure, head and heart very much at odds.

If only Marcus could be here to share all this, but then, if Marcus were still alive, she would not be here. *Had she not picked up that knife*, Marcus would be alive and they would probably be living somewhere in the Highlands of Scotland. She glanced fondly at the framed photo of her dear husband that stood on the side table next to where she sat. Suzi had taken it when she was still at school, a proper studio portrait with soft focus. It was quite the loveliest picture she had of him, the silver haired scientist, highly regarded, renowned even, in the pharmaceutical world. His gaze, his smile, were unalloyed gentleness. She felt a tension in her throat. The feelings now triggered by Marcus' eyes looking straight into her soul, made up variably of love, horror, grief and guilt (no maybe guilt was too strong, but certainly regret) that swept through her at such times were in a tangle she consistently failed to unravel.

Unwilling to allow her emotions get the better of her, she glanced at the sheet of paper Natalie had given to her. **'Nowhere to go'** it was headed. Putting on her reading glasses that hung on a chain around her neck, an 'ageing accessory' (so her London optician had warned her) to which she had finally succumbed in her constant efforts to live with restricted mobility, she read:

Residents of Appley Green have been aware of the Travellers living on council land between the church and Heatherwood Common for the past week or so. This group of people, true Romani / Romany Gypsies, have been law-abiding and peaceful during their stay, apart from one or two minor incidents, which members of the settled community have **deliberately exaggerated**.

They were issued an Eviction Order on Thursday of last week and – did you know? They have no other site to go to yet they are simply being 'moved on'. If you've made a complaint – then I urge you to think again. Imagine you and your family being cast away, onto the road with **nowhere to go**. *Travellers who must be on the move need proper transit sites in order to earn a living.*

Welfare checks should be made before an Eviction Order is served and this could not have been done as **a woman gave birth on the site on the very same evening.**

How will future generations look back on the way we treat these people?

The same way we look back on facts such as these?

- *In 18th Century England it was illegal to be born a Romani – they were persecuted. More recently than this the penalty for being a Gypsy was death.*
- *In 1920 Gypsy women were forcibly sterilised, seen as 'vermin' and a 'disease'.*
- *Before World War II in Germany it was not illegal to murder Romani, who were killed like wild animals, hunted down, with forests set on fire to drive them out.*
- *About a million Roma were exterminated but are not recorded in census data.*

ARE WE ANY BETTER?
Help give these people a chance – join in the debate,
find out more and sign a petition to get the council to
change their mind.
Appley Green Village Hall, 7.30 this Monday

Kay knew very little about Romany culture and how Gypsies live in this country, or indeed this horrendous victimisation in Europe during the war years, but something in this cry for help from young Natalie, younger than both her own daughters, gave her an emotional jolt. Could she just ignore it? She put down the piece of paper, knowing she could not tear it up, would not scrunch it and throw it in the bin. She'd said that Natalie could come around sometime to bring her up to speed, but maybe … maybe, it would be better to hear others' views as well at this meeting. She was a part of this community now. It would be impossible to live here and ignore such a hot potato.

She could call Suzi back now so hauled herself up, promising herself to get a few portable phones strategically placed around the house. Or, would it be more cost effective to use a mobile all the time, she wondered, and just forget the landline? It really hinged on how long she would be incapacitated. She sat on the chair placed conveniently next to the phone in the galleried hallway, and dialled Suzi's mobile number, mesmerised by the carpet of worrying orange and brown swirls that she must surely remove soon to renovate the original oak parquet floor she knew lay beneath. As usual, no reply – maybe tied up in a meeting on a project or a shoot, but she would see the 'Missed call'. Sure enough, just as she had made her ponderous way to the kitchen, the phone rang and she performed an about-turn as fast as she could muster, bracing herself for some urgent issue, anything from a burst boiler to boyfriend infidelity, although there seemed to be no one special in Suzi's life at the moment. Perhaps she'd lost her job, or rather her commission with Eugene, self-employed as she was. Had Kay not propped her up financially by buying her the flat, (partly as an investment), she would possibly have been on the streets, or even more miserably, living here with her and with no work. Her life was fragile.

"Can I book a visit?" asked her daughter, voices, scuffling and banging in the background. "Next week-end for a few days?"

Kay was not just relieved but overjoyed that Suzi was planning to come over again so soon. They had been a comfort to each other over the past eighteen months; more often than not by deflecting the underlying grief they shared, rarely giving way to tears.

"How lovely. Of course you can, sweetheart, but there'll be work to do, you realise? This is very far from being a holiday zone …"

"I know, I know. I'll dance attendance on you, mother – cook, clean, shop, decorate, garden … whatever. I'd like to." Had Suzi's feigned cheerfulness become a habit, she wondered? Maybe it was a good coping strategy, better than wallowing in a morbidity that, in the circumstances, would have been excusable.

But it left Kay surprised, almost suspicious. "There's no problem with the flat is there? Landlord OK?"

"Uh? How d'you mean?""

"What about work?" broached Kay, gently.

"I can take time off – come on Saturday and go back on Monday or Tuesday."

They booked the days in their respective diaries. Kay looked at the pages, already beginning to fill up. Perhaps her own coping strategy was to throw herself into practical considerations. Plumber, roof tiler, doctor, hospital, physiotherapist – and a note to place an ad for a gardener, although if she asked around, maybe this would not be necessary. Word of mouth would probably do it.

Occupied with various tasks about the house, afternoon merged seamlessly into evening such that she had to finish off her micro-waved Thai chicken curry quickly when she realised it was close to seven o'clock. Having printed off a map from the Internet to precisely locate the Village Hall by postcode, she calculated she would need about twenty minutes to get into the village and find it.

Regally poised, she felt, in her battery-powered scooter, she drove down the garden path, paved with evenly connected flags. It led from the front porch of the Arts and Crafts style, red-bricked house (which, with its many spacious rooms and high ceilings, Suzi called a mansion) cutting through the front lawns to join up with the driveway that gave access to the pavement of a quiet road. This well-constructed pathway that curled its way right round the house, branching off at intervals to the double garage and garden sheds, was, in the process of selecting her new home, a vital feature. But then she stopped and wondered how she could turn back. Had she locked the back door? Certain she had, she was compelled to double-check, a feeling of panic rippling through her. No way would she risk leaving her house insecure, vulnerable to thieves. Once bitten, twice shy ... Someone could be lurking in there when she returned later, when it would be pitch black and no one would hear her cries for help, as she lay on the floor, coshed over the head, unable to use her phone ... or, worse still, unconscious, blood gushing from an open wound, *blood everywhere* ... Gone were the old days when you could famously leave your back door open with apparent impunity.

She climbed out of the vehicle, thankful that at least she was not overweight and reasonably agile in that respect. She reached for her walking stick strapped to it. It offered less support than the frame she used indoors and, in fact, she was beginning to realise she used both aids now rather to give her confidence than truly to lean on. She took a deep breath, knowing she would have to go round the back ... No, she would open the front door, and go through the house. That would make more sense.

Cautiously she made her way, in a curious hop-step, quite unsynchronised with her stick, vaguely noting clumps of lavender and heather bordering the path, subliminally looking

10

forward to their scent and colour later in the season. She reached in the right pocket of her red wool jacket for her bunch of keys. She had learned to wear garments with large pockets, (preferably buttoned or zipped for security), as it was easier than relying on a bag, easily mislaid and ripped from your shoulder by muggers. If anyone wants my credit card, phone or cash, they would have to take me as well, she reasoned. She would have a turning area built halfway down the garden path, a small lay-by, to enable such turnabouts. Once inside she grabbed her frame and trudged to the back door, which she found to be secure, locked and bolted, top and bottom.

"Silly woman!" she said loudly. A burglar alarm, she thought, that's what I need, realising that living in the country she might be just as vulnerable as in the city, perhaps more so.

Once past the primary school, nearing the triangular village green, Appley Green's pride and joy, overlooked by upmarket country residences, she looked at her watch. Now she might be late and really wanted to avoid 'making an entrance'. Unsure if there would be a ramp at the door, though there certainly should be, she did not know what her mode of arrival would be, staggering in with her stick, grabbing any person or object within reach for support; or 'driving' in. Either way, heads would turn.

Around the steps leading up to the door was a sea of gravel, like her own driveway, which slowed her scooter, wheels struggling, normally with a top speed of eight miles per hour, to less than crawling pace. Planners and architects, or whoever hold responsibility, don't think these things through, she thought. One day I'll write a book about all these minefields and pitfalls. Alongside the official Parish Council notice of the meeting, one of Natalie's flyers was pinned to the outer door which was at least encouraging affirmation that she was in the right place, albeit late, and yes, there was a ramp. But she knew proceedings would be under way.

2

With the help of a rather surly, burly, weather-beaten man, who was minding the door on the inside, she managed to push the double-doors open, only to realise she need not have worried about attracting attention or even being noticed. The air was already hot and heavy with rhetoric, accusations being hurled across the hall, reciprocated with denials, abusive language and fists being punched in the air. No wonder the locals were 'up in arms' as Natalie had put it. The behaviour and noise levels of this motley throng resembled an uncontrollable class of teenagers, the analogy possibly doing teenagers a disservice.

She sat at the back of the hall, struggling to see over the mass of bobbing heads, straining her ears to sift out a few salient points from the hubbub.

There was a panel of three on the stage and an empty chair. Natalie was the only person she recognised and Kay was intrigued to know who the two men were. Were they for or against? Councillors, Gypsies or villagers?

Just a few feet from where Kay sat at the back, a man, tall and wide, stood up, raising his hand.

He projected his voice to the utmost, Brian Blessed-like. "This free for all is going to get us nowhere …," he boomed. He could definitely play Shakespeare.

"Quite right …" squeaked a woman with a lavender pashmina draped around her neck, who jumped up briefly like a jack-in-the-box at the front, making her contribution somewhat debatable, if not ironic, Kay felt, holding back a chuckle.

"Well, for God's sake, you lot up there on the podium, take charge and bring this rabble to order," continued the man with the cavernously loud mouth.

Natalie won't stand for that, calling her beloved nomadic community a 'rabble', thought Kay. With the detachment of a simple observer, she found herself getting rather excited. So this was real life, a veritable parochial drama. This would be something to tell Suzi about!

Natalie called out above the noise, "Unfortunately, our Parish councillor who was to chair the meeting has been called away, so …"

A threadbare man with a shock of white hair leaped up onto the stage in an alarmingly anarchic, age-defying fashion, confronting the auditorium. "The whole thing doesn't need debate – they're bloody outlaws – shouldn't be living on land, paying no taxes, thieving, making a thorough disturbance, frightening shopkeepers, flouting the law," he bellowed with great passion. "We'd all like to own a plot of country land and set up home, be it house or caravan. The point is have they ever heard of Planning Permission? Like the rest of us. Have they? Eh? Answer me that!"

There were cheers of approval and Kay realised that maybe the local residents who had bothered to turn out, were actually outnumbering those from the Travelling community. She spotted a close neighbour who had called to see her within an hour of her arrival in Appley Green.

Natalie stood up and did manage to halt the noise surprisingly quickly. The locals must know of her agenda behind this meeting – it was her name at the foot of the flyer. Good for her, thought Kay. A bright, tough little cookie she is. So young – she would go far.

"Of course they make planning applications …" retorted Natalie, scornfully. "You've all read my leaflet, I hope. If not, then why not?" She reminds me of a youthful version of my old history teacher, thought Kay. "These Travellers, not settled on a permanent site, have come here for generations, to do seasonal work on the land, picking hops, strawberries,

14

potatoes, helping with the harvest .... Not so much of that work is there for them these days, but many of them don't know how else to live! What is open to their grandchildren, the itinerant people of today? Horse-dealing? Basket-making? Tree surgery maybe, but fortune-telling, making clothes pegs, dancing for our entertainment in the village square? I don't think so!! But, to travel, to move on – it's in their blood. And, I would remind you that the right to a nomadic way of life is today enshrined in the European Convention of Human Rights." Kay felt the hairs on the back of her neck rise as she heard these words. Human Rights, Animal Rights, Activists, angry, threatening ... she must not get too involved in this fracas ... "How many of you have actually talked to any of the local Gypsy population?"

The hall fell quiet.

Natalie paused and then asked, "And how many of you here this evening are from the Travelling community in question?"

Kay became transfixed by the drama as it unfolded. No hand went up, no voice responded, until someone piped up, "No surprise there. They know they're guilty!"

Natalie acknowledged the comment with a shake of her head. "No. Mostly, they are shy of defending themselves and, let's face it, they would be outnumbered and ... well, wouldn't you be intimidated if you were them? Look around you and listen to yourselves. Baying for blood! No wonder no one from their group came forward to join us."

There were rumblings of disagreement but Natalie had their attention and barely paused for breath. "Since the 1994 Act repealed the 1968 Caravan Sites Act and local authorities no longer have to provide sites for Gypsies, these people just drift from one unauthorised place to another, criminalised, unable to stay for longer than four weeks more often than not. Can you imagine what that's like? For finding work? For the children? Their schooling?"

"Why should they use our schools at all? They don't pay taxes …" shouted out a smart man in the middle of the hall, who Kay thought looked as if he might work in a bank.

"That's where you're quite wrong," replied Natalie, coolly. "Those who can earn a living mostly *do* pay council tax, but there are problems admittedly for those on the move. How would you go about that if you were never in the same place long enough to fill in the forms? And if you couldn't read or write? And, as for income tax, some Travellers rely on benefits because no one will employ or pay them – people like *you* probably." Murmurings of protest. Natalie threw out her hands in a beseeching gesture. "Well, what would you do in their situation? Maybe, I mean just maybe, they need to eat when they are hungry! Perhaps they need to put some sort of decent clothing on their backs! Or would you prefer they raid our cupboards, steal to survive, to put food into their children's mouths. I'm not saying that they *do* steal, as I have absolutely no evidence for that, but perhaps, then in a sense stealing would not be such a crime."

"Oh right! Law of the jungle? Free for all? Anarchy?" someone shouted.

"I've seen some of 'em drive around in big cars …" called out a large, young, blonde woman.

"Some form of reasonably powerful transport is an absolute necessity to pull their homes, just as horses used to be …" put in Natalie, dismissively, "These people are resourceful. They have to be to survive, and yes, some Travellers are well-off, those who deal in scrap-metal successfully, for example, can do very well – although then they and their wares get blamed for being a blot on the landscape – but, anyway, not the ones around here at the moment. No wealthy Gypsies here, not at this time of the year …"

The blonde cut in, "Well they shouldn't be allowed to 'ave kids if they can't afford to feed 'em …" A palpable silence descended like an electrically charged soup, thick, stifling, as if people's feelings for humanity had suddenly been

16

swallowed up and drowned. Kay sensed a collective recall of the words in Natalie's flyer – "women forcibly sterilised."

Natalie, to her credit, made good use of this quiet and Kay watched her as she went on, striking hard, "Mm. Himmler ordered extermination in 1941 of what were seen as a 'defective element of the population' – 250 Gypsy children were used to test cyanide gas." Intakes of breath around the hall were audible. If she carries on like this, mused Kay, there'll be a witch-hunt for any Germans living around here, never mind the Gypsies. "During wartime there was persecution, but more recent 'ethnic cleansing' in Switzerland, saw to it that Gypsy children were forcibly removed from parents, from families where bonds were – and *still are* among the Romany people - so strong, much stronger than you or I know about. Yes, until the mid-seventies, well within the lifetime of most of you here in this hall, they were kidnapped, put into orphanages and fostered. Just because they were *born Gypsy*. In this age of anti-discrimination and equal opportunity for all, how can anyone carry on this racism against a people who actually mean no harm, but who do want to preserve their culture, their way of life?"

Kay vaguely glimpsed out of the corner of her eyes, to her right, the arrival of a couple of men, the younger of the two newcomers with a couple of cameras dangling between the fronts of his open brown leather jacket.

One of the men on the stage with Natalie stood up and cleared his throat. "David McDaniel, Planning Department. I'd like to say a few words to bring this meeting back to the immediate matter in hand and, indeed, how the law stands *today*, before we get overly emotional." Kay watched with interest at the sharp look he threw towards Natalie who met his glare without flinching. "Our Gypsy Liaison Officers do try and mediate in these matters and, as Natalie is fully aware, we have policies that go a long way to try and assess their needs, integrate these people into the community, even offering them housing, which more often than not they decline. Visits were made, several in fact, in accordance with

17

the procedures, prior to the Eviction Notice being served. When a group of Travellers has nowhere else to go, these officers offer leniency, tolerance and time, but in this case there were half a dozen complaints from the local *residents* ."

Cheers from the hall and Mr McDaniel raised his hand to quell their enthusiasm. Natalie sat, jaw clenched, arms folded. "I am told by our Legal Department that there was non-compliance with the Code, as follows," and he took a piece of paper from his jacket pocket and unfolded it. "A *fight* broke out on the camp leading to *disorder* of such a kind that the police were called in and the person who reported it felt her own *safety was at risk*; there were reports of *unroadworthy vehicles* cluttering up the lane leading to the unauthorised encampment, causing a *nuisance* to motorists; dogs roaming *loose*; alleged *thefts* from the village shop; general *litter* flying from the direction of the site; and *abusive* language towards the residents living adjacent to the site …"

Natalie jumped up from her seat, anger burning in her eyes. "So, if a fight were to break out on the streets, as happens any night in any city, is the answer to eject those responsible to another town or city? Is that how the law works? And the person who reported this, was he or she actually threatened or harmed? And did you find out if they were for some reason prejudiced, or possibly worried about the value of their property being affected? Were the owners of these vehicles you mentioned being deliberately obstructive or were they *unable*, due to lack of resources and money, to get the broken down vans moved? Maybe they can't afford a breakdown service to call upon! The rest of your list could be just hearsay born of the spiteful blood that runs through the veins of the people around here!" Oh, my god, thought Kay, she's going to get herself lynched by the villagers. Natalie, my dear girl, calm down, you young hothead. But she went on, a girl with a mission if ever there was one, "And in your so-called welfare checks, how come, I would really like to know, you missed a heavily pregnant woman since, I believe your rules are that no evictions should take place in the six weeks before the expected date of delivery? And she gave birth on the very day they were asked to move on!"

As she watched David McDaniel wither slightly, Kay decided this girl would make an excellent barrister one day, as she reminded herself of the fact that she was practically in a minority of one in this hall. No wonder she was laying it on with a spade to put her case across.

David shook his head. "I was not involved in the Eviction so I'd have to look into this. I …" he faltered, "I can't think how this happened. Presumably the Gypsies themselves did not inform the GLO of this fact. They would've had the opportunity many times over …"

"Or," cried Natalie, with relentless venom, "perhaps, an itinerant population does not fit in with your concept of urban planning. The encroachment on green-belt land is out of the question, as far as you're concerned, even though a so-called 'unsightly' encampment really does no *permanent* damage to the environment, in fact nothing at all compared with, say, a quarry, gas works, or chemicals factory …" Sarcastic jeers. "Nomads are not part of your plans for modernity, are they?"

"My dear, you've been reading too many text-books."

Kay watched Natalie's face. Oh dear. Big mistake. "How *dare* you *patronise* me!" The audience seemed now almost hypnotised by the level of drama; in theory on the side of the Planner, but warming towards Natalie and the heat of her invective. They were all at sea.

She turned away from Mr McDaniel, with great dignity as if he had now shown his true colours and was unworthy of her attention or respect. The two men standing close to Kay were whispering animatedly to each other, nudging, pointing, raising eyebrows, consulting their watches, taking video, as well as still photographs, capturing every word.

"Thank you all for coming. Please think carefully about the points raised this evening. Everyone can do their bit to help by giving them a chance – and by listening to their point of view. The petition needs to be signed now to stop these people being heartlessly moved on. The next meeting will be in one week's time, I believe," she glanced at the others on stage, "The hall is free, Ken?" She turned to a man who had taken the absentee's chair, possibly the caretaker or whoever keeps the bookings. He nodded with a blank, seriously impartial expression, not even needing to look it up. Village Hall not exactly a hive of activity then. Poor Natalie, thought Kay, as she watched her hold up a clipboard with paper attached and hand it down to the front row. She really has very little support. Actually none.

Well, what will the outcome of that be, wondered Kay?

3

"That'll be forty pence for the week, then," said Mr Patel, who ran the local Post Office and village shop. Kay handed him the card she had designed on her Mac computer, using Photoshop and Quark Xpress. It was simple, bold, colourful with a hint of vegetable.

He held it up. "Oh, very nice! Have your grandchildren been busy?"

Kay tried not to dislike Mr Patel, for fear it showed and drew forth accusations of racism. She forced a smile, even a small laugh. "No, no, I'm not blessed with grandchildren yet." But then, it was quite possible for someone in their mid fifties to have grandchildren old enough to do graphic design, if both she and her progeny had been fruitful at an early age, which in her case was not so.

"Oh dear," he said, apparently sympathetic to her double disadvantage – crippled and all alone. "Will it be just one week?" asked, adding hopefully, "or for the month?"

"Well, perhaps you can advise me?" Mr Patel assumed an attentive, almost conspiratorial air, raised eyebrows, pursed lips, but said nothing. "So, what do you think? How quickly do you think I will get a satisfactory response?"

It was clear he had not read the card, which he quickly remedied. He then began stroking his chin, pensively.

"Most people living here are away during the day working in the towns and cities, or, like yourself, madam, too *old* for that kind of work!"

He's probably a wonderful father, possibly grandfather, son, brother, uncle, fulfilling these roles admirably within his extended family. Is *that* racist, she silently mused? Am I pre-judging, building him into a stereotype? It's just the impression I'm getting from his words and manner, which surely is not the same thing at all, she confidently assured herself.

"Right, well – what a salesman you are, Mr Patel. That has persuaded me. Four weeks please," she said, handing him a two-pound coin. "Your charge is very reasonable - please keep the change."

Now he looked offended, or was he confused? Did he see this as an act of charity – because of the colour of his skin? She'd never felt this strange sense of unease in the complicated hotchpotch of multi-cultural London. His accent and manner somehow belonged to first generation Asian immigrants. It was like turning back the clock at least twenty years.

Then, something of a relief for Kay, a huge smile broke out on his face. "I've never been called a 'salesman' before," he said, his brown eyes suddenly merry. "We just provide a service here, you know, Mrs Patel and I, with the Post Office and papers, mostly," he pointed to the counter in the corner where his wife sat behind a glass screen. They gave each other a little wave across the empty shop.

"Of course," said Kay, now feeling the need to sit down, to get back to her scooter parked outside. "And a very important role you play in the community I'm sure."

"Oh really! You think so, madam. Please," and Mr Patel rushed to the back of the shop with astonishing speed, returning with a chair and Kay felt a trap being laid into which she was about to fall, but could not figure what the purpose of this was.

"Take a seat for moment and make yourself comfortable – I can see it is hard for the older person to stand for long," said the well-meaning man, who Kay figured was younger than her, but definitely the wrong side of fifty. "You see, we have a petition for good people, like yourself, to sign ..."

"Oh? For the Gypsies?"

"No no, my words, we would never be in support of those people, not good British citizens like us, like you and me, madam," he was shaking his head and, Kay noticed, his wife's head was in perfect synchronicity. "This is to save our business here, our livelihood if you please, to save the much-needed Post Office of Appley Green, which may be closed if we do not … well, put up a fight and rally and make sure that we are not one of the ones to be consigned to oblivion."

She took the clipboard and pen from him and added her signature. "I'm happy to sign, but …" Kay was rewinding his words in her head. "The Gypsies. Do you mind if I ask you, Mr Patel, what you have got against them?"

He raised his shoulders, put his head on one side, threw his hands up in the air, all in a most theatrical fashion and, entirely predictably, said, "Where to begin?"

"Well, perhaps … what have they done that you find so objectionable?"

"They come in here and buy small things, you know. Like two stamps, or a bottle of milk and the whole family are in here with children running their … dirty fingers … along the magazines there and trying to distract me so they can put chocolate bars in their pockets. But I would catch them." He pointed to his own eyes. "I keep careful look-out, see!"

"So did you call the police?"

"No, no. Not want any trouble. I did not let them take a single thing!"

"Well, good for you, Mr Patel, and what else have they done – or *not* done?" She looked him straight in the eye.

"Their site is a mess – have you seen it? The site? It's a sight all right – ha-ha!"

"Is it really? I haven't actually seen but intend to," said Kay, rising from her seat. "It was … interesting talking to you. Good luck with your petition." She would make a detour on her way home she decided.

"Nice to meet you. Please call again and thank you for your support."

23

Within two days Kay had received phone calls from two men about the gardening job and saw no point in delaying; so she invited them round for a chat, then worried in case she was being naïve, inviting total strangers into her home when she would be alone. She could have waited until Suzi was there but now it was done so she'd just have to see it through by herself.

The first candidate arrived promptly at ten o'clock. An "old boy with bits of dinner down his pullover" as Kay later described him to Suzi, "who walked stiffly on his pins, puffing and wheezing, but had worked his allotment for fifty years – at least" and could do with a "bit extra cash in hand" (his words) to help pay for his wife's new orthopaedic bed. She sympathised with him on so many levels that it was hard not to offer him the job there and then, but seriously doubted he was physically up to it. Head ruling heart on this occasion, she said gently she would get back to him once she had seen all the other applicants.

The second one, a stringy adolescent wearing a baseball cap, came later in the day, after his shift at Mcdonalds in the local town.

Claiming to be eighteen, he looked at least four years younger. "I wanna learn about growin' stuff an' 'at," he said.

"I see. Have you done much gardening then?"

"Nah, not really. Fancy a change, though."

"Tell me a bit about what you've done …"

"What? Gardenin' like?" he asked, as if surprised. Kay nodded and his gaze shifted around the sitting room as if hoping that the ceiling or the walls might, by some miracle, give up some ideas.

"What interests you in a garden?"

He screwed up his face thoughtfully. "Well, I like a nice lawn, and flowers and stuff. You know."

Kay made up her mind quickly. "Thank you so much for coming. Look, I'll let you know when I've seen the other applicants."

24

That afternoon Natalie came to visit, without warning, but not unexpectedly. Soon they were sitting down at the kitchen table with tea and some flapjacks from the village bakery, rather heavy and sticky compared with the nutty, seedy ones she used to make herself.

"I didn't really know whether to expect this follow up visit, as I …" began Kay.

"Must make sure you're in the picture, as a newcomer to the village …"

"… I was at the meeting. At the back."

"Wow, thanks for going – I guess it can't have been easy, I mean just the getting there … what happened to your legs?"

Kay liked her directness. "Long story. A domestic accident, shall we say," she replied, swallowing hard and looking away, knowing that she had no wish to expand. "But you're not here to talk about that. How did you get so involved in the Gypsy situation? I went to see the site for myself yesterday … it's … they're still there, then."

Kay thought back to the image of the site – a first impression that was, overall, depressing. She had held back, feeling like a snooper and did not get a close view. She could make out a couple of young women, poorly dressed in old jeans and fleeces, sitting on the steps of a caravan at the end of a line, smoking. Their faces were pale, hair drawn back. Some bags of rubbish were stowed behind but nothing untoward about that. A young mongrel dog was sniffing around and the women shouted at it. A small boy appeared from inside the trailer, looked up and pointed to Kay's small vehicle and at that point she knew she must leave.

"They've dug their heels in now," said Natalie with a grin, over the rim of her mug. "I'm coming at it from two angles really. Born and bred Appley Green, I've seen Gypsies come and go ever since I can remember. They're attracted, so it's said, by the name, Appleby being an old traditional fair up in Cumbria, though there's no real connection. I've seen Romany, New Age Travellers, fairground, even Circus Showmen once or twice when I was very little … All different,

I found – but, anyway, I would literally 'run off with Gypsies', play with the children and got thoroughly told off for it. I could never understand *why* because the Gypsy kids were my best friends ..."

"As a parent, I think I can understand why your parents would have ... discouraged you ..."

Natalie glowered at her. "Can you? But I bet you've never known a Gypsy family, talked to them, or seen the inside of their trailers."

"True," conceded Kay. "As far as I know ..."

"Some of them even had *vardos*, those old-fashioned wagons ..."

She raised her eyebrows. "What? Horse-drawn and painted?"

She nodded. "Yes. There were one or two just ten years ago that kept up the tradition."

"But, now ..."

"In many ways, just the same people, but don't look so romantic, do they, in their blot-on-the-landscape caravans that you associate with cheap holidays?"

"But surely the people, too, are different in the modern world?"

"Kind of. They have to be. But the yearning to move around, to travel, is passed down from one generation to the next and only a small number make the change to become *Gorgios*. It breaks up families. And being forced to move on is not the same as travelling in search of seasonal work."

"*Gorgios?*"

"Non-Gypsy. Settled people. You and me."

"So what's your other angle?"

Natalie smiled, perhaps pleased that Kay was paying attention. "I'm studying the Travellers as part of my Uni course in Social Anthropology ..."

"Well, you're clearly well-read on the subject ..."

"As David McDaniel was so eager to point out!" A short laugh failed to disguise her contempt. After a pause, she added, "I have to resort to shocking facts to get people to listen."

Kay considered this. "I can understand that."

"And they are facts. Not spin. I could give you a pile more!"

Kay nodded. "Are you enjoying your course?"

"I really am. Gives a broader picture. Aside from the Gypsy thing, I'm doing a placement in South Africa, or possibly Australia, next year, it's not fixed yet."

"Young people have so many wonderful opportunities these days. When I was your age, even with a degree, it was pretty much, secretary? Or, teacher, which is it to be? I'm sure there must've been other career paths, but my school wasn't very helpful in opening up the mind, I'm afraid."

"So, did you work?"

"Mm. Once my two daughters were old enough I got into public relations and marketing in the IT industry. Had my own business ... but back to you, Natalie. So you came to be the Gypsies' champion, but it must've been an uphill battle. And did none of your friends, little *Gorgios,* join you?"

Natalie shook her head. "I ... I was bullied at school, really had no friends ... aah, poor me!"

"Do you know why you were bullied?"

She screwed up her nose thoughtfully. "Couldn't read or write very well. Could talk all right, though!! Dyslexia they later found out, but not until I was in my teens, when I was given special help, but ..."

"So you had a lot of catching up to do, just when you should've been out having fun ..."

"You got it. So, my true friends were members of the Travelling community, who I would say goodbye to for months, never sure if I'd ever see them again. They understood about battling with print, as many children, adults too, never saw the need for it and found schoolwork difficult because of the constant moving on. They do a lot more these days, but ..."

"Ah, yes, the council? Are they all bad?"

"No, they're not. To be fair. But this time they did a very *bad* thing," Natalie looked down, biting her lip, and Kay realised that Natalie's eyes had filled with tears.

"What? The birth incident?"

She nodded, twirling strands of hair between her fingers. "Someone let me – and them – down. Seriously."

"Who was that?"

"Max, Gypsy Liaison Officer. That's his title. Poacher turned gamekeeper, more like. He should've been more thorough, seen … anyway I don't want to talk about that. Actually." She sniffed, pulled a tissue from her pocket and had a good blow. Something more going on here, thought Kay, watching Natalie's bottom lip tremble, the corners of her mouth turn down.

"I wish there was something I could do to help."

Natalie paused with a sigh. "Well I guess you signed the petition. It hasn't come back to me yet."

"I did, and yet … do you know Natalie, after the meeting I still wasn't sure if it was the right thing to do. Local people seemed so worked up, so angry …" And Kay had to silently question in her heart if she would want a group of Gypsies living in the field adjacent to her own garden.

"People. Mm. People." She sounded weary. "Trust me, you did the right thing. I heard that there's another petition going round – anti-Gypsy, opposing them being here at all! Not that I'm surprised. Anyway," she said brightly, "How're you settling in, generally …?"

"But who's spearheading that one?"

Natalie shrugged.

Kay was thinking. "Would you like me to check out the legal situation on the anti-Gypsy petition for you? Sounds racist to me. I have a very good solicitor." And, maybe thought Kay, I could make an anonymous report to the police.

"Thanks, but it's OK. I need to do this myself anyhow. I'll check it out. I know someone I could ask. Anyway, how *are* you getting on – I bet you came here for peace and quiet, didn't you?" Natalie did her impish grin.

"Well, with my … predicament," said Kay, with a hand on her right hip, and pointing to her left leg with a reproving glare, as if it did not belong to her, "everything is pretty slow, and I get very cranky and frustrated! Having to employ a gardener, for instance. I used to love gardening and it's a big part of moving here, to grow things. I can't seem to find the right person, either, so that's a bit of a priority, more than the house, if I'm honest."

"Oh," cut in Natalie, smoothly. "I know someone who'd be perfect."

A Gypsy, of course, thought Kay, her mind still harbouring memories of an old neighbour intimidated by men who tarmacked her drive, covering far more ground than agreed and demanding vast sums of instant cash. They claimed loudly to be Gypsies and having got their money, were never traced. But she had known it was wrong to think like that. *If* they were truly Gypsies, she told herself, they might have kept that to themselves, knowing how shunned they were by residential middle-England. Also, if they *were* Gypsies, not all Gypsies are tarred with the same brush – oh ha-ha. There are plenty of conmen in society anyway. Good and bad in all walks of life. But, surely, if they were *Gypsies* they would've seized the opportunity to prove that their bad reputation was false, but … and then she heard the same story from another person in the neighbourhood with the details practically identical. They'd said they had some tarmac 'left over from a previous job', then proceeded to do more than agreed and ended up marching the poor home-owners down to a cash-point who did as they were ordered through sheer fear …

Natalie was scribbling on a piece of paper, which she then handed to Kay. "Dunstan. There you go - his full name and telephone number. I'm sure he'd love to help and … He's a really nice guy. You'll … *love* him," she said, mischief in her eyes. Oh, thought Kay, very Lady Chatterley. "I shall be going

29

away next week, travelling in Europe, then back to Uni and I must get this mess sorted before then ..."

Alarm bells resounded inside Kay's head. "Is that likely?" asked Kay. "You really think you can turn this perennial problem around in a week, Natalie?"

"Well, I don't know. I'm trying really hard to get some Travellers to come forward on Monday and speak up for themselves, but ..."

"Have you asked your local MP to the meeting?"

Natalie looked at Kay, open-mouthed. "Our local MP is *Conservative*! They're the cause of the trouble – the lack of sites."

"OK, but maybe he could help. His presence might encourage others to come, who might support. Who's his opposition?"

"Hey, that's not such a bad idea. Cool! Now, come on Kay, who else ...?"

Soon they had drawn up a list, pooling Kay's experience and ideas with Natalie's local knowledge.

"Thanks a bunch for your help. You've listened to me more than the rest of the local mob put together in the past ten years – well, slight exaggeration," said Natalie, gathering up her canvas bag and its contents. Moving to the door, with Kay following her as fast as she could, she added, "You will keep an eye on things, when I'm not here, won't you?" She squeezed Kay's arm. "I really feel I can count on you as my *ally*."

Kay heard herself saying, "Of *course* you can. Anything I can do. Let's hope we get some kind of amicable agreement before you ... disappear ..."

As Kay closed the door, she leaned back on it, feeling drained.

"Oh, bloody hell," she muttered, "I'm being sucked in, I can feel it. I don't want this. I don't, but what can I do now? Too late, too late. Committed. Lumbered."

She looked at the name and number Natalie had written down for her. Well, she would see this man, see if he showed promise as a viable contender. She could at least try him out. Natalie wouldn't recommend anyone who was – unsafe, would she? A trial period would sort out his ability. Then, she could rest easy – she would have done her bit so to speak, and could, with a clear conscience back off from total commitment of managing the mission by proxy, with Natalie back in academia. Good plan.

It was arranged. He sounded normal enough on the phone, "willing to discuss" and readily agreed to visit the following morning, and "would look forward to it". Keen, or what, thought Kay, not sure if that made her pleased and impressed, or suspicious?

That afternoon, transport arrived to take her to Bloomstock Community Hospital fifteen miles away for physiotherapy, from which she was anxious to derive immediate benefit. She threw herself into the stretching and bending with gusto.

"Are there some daily exercises I can do at home?" she asked.

The physiotherapist gave her a sheet of paper. "Sure. That's the best thing. Regularity. But don't overdo it. Stick to what's recommended, and I'll see you again in a month."

Kay almost snatched it from her hand and the young woman laughed. "You're enthusiastic!"

"I will do *anything* to get out of these shackles! I have things to do, places to go, people to see …!"

"You're doing really well …" Kay heard her say, as she disappeared down the corridor in a wheelchair pushed by a hospital porter as fast as she could make him go.

Friday morning, Kay's alarm went off at seven and she turned on the radio to listen to the News and the *Today* programme that routinely accompanied her ablutions. She climbed out of bed, reaching for her upstairs walking aid, to go to the loo and switched on her kettle, set up so she could make a morning cup of tea without having to go downstairs first. It was essential to give her a kick-start first thing.

As she struggled to pull on a pair of socks, the stiffness of new jeans making it doubly difficult, she heard the words, "Appley Green ... serious implications ... Travellers being moved on ... accusations that a young woman has been distributing material that could cause racial discontent ..."

"What? What? Natalie?" On the national news, someone being interviewed. She hurried to the bedside to turn up the volume, tripping up over the edge of her duvet in her haste, flopping onto the bed. "But, you stupid man, she's doing the complete opposite. Who on earth is behind this rubbish?"

The interviewer was asking about the Human Rights issue involved "in this case where Travellers who are occupying an unauthorised site have refused to comply with an Eviction Order ..." Who was he interviewing? Damn it, she would need to play this back from the BBC website later. "The literature she has been giving to the public ... has prompted complaints from the residents that her inflammatory words are stirring up trouble ... and there is a possibility that the police will have to apply force."

But this is madness, thought Kay, so hopping mad, she wanted to cry out and scream at somebody. The world has, officially, gone insane. It was a brief item and, apparently, apart from the interviewer trying to be even-handed, nobody had spoken up to contradict the speaker. Now they were onto Baghdad.

Once downstairs, she could see her newspapers on the doormat. In addition to the daily newspaper, there was a local paper, the front page emblazoned with caravans, a group of sullen-looking people, black bags of rubbish and some old fridges and washing machines. Unable to bend over to reach it she kicked it along the floor to the kitchen and found some barbecue tongs in the drawer, finally plucking it in its jaws. Everything was such a trial, she could feel her blood pressure rise.

Next to the picture she saw an article written by a man, whose photo was inset, a local landowner, with a surname that seemed familiar. A celebrity? Someone she knows? She racked her brain as she read on. "Not the same as years ago … cluttering up the countryside … mess … dogs out of control … broken down vehicles just left to rot and residents living in fear of their lives … nomads with a chip on their shoulder – no wonder they've been evicted!"

When Dunstan Smith arrived on her doorstep, Kay knew at once that something in her life was about to change. Something significant, emotionally charged that arguably was to do with the fact he was a man, about her age. It was one of those defining moments when you meet someone and feel that you have found what you did not even know you had been looking for. It took her by surprise for surely her loyalty and affection would always rest with the memory of Marcus.

Once in the conservatory, he instantly strode to one of the many the windows to survey his potential 'workplace'. He wore a dark suit that fitted, fitted just right. Neither too tight around the hips, nor baggy and shapeless, it sat squarely and symmetrically on his broad shoulders. He turned with a smile above a white shirt and turquoise and brown silk tie that caused her pulse to suddenly race. Alone with a stranger in the house, a weird fusion of fear and attraction shot through her.

He wasn't at all what she had expected. "You look very smart for a gardener," she heard herself blurt out, immediately wishing she hadn't. Maybe not old enough to be retired, she guessed, but heading that way, greying, more so at the temples and an otherwise thick head of wavy hair thinning slightly on the crown.

Again he smiled, offering no explanation. "How many hours a week are you thinking of?" he asked.

"Please sit down," she offered, indicating a solid, wicker chair, the best one. "Well, it's so hard to say. There's a limit as to how much I want to pay but this garden is an important

33

project to me, particularly the edible produce. Eventually, as my injuries improve, I hope to be able to do more myself ..."

"So, it's temporary, then – until you're up and running?" Kay was trying to detect an accent. There was a musical lilt, not quite Irish. He spoke clearly, a manly voice, not loud, but in his question there was a doubtful edge.

"Just a matter of degree ... probably," she reassured him, bit by bit feeling more relaxed. "More work to do at the beginning to get the plot into shape, and during the summer obviously ..."

"Could make your organic veg expensive?" he ventured, his amber eyes twinkling. Who was doing this interview, she began to wonder?

Did he mean his wages would need to be sufficient to keep him in his accustomed life style, in which case, she would have to see him to the door right now? She didn't want home grown to save money, but what she would be willing to pay wouldn't keep him in shoes, or even socks. Or, was he talking relatively? Compared to buying organic vegetables from the market?

"It's the satisfaction – from growing your own ..."

"Especially if someone else is doing the hard labour, eh?" He laughed.

"But if I could, believe me, I would. And, I will!"

"Tell me a bit about your plans, then," he said, leaning forward, elbows resting on his knees, his strong fingers interlocked. She must remember to ask him, given the chance, what was motivating him to do this kind of work.

She outlined her vision of basic and more exotic fruit and vegetables, as well tidying up and maintaining the lawn and borders. He appeared to be listening carefully, nodding intermittently, but giving nothing away.

"Do you have a greenhouse?" he asked. "I'd need to move fast to catch this year's growing season."

"Not yet, but clearly we'll need one if we're to grow certain things from seed ..." *We? We?* What was she saying? She had already installed him ... "I mean ..."

34

"Tools?"

"I'll get whatever is needed. Get it delivered."

"I'd enjoy this," he said simply. His head turned slightly and she noted his perfect profile, a straight nose, features evenly proportioned.

She smiled. "Well, good."

"The wages are not that important to me," he said, with a shrug. "More a hobby but ... perhaps a share of the produce could be negotiated?" Now he spoke with businesslike authority.

Kay's heart leapt. This was perfect, there was always too much, even from her modest garden in Richmond – French beans running riot; rhubarb made into crumbles, coulis, cake, bars, jam, pies, till you were so sick of the sweet-sharpness it made your teeth go on edge just to think of it; the freezer full of sliced courgettes that, frankly, thawed into discs of seaweed coated jelly ...

This man could not be a Gypsy. She had been so wrong to jump to that conclusion and now, it would be rude to ask, suggest or even privately suspect such a thing. Not that there was anything wrong with that ...

"I know people who could use some extra vegetables," so maybe he knows some Gypsies, like Natalie does, which would make sense, "but this would be an incentive for me to do well for you."

Kay nodded eagerly. "To be productive, instead of just putting in the hours."

"Exactly. And I would only expect maybe a few pounds a month, depending on the amount of work, which will vary. I can see that."

They spoke simultaneously. "Would you like a cup of coffee?" offered Kay, wishing to seal some sort of deal which she knew would work out well, even though she had not even asked about his experience, or for references yet, as he asked, "Can we go outside now?"

Kay laughed. "Yes, let's do that first, see the garden close-up ... then you can estimate the hours ..."

When Suzi arrived on Saturday morning, Kay felt alive, better able to bury darker thoughts of the past, buzzing with her news. Uproar at the Gypsy meeting, Natalie, the media coverage, the Post Office campaign, new exercises which Suzi must make her do every day she was here, and her new find, the somewhat mysterious Dunstan.

"He is so *right* for what I need here. This man, Suzi, is perfection!"

"But he could be a Gypsy? You thought so at first?"

So what? she wanted to yell at her, feeling unaccountably furious with her daughter. "Well, if he is, he is as far removed from any stereotype as you could get … He appears to be a genuinely nice man with time on his hands, a keen interest in growing stuff, so rather than get an allotment, for which there is probably a horrendous waiting list anyway …"

"But you suspect he has some strong link? With Gypsies?"

"Probably, because Natalie put him forward, and the fact he wants to pass on spare produce from the garden, but …"

"Well, from what you've told me, you must be barking mad, mother!"

"Well, thank you, dear."

"If he has these connections – aren't you making yourself vulnerable?"

Kay stopped for a moment. One thing she must avoid was inviting danger. "I … I can tell, instinctively, that he is a good guy and Natalie would never …"

"But that's not the point," said Suzi, earnestly. "Can't you see? You've just moved here and you know how long it takes to be accepted in any village. Now all these locals, who are so anti-Gypsy, will see you employing this man and be against you. Actions like this speak louder than words and it's like putting up two fingers to them, a provocative thing to do." Suddenly her younger daughter sounded frighteningly wise.

"Oh, rot," said Kay. "I'm not going to be bullied!"

"Well, I hope you don't regret it …"

Kay was suddenly deflated. Earlier, she had literally felt as if some hormone or drug was streaming through her brain, lifting her into a new realm of happiness, something she had not felt since before the 'incident' and its aftermath. Now she felt as if someone had come along and siphoned it off, leaving a painful void.

She took herself off to the kitchen for a while to calm down, to cool off, angry with Suzi for upsetting things, turning everything upside down and inside out. She put a butternut squash, bought from the supermarket, into the oven to soften the skin ready for peeling and chopping for one of her favourite soups, and imagined picking fresh squashes maybe even this summer and her spirits rose again.

As she busied herself with tasks – emptying the dishwasher, placing a frozen baguette into the hot oven, softening a chopped onion and spices in a pan with some olive oil – she could hear Suzi upstairs, having a bath, then making up a bed in the spare room. She would focus attention on her daughter when she came down, and guard against mentioning too much about her own life. She diced the squash and tipped the pieces into the pan, savouring the aroma, then made up some stock.

When Suzi finally entered the kitchen she said, "Everything all right? Bedroom OK?"

"Lovely," replied Suzi, briefly.

"I'm managing to actually produce something home-made, cause for minor celebration, I feel. I'm on the mend, I'm on the mend, I'm on the me-end …," she sang in a kind of off-key, operatic style.

Suzi nodded, arms folded. "Good. Fantastic …"

"But, how are *you*? Work OK?"

"Mum, before we eat, there's something I must tell you. I'm not actually all that hungry, to be honest …"

Kay froze. *The problem*. The reason for her visit. She was pregnant? Or ill? Which would be the more crushing news?

"I suspected last week-end … I was five days late and knew …"

Kay said nothing, waiting, with a wooden spoon suspended in mid-air, over her hot pan of sputtering, spicy soup.

"I did the pregnancy test when I got back on Sunday and ... it was positive. I'm pregnant." She spoke in a matter of fact tone, without emotion, which made it difficult for Kay to know how to respond, react, what to say. Better than illness, she decided, realising that sometimes you actually need to be put to the test to know your own feelings. Maybe Suzi was delighted? This was so unlikely, Kay was able to move on from that thought pretty smartish.

"OK. So how d'you feel about that, then?" she asked, to be sure.

"Not exactly over the moon ..." A deliberate understatement, Kay could tell.

"So, who's the father? I didn't know you were ..."

"That's the problem. I don't know ..."

Kay closed her eyes, feeling for a moment quite sick, the smell of the soup suddenly unbearable.

"You don't *know*?" repeated Kay back to her. "Surely, darling, you ..."

"I'm not in a serious relationship ..." Kay stirred the steamy gloop that had begun to thicken at the bottom of the pan. Recreational sex, is it, thought Kay, like drugs? Is this how our daughter has turned out, Marcus? She thought Suzi had more self-respect.

"It's not as bad as it sounds, Mum," said Suzi with a little dismissive laugh, as if this was no big deal. "I thought I should tell you. I mean, I could've just kept quiet, but knew I couldn't keep it to myself and I haven't even told any of my friends ..."

"Well, presumably you'll have to, eventually ..." said Kay, forcing a short, nervous laugh as she half-propped herself up against the kitchen table, but she could already see Suzi shaking her head. "What, you mean ...?"

38

"Well, I can't go ahead with it, can I?" she said, brightly. "Bring an unwanted child into the world? In my view, that's more immoral than … the alternative."

Would either of them come out with the word? Abortion? Yes, people had abortions for a variety of reasons, she wasn't inflexible about that, but …

"Pregnancies are often, shall we say, 'inconvenient'. Babies come along unexpectedly sometimes – and people manage, although I have to say it does sound as if you've been pretty careless … and that's putting it mildly. Oh, Suzi, I mean, didn't you take precautions? Apart from the fact that you are … sleeping around? I find this all very worrying … How can you not *know*?"

Suzi was pacing around the kitchen now, fiddling with the mug-tree, folding up the tea towel lying on the counter top, opening and closing the cutlery drawer for no reason.

"OK. I made a mistake – or two. Mum, this is not what I need right now," she said, suddenly still and looking straight at her. "I've fixed to have an abortion. It will happen as soon as possible. Believe me."

When she first received the news, Kay had wondered, if what her daughter was unconsciously, or maybe deliberately, seeking was persuasion to have the baby, assurances that she had her mother's support, emotional and practical, even financial, to keep it. But no, it was absolutely clear from the fiercely determined expression on her face, she had made up her mind.

"Suzi, it's your life."

Suzi heaved a big sigh. "I really wish I hadn't told you now. You've got enough on your plate. It's not as if there's anything you can do …"

"Well, let me know if there *is* some way I can help. Do you want me to come with you?" Surely, she must be there to support her daughter, yet Kay could not help thinking how problematic that would be, just getting to the station, struggling to the taxi rank at Waterloo.

"No, no, I'll be fine. I'm going private, don't need to stay overnight or anything ..."

"I'm glad you told me – I mean I guess if you hadn't I would never have known, but if I'd somehow found out later, I would have been sad that you didn't confide ..." She could feel she was rambling. "Are you absolutely sure?"

"Absolutely certain sure."

"Well, are you going to risk some of this?" asked Kay, forcing a smile, determined Suzi was not going to wreck her mood for a moment longer. "Come on, let's eat!"

Things were a little tense between them and Kay was not surprised when Suzi, after helping out with hanging curtains, pictures and mirrors, and moving around some furniture in the sitting room, decided to return to London that evening.

"Thanks for your help – can't think *what* I would have done without you," she said, giving her daughter a hug, as she was about to go through the front door to the taxi she had booked to take her to the station. "And let me know – how you get on." Suzi nodded and left, leaving Kay sure in the knowledge that, although she would always love her dearly, she would never feel quite the same about her daughter again. Not so much the casual sex – concurrent sexual partners, and how many for heaven's sake? But for her to have been so careless, almost flippant, about creating and then discarding new life, she found that deeply distressing.

The TV News' bleak view of the world, what with mayhem in Iraq, ASBOs and global warming, seemed to contribute to Kay's feeling of overwhelming helplessness. She wanted so much to be positive, to piece together the shards of her life. All I wanted was a pleasant retirement in the country, she thought, browsing around antique shops, joining an art class, friends round for tea, trips to the nearest theatre wherever that may be, testing out the local eateries at least once a week ... Her life seemed to be steering a course of its own, far removed from her plan.

But at least there was something where maybe she could take control, have some effect, important, she knew, for good mental health. She decided to seek out the Liaison Officer who had evidently given Natalie and her mission such grief, and give him a piece of her mind first thing on Monday morning.

4

When Kay woke up on Monday morning, she recalled her resolve of Saturday evening, but somehow could not summon up the requisite energy. The rigorous exercise regimen she had set herself was, she reluctantly acknowledged, making her body feel leaden and this feeling, combined with a head still swimming with homeless Gypsies and fatherless embryos, was not altogether conducive to feelings of repose or likely to motivate her into some purposeful activity. In other words she wanted to 'slob out', as Suzi would've put it.

A TV breakfast-time programme moved seamlessly into a chat show, followed by a bacon sandwich and toast and marmalade with coffee in bed, an indulgence she felt she was entitled to now and again. Then she picked up Laura Ashley's biography she had been meaning to read for about two years but was soon distracted by a pile of cards friends had sent wishing her well in her new home and reassuring her that they would be coming to stay in the summer. It gave her a nice warm feeling. Everyone needs people, she thought, to belong to a group of people and she must make sure she never loses touch ...

As would occasionally happen to her after one of her bad nights filled with nightmares, she had slipped into what she believed was called a 'duvet day'. By lunchtime she was beginning to feel more at one with the world, reminding herself how lucky she was to be alive. To think about the 'incident' wasn't morbid, or a sign of negativity, she felt. Rather it helped her to put things in perspective, such that she valued each and every day of recent years and relatively petty things did not seem to matter as they once did. Who cared that areas of the house were still like a skip and needed refurbishing, if she was fed and warm? So long as she could see, hear, eat, drink and otherwise enjoy robust health, what did it matter that one leg and one hip were not so good? To look back was a recognition that the rest of her life should be regarded as bonus years, a phase of life of which dear Marcus had been unfairly robbed, just when he was starting to make plans for retirement himself. He always said he would like to move to Scotland, close to his family, those that were still alive, with a second home in France, whereas she had no real inclination to move so far away from their daughters and friends. France, even with the very real attractions of fresh vegetables and vineyards, would be too hot for comfort during most of the summer, so she was left wondering where they would have ended up, had they been together. The fact that she had got her way was tainted with guilt, with the other awful, unbearable fact that somehow she was to blame for what happened forever hanging over her. Still she had the grimmest dreams from time to time, but she was learning to live with that. The reality of his violent death, her emotional *tsunami*, was gradually subsiding into a gentle ebb and flow, tidal waves knocking her back from time to time until calm and repose were once more restored.

Tonight there will be the second meeting in the village hall. Should she go? Should she get up now and have a bath? Speak to Suzi, even though her daughter seemed to be handling her unwanted pregnancy with a fearsomely independent spirit? Or call a few old friends to firm up some dates? Somehow decisions were difficult today. It was just one of those days. She wondered if Natalie had managed to get some Travellers to attend the meeting tonight and tried to call her but her mobile was switched off. She sent her a text.

Then she remembered about this Gypsy Liaison person. Yes, if she did nothing else today, she would call him. She really wanted to get a clear picture of the rights and wrongs of the Eviction.

After making enquiries at the main Council Offices switchboard, she was put through to Max Leatherson. She gave her name and went on, "I'm new to the area and would dearly like a better understanding of the situation regarding the Travellers who have recently moved in to Appley Green," she said.

"They are occupying land that is unauthorised, since they don't own it, no planning application has been even made, nor has it been provided as a transit site, so ..." He sounded much older than she had expected – possibly middle-aged. For some reason she had assumed he was of an age similar to Natalie.

"And where are they supposed to go to?"

"Currently there is a shortage of stopping off places, so all we can do is be tolerant and wait until we hear of a suitable place for them to go." Of course, she should have thought, this kind of mediation role would require a degree of maturity, a lot of life experience.

"But you've issued an Eviction Order."

"Yes. We were obliged to because claims by local residents showed that they breached the Code in a number of ways," he sighed, "so the Travellers've really done themselves no favours. I paid several visits, tried to negotiate in a reasonable way, as we take each case on its merits, until the matter is taken to Court. Thankfully, those days when six police cars turn up all guns blazing to turf two families off a piece of land, are a thing of the past – I hope! Anyway, it was decided not to enforce the Eviction – as yet, but ..."

After this he began to sound as if he were reading from a public relations hand-sheet, as he continued, his spiel liberally peppered with ameliorative terms like 'evaluation and agreement', 'preserve the peace', 'common humanity' and 'personal circumstances'. He was word perfect.

As he spoke, Kay's mobile received a message and she casually reached across to read it. It was from Natalie. "Have been arrested. Will call later." *Arrested?* She thought back to the item on the radio ...

Desperate to trip him up, she could wait no longer. "You undertake welfare checks I believe and no way would you attempt to evict a group of Gypsies if one of the women was in the last few weeks of pregnancy? Is that correct?"

"Absolutely. We have the Children Act to consider. Such checks were made."

"And yet a young woman *gave birth* on the very day you issued the Eviction."

There was a pause and she could hear a rustle of papers being turned over.

"Are you sure about this? I was never given this information apart from a rumour. No one from the site has come forward about it. How did you hear about the woman?"

She wasn't sure she wanted Natalie to get to hear about this phone-call. It would look as if she had not believed her, which was not the case.

"Oh, in the village," she replied, feeling she needed to be equipped with more information to argue effectively. "Will you be attending the meeting tonight? I don't recall seeing you there last week – as a spokesperson, I mean."

"Ah, I see. Natalie. To be honest, Mrs Brackenbridge, I have to be a bit wary of taking sides in a public place. My own parents were Romany Gypsies and frankly, I was ashamed of their behaviour recently at the site in question, although I know all too well that *Gorgios* are quick to accuse. I … I'm shocked by this news. I know these people. And this woman who you say gave birth?"

"Don't know any more, I'm afraid, but if you come along to the meeting … well, maybe you could get to the bottom of it. And Natalie could use your support. She seems to have the village and its dog against her …" and is in police custody as we speak, she stopped herself from saying.

"Mm. But that's my problem, you see. She's extreme and all credit to her, she is the Travellers' champion, always has been, but in my job, I have to be a bit impartial y'see …"

Kay had to smile and did wonder whether to pass on Natalie's news, but decided against this. "Yes, I do see.

Thanks for your help. I hope we meet, anyway – this evening."

"Thanks for your call and your interest."

Wondering, as the hall filled up, if Dunstan was somewhere amongst the tangle of folk, Kay noticed that on each seat was an agenda with names of the people on the stage, sitting behind trestle tables. But *where was Natalie?* Surely not still being held for questioning, thought Kay. After trying several times to contact her that afternoon she had conceded defeat. Now it agitated her to think that she should have made enquiries and gone along to support her, to vouch for her …

She looked at the agenda. There were some *big* names this time: the local Labour candidate, Dennis Corner, she read with some satisfaction; Elsie Randles, billed as a spokesperson from the Travellers; a policeman, Dave Martin, and, as Kay recognised as another small personal triumph, Max Leatherson, from the County Council. Dennis Corner had been voted to man the gavel to keep proceedings in order, he said, and opened the meeting with a speech *in support*, stressing Human Rights and the need to cater for families in the community, no matter of what ethnic group or culture. Devious little minx, thought Kay with a smile – no doubt helping to steer him into the position of Chair! He even aired his knowledge, moving on from the Conservative Party's 1994 repeal of the Caravan Sites Act of 1968, to quote chunks from history books on the Romany people and how they came to this country about six hundred years ago, originating from India.

He went on, "The Housing Act 2004 compels District Authorities to measure Travellers' accommodation needs and plans to meet those needs. The guidance from the government on this process is that a group of neighbouring authorities work together." Now that is interesting, thought Kay, new and well presented by a man who was used to giving speeches, but, frankly, some would find it all a bit dry.

She felt this meeting needed some fire and passion. It still needed Natalie.

Dennis Corner must have brought along a cohort of supporters, as there was an outburst of clapping from a cluster of people about halfway back in the hall.

Kay then sat up straight as she spotted Natalie discreetly making her way along the side of the hall to take her chair on the stage. She breathed a sigh of relief. It went without saying that the cheers would not have been for her arrival …

Dave Martin then explained the particular dilemmas faced by the police force and Max stood up repeating much of what Kay had heard on the phone. Wow, thought Kay, so far so good. What a turnaround! Her own allegiance was becoming more sharply defined.

The focus shifted to Natalie, who had had a quick confab with Dennis and was now bursting to speak. Unable to sit still, she sprang up from her seat as soon as Max had sat down. "Everyone, thank you for coming. Apologies for my late arrival – I was … detained. We still have to hear from Elsie, who is from the nearest authorised site at Upthill. No one from the unauthorised site would come forward, I'm sorry to say."

"We all know why!" called out a man in the front row. Why was it that as soon as Natalie appears, the temperature rises?

"Yes," she replied, gritting her teeth. "We do. Because they're terrified."

Sensing the first signs of disorder, perhaps, the politician stood up to defuse the situation.

"We shall certainly hear from Elsie, but we can take some questions now, from the floor."

"Hold on!" cried Natalie, "I need to say about the petition. The response was pathetic and outnumbered by another one …"

Kay groaned. Oh damn it. She had forgotten and she really intended to report the 'other one' to the police … so much for her 'duvet day'. She vowed to make more effort not to give in to these melancholic moods again. They were self-indulgent, unproductive.

But the policeman stood up. "If I could just intervene," he said, firmly but politely, "We stopped the anti-Gypsy petition, under the Incitement to Racial Hatred laws, but there were a good number of signatures on it, I have to say ... er, actually, no forget I said that." Kay raised her eyebrows as she observed him go red in the face, aware of the press, of the probable *faux pas* he had just uttered. "Just pointing out that I can confirm that the signatories did outnumber the one in support of the Travellers in question."

"Well, everyone, now's the chance to do something about it. Please, if you haven't signed, then please can you do it before you leave this evening, if you have an ounce of humanity in you!"

A man, probably in his fifties, tall, distinguished, at the back of the hall, had stood up to speak, opening with the statement, "As you are aware ..." then declaring himself to be the owner of land adjacent to the unauthorised site. Kay swivelled to see the person speaking with a rather gravely, upper-crust voice.

"Yes, sir," said the politician. Clearly this gent commanded respect.

"Every year, we go through this charade, as Travellers arrive from somewhere on their way to somewhere else ... I'm sorry, but I do feel that for these people their time is over. In the modern world there is simply no place for a nomadic way of life. Immigrants from Eastern Europe do the kind of work on the land that was once their sole province, flexible and ready to move wherever the work is, to work hard for small wages and glad of them."

Natalie jumped up, raising an arm, clearly mad at him. "Are you saying it's all right for *them*, but ..."

"*They* don't appear to demand to live in caravans around the countryside and on green-belt ..."

"That is so unfair! So unjust! Living in groups preserves the strong family tradition, you know that. It's their choice!

Their right! Our Travellers should have the support of the British people. Past generations of Gypsies have scraped together a meagre living, giving their cheap labour to agriculture. And rural crafts that once were actually needed. We should do everything to help them apply their transferable skills into other areas, not roll over and just give in ..."

"Natalie. Please." He paused and there was a silence as if any living thing in that room had temporarily yet indefinitely held its breath. Nothing stirred. He continued, "I know you would like me to open up one of my fields and wave the Travellers in with a big Welcome banner, but the fact is, as you very well know, I have no work for them and it would be illegal for me to have them on my land unless they are actively involved in working on the land. I simply have no produce that requires to be manually picked and I use contractors with highly sophisticated plant and machinery." His voice was ringing a faint bell in Kay's head.

"You could have held on to a few fields of potatoes, or strawberries, instead of turning the whole area into a yellow and purple patchwork of rape and linseed," Natalie threw at him.

"As an act of charity maybe, but as a realistic economic future for me – and, indeed for them, no ..."

"If they had somewhere to live they could ... I don't know ... modernise, develop recycling businesses, things that are more relevant to today's needs, but they have *nowhere to go, nowhere to live, nowhere to be – let alone belong.*"

Eventually, after a further five minutes, the politician-chairman coughed loudly and invited questions from the rest of the hall, which still seemed mesmerised.

Just as it dawned on Kay that the voice of this highly respected, eloquent, unyielding, and – now she could get a full squint at him standing – tweedily dressed, landowner, was the voice she had heard on the early morning radio programme when his words had been less restrained, she heard a woman next to her say to her companion, "It's always good sport to watch Natalie and her Dad go at it hammer and tongs ..."

Elsie Randles from the Upthill site stood up to speak but Kay was distracted. The face, of course, was the face that had been on the front page of the local paper. My God, how could a father be so far removed from his own child? She knew what it was to have a difference of viewpoint, a sharp exchange, a private family debate, and what the generation gap felt like, but this? It was quite bizarre, off the scale. Publicly speaking against his daughter, on the radio, in the press and now here in the bosom of their local community where everyone appeared to know them … and this was just the media she knew of, possibly the tip of a much wider, far-reaching awareness.

Once the meeting was closed, Natalie looked both angry and tearful as she strode to the back of the hall, passing close to where Kay was sitting.

Kay called over to her. "Natalie! What happened?"

She came over to Kay but did not respond with her usual bright smile. "I'm OK," she said. "Just a misinterpretation of my flyer – deliberate though, if you know what I mean. People can be not just thick, but actually, quite vindictive … anyway, thanks a lot for your help and support, Kay. See you later …"

People? 'Thick' and 'vindictive'. Was this somewhat harsh view of her opponents meant to include her own father?

5

Very soon Natalie would be heading off, and Kay anticipated something of an update winging its way in her direction, possibly an attempted handover of the reins, a passing of the baton, but she heard nothing. She sent her a text, asking what the outcome of the petition finally was. She was desperately curious to find out more about her father, too.

She decided to take a recce to try and find out more at the site. She would need to be discreet. It was a drizzly day, wet enough to put her scooter's waterproof cover on, with few people about. What had really sold the village to her was its absence of a main thoroughfare cutting through the community, as well as the stunningly picturesque heath and woodland that surrounded it. Other places she had investigated were ribbon developments or beautiful hamlets desecrated by the din and fumes of traffic. Steering her way along a road bordered by tall dark Scots pine trees and slender silver birches that formed a lacy canopy above her, and cocooned in transparent plastic, she passed bungalows and houses of varying styles and ages whose owners she planned to get to know better in due course. As she rounded a left bend, she realised this quiet B road must run parallel to the public footpath that ran alongside her back garden, which she decided to explore on the way back home.

It occurred to her, also, that if she did not manage to speak to Natalie to quiz her on this extraordinary relationship she had with her father, she would be forced to gossip in the village until she found out, or quite possibly die of curiosity. Talking about her behind her back did not seem ethical, somehow (besides which the grapevine was notoriously unreliable).

The site looked Spartan and drab, grey skies and rain clouds not helping and keeping everyone inside this time, but everything seemed peaceful, which made her wonder what all the fuss was about. Had they been occupying a station car park or school playing field, she could have understood the objections. Maybe some residents leading safe but isolated lives fantasised about taking to the open road with *their* extended family and felt jealous; on a bright sunny day, she could see it might have a certain appeal to restless, repressed spirits.

Then she began to consider how on earth the Travellers manage basic human needs, with no obvious facilities for washing bodies or clothes, as you might have on a campsite for the Caravan Club, for example or for touring caravans and tents in France, thinking back to when Marcus and she had taken Suzi and Claudia on such holidays when they were both quite young children. That was *le camping* in style, shower blocks, washing up places and even laundry rooms always spotless and well equipped, with plenty of hot water and space. And, above all the breeze would be balmy, the sun shone brightly and at night everyone felt tempted to sleep under the stars and be lulled to sleep by the rhythmic click of cicadas. But this was England in spring and the ground was muddy. The small caravans – trailers, she noticed Natalie would call them – were poor quality, although she had heard that on some permanent sites they could be very luxurious, soft, carpeted, pale upholstery, warm, with TV and all mod cons. She noticed they were linked together with cabling that seemed to run in one window and out of another along to the next. The connectivity gave them a kind of symbolic solidarity, strung together like a giant charm bracelet. All for one, one for all.

On the way home, she called into the Post Office.

"Good afternoon, Mr Patel, how's your petition coming along?" It gave her a warm feeling of belonging to a community to do this, although their cause did not fill her with passion.

"Always need more people to sign, but we keep trying. The pensioners will miss us when we're gone." Kay could see his point, and appreciate his fight for survival, but her business head suggested that to subsidise Post Offices to eternity might not be the best way forward. Maybe they could diversify? Maybe the local government could help set up a Day Centre for the village, which it did not seem to have, until it became self-funding, where pensioners could be assisted to do their banking online, as she did, and use cash-points. That might be a worthwhile investment to inject some life into an ageing rural community. She began to feel another 'good cause' coming on and gave herself a little shake. No, no, no. Stop it.

Before heading back she called in to the small library, surprised that the population could justify it. It was actually quite busy, with the librarian actively helping people. Their notice board was a joy to behold. Farmers' Market, Art classes, Local History Society, Car-Boot Sales, Chiropody, Yoga and Tai Chi for the over fifties, Line Dancing, Book club, even Baby-sitting services, Nurseries and a Playgroup, indicating that there were a few young adults living here albeit they would doubtless work outside the village. But all this potential activity was a welcome reminder of the kind of life she had planned. Then as her gaze moved to the right, to another pin-board headed **LOCAL NEWS**, she saw an array of laminated press-cuttings, not just recent but going back about five years, some actually from national broadsheets and no doubt revered as having put Appley Green on the map. She skimmed the headlines: *Countryside invaded by gipsies! Appley Green residents ready to do battle! Villagers watch helplessly as gipsies pour in.* Funny, she thought, how the estate agent had never mentioned this quaint rural tradition amongst all its many selling points: the 'soft swelling greensward that is the village hub'; the 'breathtakingly beautiful surrounding countryside, including a common with ancient trees'; 'antique shop'; 'art gallery and nearby garden centre'.

As she came away from the library, pockets bulging with leaflets, her mobile phone rang.

"Where have you been?" said the voice, accusingly.

"Out, around the village …"

"Well, I've been trying to get you …" It was Suzi, speaking as if her mother had no right to be out of the house, as if she should be just sitting around, waiting for her to ring – "…all day."

"You could have tried my mobile before. I don't usually switch it off, unless I'm in hospital – or meetings, which isn't very often these days …"

"OK. Well, anyway, it's all happening quicker than I thought …"

"Oh, darling, you've not miscarried have you?" asked Kay, thinking this would be an unexpected and unwanted emotional shock.

"No, no. If only. Went to the clinic and been given a pill. Have to go back in two days time for another drug which will *make* me miscarry."

"Are you all right?"

"Yes, yes, of course I am. Just relieved." Kay, too, had to silently confess she was experiencing feelings of relief. This baby, now an ovum barely fertilised, was not meant to be and it wasn't as if she was going to abort a twenty-week foetus with a familiar face. She had been a bit hard on her daughter, maybe. It was her attitude that upset her. Even now, she sounded very hard-nosed, severely practical, with no hint of emotion, doubt or regret for what might have been.

"Well, take care, my love. Look after yourself and keep me posted."

Kay took the route by public footpath, once she had worked out where it emerged on the common. The weather had cleared so she managed to fold up the sides of the cover and, ventilated by a sweep of fresh air from both sides, she felt more in touch with her surroundings. The footpath was unmade and quite narrow as she bumped along over clumps of stray heather and tufts of thick grass, her jacket sleeve occasionally brushing against tall nettles and scratchy brambles. But as she rounded a bend, she was faced by a steep dip, a hollow filled with evil-looking, peaty, black water. She stopped, literally, in her tracks. Now what? She rather pointlessly looked over her shoulder, in the full knowledge that she could not possibly turn around. Perhaps someone would come along and help her reverse the scooter, or she could phone someone. Thank goodness she had her mobile. But who? That was the question. Strangely she felt no panic, becoming used to these minor setbacks – like Suzi's careless attitude, the abortion, Natalie being arrested. How the rift between Natalie and her father could ever be healed, she could not imagine, but on the whole things seemed to find a logical resolution in the end. It was, as they say, 'all relative'. Surely most problems have a fitting solution and it was good that she was learning this, after the 'incident', that had ended in Marcus's death. Not everything had to end in tragedy.

Did she have Dunstan's number? She scrolled down the Names in her mobile. No. How far was she from her garden? She tried to gauge the distance but it was difficult, her mind had been all over the place as she travelled along, covering what might have been a third of a mile or a hundred metres. She could hear some kind of road traffic or engine noise, but it was hard to judge where this was coming from. Should she call an emergency service? If so, which one? This vehicle did not come with breakdown cover, and she would hardly qualify for police, ambulance or fire brigade. Or, did she? If she simply stayed put, she might soon become a medical case, or possibly suspected murder victim. She found herself laughing. Was this hysterics? She would shout, that's what she would do.

"Help!" she yelled as loudly as her lungs would allow. "Anyone there? Help!"

6

The dawn chorus and shafts of golden sunlight streaming in between too-small bedroom curtains combined to awaken Kay early next morning. By seven she had already made a cautious trip to survey the bottom half of the garden, managing with the aid of just her stick, which achievement infused her with great smugness. Such relatively athletic progress augured well for the future.

Nursing a cup of coffee now, she was looking through the conservatory window and narrowed her eyes. What was that on the old swing-seat? A heap of old clothes – or bedding? As she brought the somewhat formless shape into sharper focus, she could see it was actually a human being huddled there. Dunstan? Had he come in absurdly early, or slept there all night? Strange behaviour, indeed, especially after the argument they'd had as the sun went down.

She realised, once they had finally parted company at about nine o'clock when he had presumably gone home, she had been a bit hard on the poor chap. But he should have asked first. He should have sought permission and checked before … before … well, he had made such a good job of it that now she was filled with forgiveness and regret that she had shouted at him. Sworn even.

But she was stressed. She had been stuck on the path for … for about an hour, though it seemed like four. It was only afterwards, when he had finally rescued her and her trusty steed, when they were sipping hot chocolate and eating wedges of bacon and egg pie, both so hungry that she felt justified in making every mouthful maximise on calories, it was only then that she had given him the chance to explain.

He told her that he had grabbed an opportunity of using the hired machine for half a day for nothing, so took advantage.

But to rotavate a quarter of an acre of her garden without warning! So busy, so deafened by the noise, no wonder he had been blithely unaware of her cries. Having slept on it she wanted very much to tell him that, overall, by and large, all things considered, she liked his pro-active approach. She could see now that this is the way he will work best – to be given a fairly free rein, using his initiative, taking responsibility. The debate they had last night, both tired and cross, did not end close to this understanding. He must have left feeling that his heroic efforts to pluck her from a very uncertain future in the dark, drizzle and mud of the foot-path no more than fifteen metres from her own garden, must have gone unrecognised, unappreciated. Of course, she did thank him profusely for this out-of-hours act of chivalry, but when she realised what he had done to her land – without permission – she shot him down with ill-formed accusations of exceeding his remit. He had gone too far. It's not as if they had previously agreed on the final shape, design or boundaries of the plot. For him to assume control in this had felt like a stab in the back, another symptom of her failing retirement plans. Above all, she needed to be in charge of her own destiny, her own body. She needed the security of steering her own life – to plan in the desired direction.

But now – now, she wanted, more than anything, to offer both forgiveness *and* apologies. She had been wrong and she must make some requital in the form of fresh coffee and toast which she would take out to him here and now, still puzzled as to why he was taking a kip in the garden, in *her* garden, so early. He must've been up with the larks.

She approached cautiously, pushing a trolley along a crazy-paving path that bordered the lawn. It was bumpy, unlike the even slabs skirting the house, and the coffee was sloshing in the *cafetière*, two large breakfast cups rattling, the hand towel upon which she had nestled them, becoming splattered with milk. There came a point at which she had to stop, the wheels would not go round on the long, wet grass.

So focused was she on the tricky nature of this manoeuvre, longing for the day when she could stride out bearing a loaded tray, that she was no more than three metres away from the swing-seat, when she finally looked up. Three unknown, round faces with pink cheeks greeted her with staring, frightened eyes. Genuinely startled, Kay gasped. "Oh," she said, "I … I thought …"

The older face belonged to a girl, a teenager Kay guessed, who removed the brown and red scarf she had wound round her head and neck. A mane of curly, golden locks tumbled out onto her shoulders, wide eyes like polished chestnuts darting around, as if she was looking for a way out, a quick escape route. The small child and smaller toddler, possibly both boys, grinned at Kay and, without hesitation, tried to break away to come over to her, but the girl's arms reached out anxiously to pull them back towards her. The children, rather than reassured by this gesture, seemed to interpret it as one of alarm, their smiles retracting and frowns appearing on their little foreheads.

"Sorry," said the girl, with an embarrassed smile that brought two dimples to her cheeks. "We were just … takin' a rest. These two dropped off to sleep …" She sat up with the agility of youth, quickly folding and rolling up the coarse blanket that had covered them.

Kay could recognise distress when she saw it. "It's all right. I thought you were my gardener … from the house I couldn't make out what … who … and there's three of you!"

'Goldilocks' bit her lip. "Mm," was all Kay heard. As Kay watched her gather her rucksack and blanket together as if to go, she was wondering how this rather wild looking trio came to be fast asleep in her garden on this sunny but damp, spring morning. Gypsies sprang to mind, but what could have brought them here? She did not want to jump to any conclusions.

"Well you're welcome to share this coffee with me. I could get some milk for the children if you like. That is, if you have time to stop. It's a lovely morning," said Kay.

Three pairs of eyes gawped at the tray. The girl swallowed and the two children went very still, clearly understanding.

"Well, if you're sure …"

Kay couldn't wait any longer. "Look, my love, have you been here all night? I mean, are you all OK?" The girl shrank back in the seat, hugging herself and said nothing. Softly, softly, thought Kay. "My name is Kay," she offered, waiting for a response, but none came.

"Me – I'm Tom," said the little boy, the older of the two, probably about four, pointing to his own stomach to identify himself. He had short brown hair and intensely blue eyes. "S'my baby brother, Jason. He's two." He kissed his little brother, who grumbled then chortled. Now cherubs came to mind … The girl told him to "Shush." "*Kek pukker nixies*," she urged them.

"Adorable. Are they yours?" asked Kay, wondering what she was saying to them in this strange unrecognisable language.

"Well, o' course they're mine! Who else d'you think they'd belong to? You fink I *nicked* 'em?"

"No, no, no … of course not. It's just that you look too young to be the mother of two children. I thought you might be an older sister or … See now, I have a problem with my legs. If you go through that door over there," she said, pointing to the back door with its small stone porch, "you'll find the kitchen through the lobby, on the left, and there's milk in the fridge, in the door ."

The unnamed girl had frozen, she was listening so intently. "Right. Right," she replied nervously. Am I being naïve, stupid, wondered Kay, wanting to prove that I trust this stranger to go into my home? Imagine what Suzi would say? "Mum … and after all that's happened, how *could* you?" All the brochures she'd read on security in the home and the entirely plausible stories potential intruders would spin at the threshold to gain a step through it. A tape recording of a crying baby on the doorstep to persuade the home owner to open up, was one astonishing method she had heard. Maybe her sensible head should be telling this person, unwilling to even say who she was, to clear off her land, but her heart was looking at someone who needed help. To simply send them on their way was not an option. Besides curiosity was killing her.

The young mother set off, then turned back to include Tom and Jason in the trip. Perhaps, thought Kay, she was afraid they might talk in her absence. There was an aura of secrecy, of fear, about them. After all three of them had removed their trainers and stared warily at the doorway; the girl looked over her shoulder before going any further, and called out to Kay, "Should I bring the whole carton?"

"It's in a bottle. Yes."

"Oh ..."

"Bring some cups or mugs, they're on a mug-tree ..."

"A what?"

Soon they re-appeared, each of them clutching a mug and the girl carrying the unopened bottle of milk.

As they sat down again, and Kay passed them toast, and poured out the milk and coffee, the girl said. "And I am married and everything ... in case you're wondering ..."

"No, I wasn't wondering. These days, it doesn't seem to have much to do with having children ..."

The girl's eyes widened as though Kay had uttered a foul profanity or personal insult, but she said nothing. The two infants stuffed toast into their mouths as if they hadn't eaten in weeks and the milk had vanished already. Kay had to chuckle at them.

"More?" she asked.

The girl stood up. "No. Really, you've been kind. Really kind."

"Where do you live?" The silence spoke volumes and again, Kay felt that a certain directness might get results. "Are you from the Travellers, on the Common?" Then everything changed. The large brown eyes filled with tears and she drooped, looking totally sapped of energy, strange to see in someone so young. Kay went on, "I have two daughters, probably a bit older than you, I should think ... Well, how old are *you*?"

She sniffed. "Nearly twenty."

"You look tired. Were you here all night?" The girl nodded. "Must've been cold."

"Not too bad."

"What's your name?"

She sighed. "Lena. But you mustn't let on, mustn't tell anyone you've seen me, or they'll be after me and ..." Suddenly, the words were coming out fast, her voice hoarse with emotion. "I had to *jass. Jal.* Run away. I've brought shame on my family, on my community and can *never* go back. If they find me, they'd prob'ly kill me ..."

People say these things. They don't mean it. Kay put an arm round Lena's shoulders, trying to steady herself so she did not fall over, taking Lena and the two children crashing down with her, which she felt would not be helpful. "Come on, let's go inside, so you can have a bath, a sleep and whatever else you need."

"But, please, you mustn't tell anyone you've seen us. Do you truly promise? I really mean it. My life – me *chavies'* ... my children's lives – could be freatened," she urged, her face suddenly looking older.

However much she tried to chivvy them along the garden path towards the house, they held back nervously, the two little boys holding onto their mother's legs. She was surprised at the way Lena was dressed, stereotypically traditional, her long cotton skirt, of red patterned fabric – perhaps more hippie than Gypsy, but not akin to the style of young women her age in general. Jewellery as well, she noticed.

Kay held out her hand invitingly. "Let's see what we can find shall we?" she said, desperately trying to think of what she had that could be of interest. Two very young children as unexpected guests was the very last thing she had provided for in her state of both clutter and excessive space. The ample house, with its exposed beams and tall brick chimneys, was still in considerable disarray and jam-packed with potentially lethal hazards. Not 'child-friendly'.

It took them a long time to climb the stairs to the bathroom, the children on all fours as if scaling the North face of the Eiger. "They never been in a house before," explained Lena, who was clutching the banister rail rather like an old woman, one hand lifting her skirt to clear the steps.

Kay thought it might seem rude to express her shock at what Lena had just said. In this day and age, in the UK … Then her mobile told her she had received a text and she fished it quickly from her bottle-green linen jacket pocket. It was from Claudia.

To save making her own laborious way in their wake, she said, "The bathroom is down the end of the corridor on the right, third door along. Help yourself to towels in the cupboard under the wash-basin."

"Thank you," came the chorus as Kay retreated to read the message.

For six months Claudia had been travelling. After the death of her father, for a full year she had tried to carry on as normal with her teaching, but it was all too much, officially diagnosed as posttraumatic stress. She told Kay that to distance herself, geographically as well as emotionally, for a while would be best and Kay agreed to help fund her trip. It was the least she could do. The texts or e-mails began regularly enough, every two days at least, but then reduced to once a week until now, erratically she heard from her around twice a month, when she had network or access to an Internet café. The last time she'd heard from Claudia, then in Thailand, her friend was suffering from an evil tummy bug and she'd hoped she wasn't going to go down with it too … Kay was relieved to read now that she had made contact with one of Kay's former clients, a software developer, and his family who lived in Singapore and had eaten a meal together and got on well. "Oldest son fit", her text said. Nice. Kay felt good. Nothing raised her spirits more than these little networking strategies, bringing people together. It gave a sense of cohesion, of belonging to the global village and of connecting with the younger generation.

It was all very quiet upstairs and she decided to go and check how they were getting on. She could hear some movement in the box-room destined for conversion into a second en-suite shower-room. It was just opposite the main bathroom. She peeped in. The two boys were on the floor, sitting very still, awestruck, wrapped up together in Lena's old blanket, which looked as if it had been ripped off the back of a horse. They looked up and gave Kay heart-melting smiles, just moving at the sound of Lena calling out to them, "You stay there until I say. Don't you touch the *rawnie's* things …" Poor little loves, thought Kay, I must find something for them to play with, and more to the point I must find out what's going on in their lives, past, present – and future.

The bathroom door was ajar, so Kay knocked perfunctorily and gently pushed the door open. "Everything OK? Did you find …?" but her jaw fell as she saw the blood. Her fluffy white towels streaked with a lot of dark blood. The sight of it made the hairs on the back of Kay's neck rise and her own blood drain from her face down, somewhere deep into her groin. Pictures of Marcus flashed up in her head and she wanted to retch. Amazing how instantly the brain can make these emotional reactions. Connections. Associations. Was it chemical or hormonal? Not the conscious mind that's for sure, more intuitive, although already her analytical head had switched on, hard at work.

Lena looked so fearful, so worried, so guilty, that Kay hesitated, unsure of what to say or what to do. Some kind of acute suffering was in those bitter-chocolate-brown eyes and she knew she must be strong for the poor girl's sake.

"*Dordi, dordi*! It's all er … well, what the old folks call *mokadi*. Dirty! … I'm *ladged* – sorry – a mess I've made. I'm so embarrassed. My time of the month – came a bit early. Caught me by surprise, like."

Some sort of wound, *more* like, thought Kay. She was covering up, there was something about her voice that did not sound quite genuine. Had someone cut or stabbed her? But then Kay saw her hands shaking as she stood at the wash-basin, trying to rub out horrendous stains from underclothes. Menstrual blood.

"Oh, don't worry about that. I don't have the right things, but never mind ... we can sort that out. Can you manage with a few panty liners – I think I have some of those, and tissues, for now, and some spare knickers – that *might* fit." Kay laughed to try and lighten things while her emotions were now flying off to Suzi who tomorrow would be shedding her fertilised egg. The picture in her head made her feel sick and she dismissed it, or at least shelved it to be retrieved at a more suitable moment.

Lena was shaking her head, blushing bright pink. "I feel so ashamed. This is terrible, but ..."

Kay put her hand to her mouth. "Did you leave in such a hurry?" she asked, softly.

Then came the sobs, huge, heaving, stomach wrenching sobs that would prevent any words from being uttered for a long time. Some feelings of panic rippled through Kay at this point as she rushed to Tom and Jason who must've been able to hear. She didn't know who to tend to first but decided that maybe Lena would prefer to be left for a while anyway, and it wouldn't do for the children to come along and investigate the noise. Promising herself she would set up a toy-box for the odd visitor with children in tow (and future, hypothetical grandchildren), she stumbled, as fast as her leg and hip would allow, to her bedside cabinet where she had some pencils and notebooks. It wasn't much, just a distraction in the absence of building bricks, small plastic animals or cars. When her girls had been small she always kept them occupied – idle hands find mischief, she'd always say. She went in to the boys again, but need not have bothered. They had curled up together like puppies and fallen asleep, damp hair framing their faces in such an angelic fashion, Kay had to take deep, controlling breaths. It fleetingly struck her how fast she could move when she had to … which, had circumstances pushing her been different, might have flooded her grey matter with all the endorphins she could handle.

Back in the bathroom, Lena was lying in the foetal position on the tiled floor, head buried in her arms. Kay touched the door handle to make a noise, thus announcing her presence, then very softly went towards her and, almost whispering, said, "You must tell me … what has happened. What about your parents? Can I phone them?" Lena shook her head, still not looking up. "Someone else?"

"No one ," came the muffled reply.

"But you Travellers – family is everything. Even I know that – an ignorant *Gorgio* …"

At that, Lena unfurled herself and sat up, regarding Kay with some bemusement, her cheeks glistening with tears.

"If you can tell me your problems, then perhaps I can help you. If you don't, then," she shrugged, "how can I?" She gently steered her through to the most decent spare bedroom, already used by Suzi, within earshot of Tom and Jason. It was a good size, fitted out with two single beds, a cream sofa bed, sets of pine drawers, bookcases, wardrobe, small table and an en-suite bathroom leading off, somewhere either of her daughters could be almost self-contained on their sporadic visits.

Lena seemed unaware of her surroundings, lost inside her own head. Once they had sat down, Kay waited patiently until eventually, Lena said, her chin trembling, "So much, I don't know where to start …"

7

Perhaps it was timely that Natalie called to see Kay when she did that morning. Lena was overwrought and tired, eyelids heavy, and Kay suggested she have a rest before they sit down and talk over a hot meal. Although not the most obvious time of day to take a nap, Kay suspected that her sleep during the previous night on the damp, mouldering swing-seat would have been less than solid. Clean, dry, safe and warm, she soon fell into a deep sleep in the spare room, with the two boys tucked up in the other single bed.

Kay had caught sight of Natalie out of the landing window and knew she had little time to organise her 'guests' before going downstairs to let her in. Moreover, her plans to nip out to the chemist in the village were thwarted.

Her eyes were drawn to the bulging folder Natalie was carrying. "Can't stop," said Natalie, as she sped through the hall, making her way through to the sitting-room, "but thought we'd ..."

"You're off soon then?" Kay cut in.

"Away this evening, but we can keep in touch once I'm back from holiday. Uni's not a million miles away."

"So what's the situation now?"

"Travellers have gone. Moved on to another site ... unauthorised, of course."

"Where? They were still there yesterday!"

"Yep, overnight. Disappeared. They're good at that. It's their way. They'll be heading out to wherever they get to hear there's a car park or patch of land they can spend another couple of weeks or so. They know they're not welcome here."

66

"It must be hard. I mean, I know that in one way they want to be travelling to where they might seek work, but not to be forced like this, when they might find nowhere and no guarantee of earning any money. How can they re-organise themselves or ever plan for the future. Children's education? All that sort of thing …" Kay was shaking her head.

"Exactly. They need proper transit sites."

Kay laughed. "Yes, I know. Sorry, didn't mean to be preaching to the converted. What did you think of the meeting …?" she probed gently.

"What I saw of it – no surprises. Same every time. You'll need to work on Dennis Corner – he's good. On the ball."

"Yes, this more recent legislation is encouraging …" agreed Kay. "But, it seems that it's local residents who pose the real problem …."

"Yep." Natalie nodded. "Gypsies should stop *there* – wherever, out of sight, out of mind – never *here*. That's pretty much how people see it."

"What about that landowner? The one with the *same surname* as you?"

Kay folded her arms and gave her a reproving glare.

"Oh, what, my *father*? Oh, yeah, of course, you've seen him and what an ass he is. But if you can work your magic on *him*, now that *would* do it, it really would!"

"But, Natalie, your father? I mean, how can you have such different opinions and, wasn't he on the radio, talking about you? Wasn't that him?"

"So I'm told, although I didn't hear it. And it was him that got me arrested – well, you know, questioned. He never gives up … anyway …" she sighed, astoundingly unfazed, "Must go."

"Really? He did that to you?" Conceding that it is par for the course that parents and young adult children should have spats, she found this public exposure somewhat extreme.

Natalie shrugged. "Well, not arrested exactly, just questioned, but the police know me, they know I'm not, for fuck's sake – excuse me – inciting hatred against minority groups. I mean, how bloody ridiculous would that be?" Natalie's voice and language were getting stronger by the minute and Kay remembered the sleeping trio upstairs.

"Tea? Coffee? I have some home-made-from-the-bakery carrot cake – *to die for*, as you youngsters say ..."

"Sounds very tempting but I'm *out of here*, as we youngsters say ...! Thanks for your help, Kay," she said, giving her an enveloping hug, "you're a star!"

As soon as she closed the front door, Kay heard sounds of movement from the landing. She went to the foot of the wide stairway, just lightly touching walls and furniture to keep her steady, taking a moment to wonder at her progress. Maybe she should have a symbolic bonfire, a pyre to cremate all her various walking aids ... or, not wishing to be wantonly wasteful, more sensibly take them to a charity shop.

Slowly, weirdly, with feet less steady than hers, the three of them were making their way down the second flight of stairs. Tom then decided to slide down on his tummy, with little Jason doing a bottom shuffle from one step down to the next, giving himself a very bumpy ride. Lena, rucksack slung over one shoulder, blanket tucked under an arm, was hanging onto the oak banister as she made her way down after them.

"A friend called round – I hope we didn't disturb you."

"We need to get going anyhow ..."

"Your group have left the area ..."

Lena stood still, looked up, bit her lip and gave an involuntary yelp, "Oh! They've gone ..." Raising her chin, she added, "That's good."

"Good? But where does that leave you? Please ... come downstairs, and at least stay the night. You were going to tell me ... your plans ... so maybe I can help you," Kay reminded her.

She didn't then seem to need much persuading, but was uneasy, eyes darting around, fingers drumming her mouth. Once sitting down in the lounge, Lena said, "Why would you want to help me?"

"Call me mad … No. Lena, I can't let you just go off. You told me earlier that you are afraid of something. Somebody?"

No response. Kay decided to light a fire, to make the room cosy. It was still chilly outside and she had not turned on the central heating. What she called the 'lounge' was a small reception room she had not yet used, perhaps because she had strewn rugs on the floor, throws and cushions on the armchairs and sofas that had once graced her old Richmond home, a town house. It contained more reminders of her past than any other room, but with its beams and small leaded light windows, it had all the potential of being a snug bolthole. She also felt it might ease the tension to keep busy, to be actively doing something, so Lena didn't feel she was being put in the spotlight. There was little hope of her opening up until she felt comfortable and relaxed.

"I have an injury, on the mend I'm pleased to say, but still have trouble bending down. Could you just pull out one of those firelighters from the pack in that cupboard there? They're wrapped so won't make your hands smelly."

Kay carefully got down on her knees to make a fire in the inglenook fireplace, using the tongs to lift each piece of coal from the brass scuttle and then her hands to reach for a couple of logs from a basket.

Lena did not respond to any of this, apart from getting the firelighter. No curiosity about her injury, no wish to come out of her cocoon. She was totally pre-occupied with her own problems, private problems.

"Can you tell me why you ran away? That might be the best place to start."

There was a long pause, but Kay waited, taking time over her task at the grate. Eventually, Lena said, "They … oh, *dordi, dordi* … they think I did a bad thing, so bad they'll never let me back." She paused and muttered to herself, "It *traishes* me to death …" then louder, "That's it. 'S all you need to know."

"What about your mum?"

Lena shook her head. "*Mullad*," she said softly.

Kay gave her a quizzical look. "No matter what you've done, or what they think you've done, wouldn't your mother support you?" Tom came over and squatted next to her, wide eyes watching her light a match.

"I can do that," he said, proudly. He pointed.

"Can you? Well, don't ever do it unless a grown up says it's all right, OK?"

He nodded solemnly. "Burn fingers."

Kay gave him a hug, biting back the words, "Burn house down ..."

"Mind what the *rawni* says, Tom," said Lena, gently touching him on the shoulder. "My Mum died when I was about seven. Can just remember her."

"We use *coshties* ...when we light the real *yog* outside ..." supplied Tom, still watching her every move critically.

Kay gave him a puzzled look. "Sticks, he means firewood," said Lena, patiently.

"Oh, I see, that's a good idea. Perhaps I should use *coshties* too next time. You could collect some for me ... " she turned again to Lena. "Your mother, I'm sorry ... Father, then?"

"Dead too ... my mother got some kinda blood poisoning after she cut her finger cookin', and then my Dad, a couple a years on, from an accident with some farm machinery ..."

Kay frowned. "Machinery?"

"Yeah. He'd never been trained to use it or nothing, and pretended he could, to get the work and then somefing big dunno what fell on him an' crushed his back ..."

"That is so tragic," said Kay, quite appalled, but trying not to let emotions prevail at this point. After a pause, she asked, "So, what about brothers and sisters?"

"I was their first and only, brought up by grandparents who died not long ago. Just got ill and died from, like, old age an' 'at. So I was about fourteen and my Mum's sister let me have a trailer close to their family."

"What about her then? Can't you turn to your aunt?"

Lena shook her head. "Me Auntie Vera? Nah. She never liked me. She's got seven of her own to look after. I married the *mush* … the man one of her girls had her eye on and I knew she fancied him. Mind you, she can 'ave 'im. She's welcome." Kay was burning to know what she had done that was so wicked. "He was right *roshto*. So angry, he said he'd kill me …"

"Yes, but he probably didn't mean it. People say things, especially where those close to them are involved. Love, passion, anger – they get so entwined, all mix-muddled up, don't they? Even men can get over emotional …"

"But if he did mean it? Bit of a risk, uh? He's, he's … I do …but, " she stumbled over her words, wringing her hands, which Kay took to mean that she still had deep feelings for him, "but, oh *dordi,* he's got a hot temper. I'll have to keep hidden 'til I'm sure they're well away from here. Can we stay in your shed?" She looked at Kay very directly, even though her eyes were swimming with tears again.

Kay blinked. "Do I have a shed?"

"Yea. Down far end, by old dung-heap. I dunno what's in it but …"

"No, no. You can stay here until we sort out something for you …"

"What. Stay in the *kennel* … I mean house?" She said this as if it were the moon. Kay wondered if she'd heard her right.

"I have all this space, with one daughter millions of miles away, and the other so busy I shall hardly ever see her, and friends who haven't organised their diaries yet, and can wait if I ask them to anyway. I think your need is greater …"

"We can't do that. Stay here?"

"A house. Yes."

"I mean, it's like charity …"

"Not at all. You can help me. I have plenty of jobs you could do, if you don't mind a bit of tidying … No, you'd be … you'd be doing *me* a favour. But, in time, is there another group you could join? Another group of Travellers?"

Lena gave a derisory laugh. "No-o. Joseph'd find me quick as lightnin' …"

71

It was beginning to dawn on Kay exactly what she had on her hands, or what she might have. Part of her wondered if Lena had done something actually criminal, despite her denying it. After all, who wouldn't plead innocence, in the circumstances? Maybe *she'd* killed somebody. It must've been something quite serious.

"You know there are places – refuges, they're called, for women who are victims of domestic violence."

A cry came from Lena, like that of a small wounded animal. "I couldn't do that. That would be like lots of strangers, in a house, sharing stuff, nasty people. No. No. I'd sooner just travel round on foot and sleep rough like a hedge *mumper*. In fact," she said, defiantly, "yes, that's what we'll do. We can survive somehow, don't you worry about that ..." She stood up and reached for the two boys, seriously intending to walk off.

"But you have no money ..."

Lena pointed to her necklace and earrings, possibly white gold studded with diamonds, if they were the real thing. "I can hawk these, for a start, get some *lolli* for 'em quick..."

"They're beautiful. Were they a gift?"

Lena nodded but offered no more information.

"No," said Kay, speaking fast, desperately thinking how to stop her. "If you do that ... It's not fair on your little boys. Your money would soon run out. No proper shelter for them, or meals or place to sleep, or wash ... I ... Lena, I shall inform the authorities." She suddenly realised what power she had over this defenceless girl and her two children and it did not make her feel good.

"What? Who?" she said, her eyes round. "Police? Council? I'd not do anything against the law!"

Was there a law against vagrancy? Would such a lifestyle breach child protection laws? Child neglect? What would Social Services make of it, she wondered? "You'd all be so vulnerable. And for how long could you survive, without the support of your people? You must stay here. For now. But I still want to understand."

They were interrupted by a knock on the front door and Kay thought it might be carpet fitters who had said they would be calling to measure up some of the rooms downstairs. In theory, she was excited at the prospect of this, but inwardly groaned as she realised how much practical upheaval this would cause, both before and during the work.

"Ah! Sorry – I'll need to see to that, quickly. Would you like the TV on?" Kay wondered if they had TV in the trailer, their old home.

The two children looked up, clearly understanding, Tom instantly reaching for the remote control. What a strange mixture of innocence and worldly wisdom, mused Kay as she left them to her devices.

When she opened the door, a spindly woman, with white hair, stood with a clipboard and smiled beamingly. But it was one of those beatific smiles that Kay detected had been pinned on with facial muscles twitching from the effort of keeping it in place. She wore a bottle green, sensible kilt, topped with a sage, cashmere jumper and sheepskin gilet, paisley scarf loosely draped around her neck behind which was just visible a single, understated string of pearls. She was, in short, stereotypical middle-England and proud of it, making Kay realise how distant she was from that *persona* herself. In fact, the appearance of this woman made her feel quite bohemian, with her jeans, black tee-shirt with *No Fear* inscribed across her 36 inch bosom, trainers, and denim boxy jacket that was probably designed for a much younger person. But, at the risk of being labelled the proverbial mutton dressed up as lamb, she usually opted for an off the wall, arty style, long skirts or jeans, bold or dark colours (unless pure white), silk scarves, beads, all good quality but not stuffy. Since being forced into being accessorised by various orthopaedic aids, she had veered as far from the Saga convention as she had dared. Her aim was to offset the possible inference that this image might carry as one of infirmity and general wobbliness of mind and body that, she had witnessed in hospital, can come as part of the seniority package.

There was a strong whiff of perfume, like roses, and Kay noticed her face looked as if it had been plastered, left to dry in the sun, then powdered with flour. Make-up, she felt, was a necessity, but only to try and deceive the onlooker into believing there was some vestigial bloom of youth, not to look as if you were a transvestite or about to go on stage. My God, how uncharitable am I becoming, thought Kay? What chance am I giving this poor woman, who has done me no harm and deserves none of this? Am I becoming judgemental against my own sex and, in the foreseeable future, my own age group?

"Good afternoon," said the woman. Kay checked her watch. It had just turned noon. But what a stickler.

"Goodness – how time flies," said Kay, followed by a closed mouth smile, as sincere as she could make it, not sure if this person not yet worthy of an open one. "Good afternoon to you. What can I do for you?"

"I'm sure you'll be aware of the terrible times we have with the … er … *Traveller situation*," she said, her voice emphasising the words yet almost dropping to a whisper, as if she would rather avoid contaminating her mouth. Rather ironic, thought Kay, bearing in mind the fact that she was harbouring three of that number about three metres away from where this good villager was standing.

Ah, the clipboard, thought Kay, her gaze fixing on it now. "May I see what this says?"

"Of course, of course … my name is Nancy, by the way, short for Bernice," and she extended a veiny hand which Kay clasped in a firm handshake.

"Lovely to meet you, Nancy. Kay. Kay Brackenbridge." She could not ask her in, for obvious reasons, but needed to read this through here and now. There were a lot of words and her eyes slipped easily into skim-read mode she had regularly used in her PR and Marketing past, thereby absorbing vast amounts of technical information in order to render it down into something more palatable for the average software user to understand. Even now, out of habit, her mind was doing a *précis* of the acreage of densely-packed, single-space text, breaking it up into pithy paragraphs, inserting punchy sub-headings ...

The usual spiteful *clichés* were threaded together with little thought. Did these people think they were above the law, that 'democratic freedom of speech' actually *meant* that in this fraught politically correct, modern world? Against any other ethnic group, it would be deemed racially vindictive.

"I thought this petition had been stopped by the police," said Kay, passing it back.

"Oh, I don't think so. Why would they? We retired professional people – we always try to stand up for our rural way of life and ... well, you know, we just hope it will do some good. I'm sure you sympathise," she said. "Maintaining standards and so forth." Kay concluded that this must be yet another one that had sprung up spontaneously. This village really needs to get its act together.

"Well, actually my sympathies probably lie in a different direction," replied Kay, choosing her words carefully. No way would she support this, but she had no wish to be hostile towards this elderly soul who thought she was doing a socially responsible act on behalf of her fellow residents. "I can't add my name to this ..."

"Oh! Really?" Nancy said, genuinely taken aback. "Well, you do surprise me."

"Oh good. Well, I'm sorry but I must go – million things to do. Please excuse me," and she closed the door.

She returned to her sitting room to find her new charges glued to the television, watching a daytime soap.

"These people are so disgustin'," commented Lena. "House-dwellers. I shan't never, ever become like them. They have no morals."

This did not strike Kay as the best segue into a conversation upon which this young nomad's immediate comfort and well-being could hinge. This refugee-on-the-run had nowhere to go, no one to turn to, no regular income of any kind, was in need of 'feminine products', and if she tried to leave, as Kay had told her, she would inform on her. From her side, after all, it was not looking too good.

Yet somehow she liked this pride that would suddenly elevate the young woman into another world. It was a prickly independence of spirit she could relate to.

She turned channels to find CBeeBies and led Lena over to the other end of the room, where there was a quiet corner, a small sofa and desk.

"What's your happiest childhood memory?" asked Kay, on a sudden whim, as they sat down. Let's try a positive approach. Let's bond.

Lena's face lit up. "So many. When you're a little un, everything's simple," she said, "even without a Mum and Dad. I had me cousins and others in the group. We all looked out for each other ... One night Maria, a pal o' mine, was celebratin' her engagement, before being *rommed*, and at the party they arranged a *karaoke* night." Such a fusion of cultures, mused Kay, with a smile.

"Did you sing?"

"I did."

"How old were you then?"

"Eight. It was the best evening of my life."

"Did you ever do it again?"

"No. The local people complained and the police came. We never *dared* do it again." She giggled. "It was *very* noisy."

"I bet it was! Do you like music?"

"Me Mum could *gil* ... was a real singer, so I'm told, and me Dad could play the violin and piano accordion – not at the same time! They did all the old Gypsy *gillies* ... songs."

Kay raised her eyebrows – two more unbelievable stereotypes all within the hour. She now had a picture of large, gold-hoop earrings, a florally-painted wagon, – no, she corrected herself, a *vardo*.

"Some country 'n' western songs I did, an' old favourites like *Will there be any Travellers in Heaven?* You know it?" Kay confessed she did not. "My Mum used to sing it. Everyone clapped and hugged and kissed me. They said I was really good and stuff. I felt miles tall and for days after everyone would come in my trailer and ask me to sing for them and tell me I should sing at festivals, even be a pop star. But then, it all died away. People forgot. You know." She shrugged.

"What's your husband called?"

"Joseph." Her eyes went soft and dreamy.

"And what about *your* engagement. Wasn't that pretty special?"

She raised her chin and looked away. "I told you. Vera, my aunt, she was against it, 'cause her Chrissie thought she had her future all set and rosy with my Joseph. It was all in 'er 'ead. So, no one to celebrate, 'cept on his side. *They* were in favour and made it all 'appen, so then I moved to be with his family. We were promised to each other and I just shifted me trailer round to their pitch."

Kay seized on this. "So, why can't you go back to them?"

"No, no. Can't. Can't possibly, ever. They'll be looking for me, though, I know that. Him and his brothers. He'll want the boys."

"Did you rely on Joseph totally? For money?"

"Course. Husbands always provide, don't they? These days women can't get so much from hawkin' like they used to do. They get shouted at, turned away."

"What have you done – I mean, what do they think you've done that's so *wrong*?" Kay now felt like shaking her by the shoulders to make her talk, she was so frustrated. But to shout and demand and throw a tantrum would, she knew, be futile. Patience would pay in the end. She had a suspicion. "Were you unfaithful to your man? Was that it?" she asked, softly.

Hot tears were welling up, about to spill. She growled, "Aaaaah. It makes me so angry, that they should think I'd … anyhow, I never did it, so you don't need to know. It makes no difference. Trust me."

The rest of the day, despite Kay's efforts to bring them in, they spent outside, furtively looking around them. Lena said they couldn't stay in the house as it was suffocating and the children were "*traished*, just terrified" of ghosts and bogey men in the chimney. She said she worried the walls would fall down on her, but it seemed to Kay that she was unable to find the words to rationalise her fears.

For them to risk being seen outdoors, their anti-bricks-and-mortar instincts must be powerful, she reasoned, so did not argue. When Kay returned from a dash to the chemist, she explained that her gardener might turn up, something that had struck her as she made her way back to the house. But she said she would give them fair warning.

Lena looked worried. "You could phone me," she offered.

"What?" blurted Kay, puzzled.

"On my mobile. If I could charge it, that is. And it's got no credit, but you could call or text me. Call is best as I do have trouble with letters. Let me know when he's coming and we can hide somewhere – the shed, or ..."

"Well I wouldn't risk the shed, as that's somewhere he may well decide to explore," advised Kay.

"You could tell him not to, couldn't you?"

It seemed like a simple instruction, but he would want to know why and she could think of no good reason that might not actually entice him to take a look. Asbestos? Rats? Wasps' nest? Danger of roof falling on him? Dead bodies? Badger run? Weak floorboards he would simply want to fix. No, she could think of nothing plausible that might deter him, but only of reasons that would actively encourage his curiosity.

"Not really. No. We could perhaps tell him about you, ask him to keep a secret? He's going to be round here a fair bit you see..."

"*No!* Please. It won't work. If one person knows about us bein' 'ere, word'll spread like fire in the village ... You can't. You *promised* you'd tell no one ... didn't you?"

"OK, OK. You'll have to hide in a bedroom then, when he's round here."

Lena looked horrified but then resignation creamed over her face. "But what will we *do*? The boys can't look out the window, dig holes or build camps. They'll be *jawing diviou*. I don't know *what* they'll do," she said despairingly, "without the others. So *chewed* they'll be."

Kay put an arm round her shoulders to calm her obvious distress. "Don't worry, Lena. We'll find something. I'll go to the village shop for some toys, crayons, bricks, games ... Whatever you think they'd like. It's not exactly Hamleys but we'll find a few bits and pieces at least to keep them occupied until ..."

She shrugged. "I don't know. They're either outside or asleep – *normally*."

Something struck a resonant chord with Kay. People did not need to know all the minutiae of how Marcus died and it was second nature to her not to mention those details. Since the counselling sessions provided soon afterwards, she had not opened up to a single human being, including Suzi and Claudia. Always skirting round it, denying it was a big deal, believing life could now go on as *normal*, whatever that was, yet sometimes in the night as she lay alone in the middle of her king-sized bed, tossing and turning, she could envisage that one day the hissing steam building up inside her would thrust the lid off in one almighty explosion. But in Appley Green she had vowed it would make no difference what happened in her past. A clean sweep is best, a fresh page, a new start ...

For now, for today, she would accept Lena's refusal to supply more detail, as she knew she had no real intention of carrying out her threat of reporting her. She could see that for her to be placed in a hostel or a refuge would be like trapping a nightingale in a cage.

But tomorrow, to preserve her sanity, she would find out more.

8

Next morning Kay left a note for Lena stuck on the door of the bedroom where the three of them were still apparently sleeping. Unsure of Lena's literacy skills, she wrote in large letters. "Gone to village shop. Back by 9." She could hear a warning voice in the back of her head telling her that on her return, anything valuable and portable would be gone, along with Lena and the boys, but she chose not to listen.

The Post Office-come-newsagent had a very small selection of toys, the same as it had a limited range of tinned vegetables, stationery, detergents and sweets. She could feel Mr Patel watching her with hawk-eyes, as she picked up a kaleidoscope, a plastic boat for the bath, two colouring books and crayons, a toy whistle-recorder, and a bag of alphabet bricks. It practically cleaned him out. As she took the armful to the counter, walking steadily, no longer leaning on a stick, she privately felt a triumphant sense of achievement.

"Good morning Mr Patel," she said, "How are you today?"

"Just about surviving – without Mrs Patel, you see – she's gone home ..."

"Home? To ... ?"

"Yes, to Calcutta, to see family – her father is not too well – and friends. Old friends ...," he sighed. Another time, she would have pursued this, would have asked him the why, the how long for, the when did you last see your old friends, Mr Patel, but now was not the time.

"Let me see, grandchildren coming to stay?" said Mr Patel, his dark eyes twinkling. "Am I right?"

"No – not blessed in that way. Just a precaution in case I get visitors with young children."

She could sense the cogs turning inside his head. Why would this woman be rushing in here first thing in the morning to make such a purchase?

"How very sensible," he said, totalling up her bill. "Better than them playing with your ornaments." He smiled knowingly.

"Exactly. I felt the matter was quite urgent. Children expect to be amused these days."

"Ah, indeed, but then they don't have the same freedoms as we did when we were young."

Kay thought for moment. "Do you know, Mr Patel, you are so right," she agreed, supposing now that his childhood must have been in India, but not liking to ask. "They don't. We used to roam free …"

"And we survived!"

"But the traffic and strange people around – it's all changed now … anyway, lovely to talk, but must fly. Expecting my gardener and need to speak to him …"

"Ah yes, Dunstan. I heard about how he dug up your garden …"

As he said this, conveyed with some amusement, Kay went quiet and stood quite still, fast coming to terms with how village life works. Lena was right to be cautious of wagging tongues. And was the shop assistant at the chemist's counter a curious, chatty type? Now she was just being paranoid …

Once back at the house, she went into the conservatory and opened up the blinds to let the lovely morning sunshine cast its magical warmth. She was planning what to put out for breakfast, unsure of what her lodgers might prefer – toast, eggs, cereals, bananas – when she looked out to the garden, only to see Lena busily washing Tom's hair, using a cup and a bucket. What the devil ….? Perhaps she was more comfortable doing things this way. But she must reassure the girl that she was welcome to use the bathrooms – after all she had two, going on three.

As she approached them, Lena looked up and smiled as if this was the most natural thing in the world for her to be doing.

"Hello you three! Did you sleep well?"

"Yes. We did. Tom had a nice dream – he was just telling me about it …"

Kay watched as she carefully patted Tom's hair dry, thoroughly, firmly but not roughly. Lena would stroke his cheeks and softly murmur words Kay did not understand but clearly Tom did, probably to take his mind off the water, which Kay could somehow sense was as cold as the morning air. She pointed to a robin, telling Jason to watch where the little redbreast went but keep very still so as not to frighten it too far away. It was a rare, touching thing to see such love and tenderness and she felt privileged to be witness. It was clever too. She thought of impatient, young mothers she would see tugging recalcitrant toddlers round the supermarkets. Why upset things by trying to impose hot running water within confining walls?

Then her rational head began asking how she was going to be able to manage Dunstan's comings and goings so that he does not see Lena, or even know about her existence?

After discussing breakfast and telling them it would be on the table indoors in ten minutes, but they could eat it outside if they preferred, she ambled back to the house. What is to become of them? They can't stay here forever. Actually if that seemed likely, she thought, as she checked the kettle had boiled, she really would have to get them onto a council flat waiting list and register them as homeless. This would be the reality, not just a veiled threat to extract the truth from her. She must be firm.

She saw them disappear down into the thickets at the bottom of the garden, maybe following the robin, or a squirrel, of which there were plenty. The sky was clouding over now, fast becoming overcast.

Suddenly, as she turned round from the sink, there at the back door stood Dunstan, dressed in his old gardening jeans and blue denim shirt. The shock knocked her back and made her gasp.

"Hey! Sorry, didn't mean to make you jump!" he said, laughing then frowning. "I'm not that scary, am I?"

Pale sunshine of just moments before had now turned to a sudden, violent hail storm, stones like marbles gusting through the open doorway, and Kay was half-looking out of the window, whilst she said what she must, "Please come in before you get drenched – or battered," and as she was mechanically sitting him down and making coffee, her mind was in turmoil. Excusing herself, she walked as fast as she could without risk of falling over, went upstairs, scrabbled around in various pockets for her mobile so she could send a cryptic, rapid text to Lena. They had previously agreed on what should happen if this arose, but neither expected it to happen so quickly. Although she had said to Mr Patel, as a pretext to get away, that she was expecting her gardener, this was not so. In reality, she thought he was coming tomorrow, but this was clearly his *modus operandi*. "To work on a whim, as it suits him," she muttered to herself. "What's the betting Lena doesn't have her mobile on her?" They will have to push through the hedge at the bottom of the garden; make their way up via the public footpath; come in by the front door, which she must leave ajar for them; and creep upstairs; while she keeps Dunstan trapped in the kitchen. Why should this be her problem? She begins to realise that the situation is all hopeless, just ridiculous. *What is happening to her life?* While she has people working in the house – plumbers, electricians, decorators, and the rest, she will have to keep moving Lena, her boys and any tell-tale signs of their being there, from one room to another, making up stories as to why no one must go in there … *What is happening to her quiet life in the country, her retirement?*

The spring shower had ended as quickly as it had begun, giving the view outside a wonderful clarity. As she came downstairs, to find Dunstan making plans to go out into the garden with his coffee, she felt a steely determination to worm the facts from Lena and make an action plan. She must stay in control, or she was in danger of having her life spin into a vortex that would suck her down into some kind of breakdown. She was feeling stressed. It was not part of her life-plan at all.

There was no evidence as yet that Lena, Tom and Jason had made their way to the house safely, or whether Lena had got her text. Kay's mobile was in her jeans' pocket, but then she remembered that Lena could not text back as she still had no credit on her phone.

"Dunstan," she called to him, "could I have a word?"

"Sure. I wanted to tell you my plans ..."

"Yes, well, I have plans too," she cut in, a little too sharply she realised, but it had to be done. "I'm really sorry to mess you about, but just at the moment I have so many people coming to do work in the house, I would appreciate it if you could hold off the gardening for a couple of weeks or so ..."

He looked not just puzzled, but outraged. "But, how can you say that? We'll miss the whole growing season! With the wet spring, things have been delayed enough. Until you get a greenhouse, I need to get seeds going outside now, or you will have very little produce this summer. Why? Why are you saying this, Kay?"

She stood firm, risking their friendship. "There's too much ... too many people ..." she sat down, feeling actually dizzy, head in her hands. "Please, I'm sorry to change plans, but it's just for a little while ..."

"But this is the critical time of the year. I've prepared the ground. I have nowhere to bring on the seedlings I've already grown at home for you ..." Kay looked up. He'd done that for her? In two weeks? "Well, I had them spare," he admitted, "but they need to be in the ground ..."

Was two weeks' delay such an unreasonable request? "I get stressed if too many things are going on at the same time ... it's a condition I have. So many vehicles outside, strange men tramping through the house. No amount of organic vegetables are worth a nervous breakdown."

At this prognosis, he sulkily gave in, but was clearly mystified. She knew *he* knew she was not the kind of person to use emotional blackmail, or to feel prone to nervous problems over relatively petty, domestic problems. And she privately acknowledged that she had come through a lot, lot worse, not entirely unscathed, but pretty much intact all things considered. Now she sensed she might lose him altogether, which could cause even more stress, of a different kind.

"Look," she said, now desperately trying to come up with a compromise. "We'll stick to Plan A, but *please*, Dunstan, will you call beforehand and agree a time, so that I can plan my days – with military precision. That way, we won't have too many activities fighting over each other. How's that?"

An enormous smile spread across his face in the knowledge that his seedlings, outgrowing their little pots, were saved, and he nodded. Kay felt pleased with herself, that without pushing him, without the genuine threat of pulling the rug from his feet completely, he could not have capitulated so easily into this simple agreement, which was really all she needed.

She gave herself a score of 12 out of 10 for man management. Now she just had to sort out Lena.

With Lena, Tom and Jason temporarily trapped upstairs like wild rabbits in a hutch, Dunstan was allowed to proceed with some raking and planting for a couple of hours. He had brought out from his van four-inch high broad bean plants, onion sets and potatoes, which he swiftly bedded in. As Kay surveyed his work after he had gone, she felt pleased that it was all taking shape. Basic stuff, but good nonetheless.

She asked Lena what she would like most as a hot meal at lunch time, since the boys might prefer to have a main meal then rather than just before their bed time.

"Nobody's ever given me free choice like that before," she said. "You mean, like anything?"

Kay laughed. "Well, within reason. I'm not a magician! But something that's do-able with what I have in my fridge or freezer. Try me!"

Lena thought for a long time, as if this was such a special opportunity she must make the right decision. Eventually, looking up from the kaleidoscope that she had been playing with, like a child, for about ten minutes, she said.

"We like broth – you know made with lentils and peas and oxtail … "

Kay smiled at her modest choice. "That sounds really tasty – but I don't have any oxtail. Anything else you fancy?"

"I do remember my Mum used to make a bacon puddin'. It smelled like … heaven, when it was cooking and then would fill you up so you felt .. oh, so good. Like you might not want to eat again for a week, 'cept of course you did …"

Kay had already reached for a cookery book and was looking in the index. Nothing there, so she tried another, and another.

"I would watch her – she made a dough, using that … bitty fat, you know?"

"Um …"

"Looks like maggots …"

Kay scratched her head. "Bitty fat? Maggots. Ah, grated suet? Yep, OK. I remember when my Mum used to make suet puddings. Not very healthy, but I think you can get some sort of non animal variety these days …"

"Then she would like roll the dough, quite thick and lay on bacon and, I think maybe onion – she would cry when she cut this up. Great fat tears and I used to wrap my arms round her legs and ask her what was wrong … " Lena smiled at the memory and went off into her own world for a few moments, as Kay continued her search for a recipe.

"*Eureka!*" cried Kay at last as she found something in an old Women's Institute cookbook that had indeed belonged to her mother. It was crusty with old bits of flour and other unknown ingredients. Quite disgusting, but it had sentimental value. "Bacon Roly Poly – does this look right?"

Lena looked at the old-fashioned book without illustrations. "Not sure if that's the same – but anyhow I could cook that for *you*. All girls learn how to do bacon puddin' ... although I'd have to remember from just watching my Mum when I was little. Me Aunty Vera never really showed me how ..."

Kay felt doubtful. It would be easier to make her something than to feel she had watch over her in the kitchen.

"Would that be difficult to cook – in your kitchen? My Mum would cook it outside over a fire in a pan of water for a long time."

Kay smiled. "I think we can improvise ... you know, find a way," she said, wondering where she would find a piece of muslin. "But I don't think we can do this today. Another day?" This could be a simple but effective lure to discourage a sudden escape. "For now, how about toasted cheese, ham and tomato sandwiches, with chips and salad?"

Lena nodded eagerly. "Can I watch how you do that?"

As Kay pulled out the necessary items from the fridge, the phone rang.

"It's Suzi. Mum, it's terrible. I feel so bloody ill ..."

Kay abandoned the kitchen to take the portable phone to another room.

"Darling, what's happened?"

"I've done it. I've miscarried – or aborted, rather - and, it was horrible, but that's over at least. I just can't stop crying – I feel so depressed. It's not like me. I don't understand what's happening to me. Is it hormones, d'you think or what?"

Kay's guilt for having pushed her daughter's plight to the back of her mind, so pre-occupied was she with other things, stabbed her in the chest like a physical pain.

"Mum, I can't work. I can't even think straight. I'm going to the doctor in a minute, but can I come to yours for a bit?"

9

Tom helped butter the bread and Jason lined up the slices in a path across the kitchen table like flagstones, standing on a chair so he could reach.

There was no need to remind them to wash their hands first as Lena was quick to make sure they all did this, but as Kay observed, the children had no idea how to cope with taps at the kitchen sink. She noticed that Lena reminded them not to use the washing up area at all, then briefly disappearing to fetch a new bowl she had commandeered from the utility room. Lena was looking thoughtful as she ran some water into the bowl and carefully set it down on the patio just outside the kitchen door so the boys could dabble their fingers, which their mother also rubbed to get them clean.

"Is this all right?" asked Lena, looking up.

"Of course it is," replied Kay. "Easier for them than reaching ..."

"It's just that we don't normally wash hands in the same bowl as crocks – it ain't right hygienic."

"Don't worry – whatever you're happy with, my love," Kay reassured her, whilst thinking how different she was, with her almost obsessive concern for cleanliness, from the common perception.

Lena then copied what Kay did, slicing tomatoes, dicing the ham, grating cheese, then watched as the sandwich toaster was pulled from a cupboard, plugged in and switched on, with warnings from Kay not to touch as it was likely to get very hot ...

How could I *possibly* refuse Suzi, thought Kay? Naturally, she had agreed on the phone for her to come home the following day, whilst not having the faintest idea what she would do with her secret lodgers. Lena would be terrified of her hiding place being revealed to the rest of the world and of her vengeful husband finding them and maybe taking Tom and Jason away. As she imagined the meeting of these two young women, the words chalk and cheese came to mind, as did a mental picture of young men, mob-handed, raiding her home.

After a lunch involving much lip smacking and finger sucking to ensure that no crumbs were wasted, Lena made a brave effort to keep the boys upstairs in the bedroom, but it was obvious that all three of them hated being confined. By half-past two, Lena came downstairs.

"They're asleep," she said, sounding relieved to have some precious time to herself. "Tom's outgrowing daytime sleeps, but I haven't told him that yet …" She smiled at Kay and then sat on the door-mat by the back door looking outside, up at the sky, lost in her own thoughts. Kay was becoming anxious about the whole situation, about Suzi coming tomorrow and about Lena's non-existent long-term plans. If it came out eventually that she had done this thing, taken in these 'strays', she did not care a jot about what other people thought about her, but she could not help recalling how Natalie once said that, in times gone by, harbouring a Gypsy once incurred the death penalty.

She needed to get away from Lena to think and withdrew to her study to check on the schedule of workmen and her e-mails. There was one from Claudia, now in Australia, wanting to know all her news. How to begin? She began jotting a list of things she can tell and things she can't. She longed to open up and pour her heart out, to confide. Even telling someone on the other side of the world would be a catharsis, but there was the risk Claudia would tell Suzi … but then Suzi would know soon anyway. Or would she? Somehow she just could not imagine this happening. Suzi would explode at her stupidity! How much longer can she keep up with this pretence? When will Lena and her children be safe to come out of hiding?

Her head bursting with unanswered questions, she scrolled through her Inbox, seeing an e-mail from Max:

Dear Kay, I thought you would be interested to know that the complaints against the Travelling Group in Appley Green did not stand up, which has made certain members of the community furious. As they see it, the Gypsies have gone anyway to keep the peace, making martyrs of themselves and may think they are free to come and go in the future. The local population are wondering what will happen next time they, or another group, appear. This could happen again soon, as we are now entering the active season for travelling groups looking for stopping-off places. Kind regards, Max Leatherson, Gypsy Liaison Officer.

The boys played with their new toys and some play-dough Kay quickly made for them. After their tea, Lena got them washed, preferring to do this outside, using the bowl.

"Wouldn't they rather be in the bath? In the warm bathroom? You're welcome, you know. Don't feel …"

Lena was shaking her head. "No. Thank-you. It's not our way, to sit in our own dirt," she said plainly, as a statement of fact, not meaning to cause offence. "They can splash about out here without gettin' your floor wet. And besides, this is what they're used to and it would *traish* 'em to be dunked into a big trough of water."

When she saw Lena outside later scrubbing some items of clothing in a plastic bucket she must've found in her utility room, the same one she used for hair washing, she held back from questioning. Maybe she would point her in the direction of the washing machine another day.

Finally, once the boys were asleep, Kay and Lena sat down together, Lena restless, moving from chair to floor, to sofa, rising to look out of the window, but with the TV off, it was at least peaceful.

"Lena, I have a problem. It involves you," broached Kay softly, as Lena curled up in an armchair. "My daughter is coming here tomorrow. Suzi – she's a bit older than you, but I …"

Lena jumped up. "Oh, no, no. If she knows ... she won't like me being here," she cried. "She's bound to tell someone else and then before we know it ... We'll 'ave to leave. Tonight. Course, you need to 'ave people here, your family. Plain stupid of me to think this wouldn't 'appen."

"Please, Lena, you can't run away. You know that – we've been through it ... We'll just have to explain to her your situation ..."

"You think she'll understand? That we can totally trust your girl to tell no one about us?"

Kay hesitated. No, Suzi would not understand at all. No, she couldn't trust her to keep it to herself. Lena stood, looking at her wide-eyed with terror.

"The trouble is, maybe, Lena, that until I understand properly, the whole story behind this, then I cannot convince her. Do you see?" Lena nodded. "OK. I trust you, anyway. You've been kind, so I'll tell you, but I don't know about your Suzi. Maybe we could hide in your shed, just while she's here ..." Kay nodded, thinking "no way", but determined not to spoil things. "There's nothing you can do. You won't be able to change anything. The problem was, I ... I lost my *tikno*, a baby ..."

Kay sat up straight. What exactly did she mean, lost? The questioning look she gave Lena must have registered on the girl. "I gave birth to a stillborn baby ..."

The story about the Eviction clicked in Kay's head. "Ah, it was you then who gave birth on the day your group was told to move on ..."

"I didn't know about that. There were too many other things goin' on. Fightin', arguin', shoutin'. Oh *dordi,* it was awful, just awful ..."

"And your baby had died. Oh, Lena, that is so very sad. A terrible thing to happen to a woman."

Kay watched the pain in her face as she reflected on the memory. But she seemed to be coping well with a trauma that she had had time to come to terms with, not allowing herself to dissolve into tears.

91

Her voice was steady. "You see, I met this man one day. In the village where we were, not here. I was coming out the Post Office. An immigrant, Tibor, and he stopped me, perhaps seeing I had a Romany look about me. We're good at recognisin' each other. Not specially dark, but certain features I s'pose and style of clothes."

Kay nodded and smiled, actively listening, hanging on to her every word.

"Tibor is a Czech man, *jalling the drom*, travellin' around, looking for Roma people and I spoke to 'im for a bit in the village. We walked along together, as he told me about how his family had been turned away at Prague airport on orders from British immigration. Not *allowed* to leave their country! They had to go back home, well actually to go back to ... to nothin'. After a few years, they gave up tryin' to leave, and then he described to me how they're treated in their own country. Worse than here! Much worse. He was bullied, beaten and knifed ..."

Kay shuddered. The mention of knives immediately brought with it the glint of steel, pierced flesh, fresh spurting blood, scarlet on white ... She took deep breaths and closed her eyes, feeling dizzy.

"Oh, are you all right?" asked Lena, concerned, leaning over to touch Kay's arm. Kay jumped.

"Yes, yes, just me being silly. Squeamish ..."

"Well, he tried again, but on his own this time, without his family and the plan was to join a group of cousins, who had left years ago, but he had no idea where they were, just their names. He was travellin' around, homeless, sleeping rough, tryin' to track 'em down."

"And were you able to help him?"

"Said I'd try. Make enquiries, get messages across to other families when we meet at festivals and fairs and that, and agreed to meet 'im again to let 'im know if anyone else could help. But he said to just be a bit careful and not let people know he was around. Some reason. I don't know."

"Maybe he'd entered illegally and the authorities would probably send him back if they found him …" suggested Kay. "So, on the one hand you had to try and find his relatives, but not let on he was on the loose?"

"Mm. I felt really sorry for him. He had nothin' so I smuggled *scran* and some money to him. But, people saw me talkin' to this stranger and, unknown to me at the time, there was gossip. Word got to Joseph. He was shamed and angry and when I found myself *shuvvali*, you know, pregnant, he accused me of being unfaithful and freatened to beat me and kick me out. I pleaded with him and said that I'd never gone with Tibor, I'd never do that …"

"Did he believe you in the end?" Kay asked, predicting what the answer would be.

Then Lena's chin wobbled and her hand went to her mouth. "The baby, you know … it was a little girl, " she said, her eyes now watery again. "My *tickni*. A bit blue and so small, but perfect – mine and Joseph's. But … couldn't believe it at first … that there was no breath, not a flicker of life …"

Kay wanted to give her a hug, but it was difficult as Lena had drawn her knees up to her chin and wrapped her arms around them, so Kay just sat forward to listen.

"Where did you have the baby? In your trailer?"

"No. Me Aunty Vera did at least get someone to get me to hospital. It all happened so quick though! She didn't want me there, making a mess and causing trouble …" There was a long pause and Kay waited. "I called her Abigail."

"Sweet name. How long were you in hospital?"

"A day – half a day really. I left soon as I could. Couldn't face bein' in that place at night … Hated it in there … They offered a funeral, but it was expensive and there was no time, so I … just let them take her away …." Her voice was hoarse, fading away. "That was *hard*. You know, we do big funerals. It's our way of payin' proper respect – wakes go on for days and nights. And my little girl, my little angel, was probably dumped in some incinerator …" Kay could see nothing but a bereaved mother utterly distraught, a mother who was now

93

picturing the unwanted detail, the still tiny form of her little girl, the afterbirth, and feeling again the crushing pain of disappointment, grief – and loneliness. The horror of the memory, like a knife twisting in a festering wound ... knives again, always knives ... It was all she could do to stop herself breaking down, she felt so keenly for Lena. It brought back the time when she and Marcus were trying for a third child, hoping for a boy, when Marcus suddenly announced that he did not want any more children and planned to have a vasectomy. He would not discuss or be persuaded. It was a *fait accompli*, leaving Kay feeling bereft, knowing she would never have another child, let alone a son. But this was far, far worse.

"So I got back to the site and I ... I had everyone flyin' at me," she went on, finding it hard to get the words out. "Joseph reminded me he'd been away from us for about six weeks doing some seasonal work with another group about nine months ago – June last year. 'e wouldn't believe the baby was premature and was actually conceived in August! Said I'd got *bori* – big – with Tibor! He wouldn't listen to me, just shouted and then he raised his hand – just stopped himself. He said he couldn't be trusted with me in his sight and I had better *go*."

"So he thought you'd gone the full nine months and that you'd become pregnant by another man, by this Tibor? But the midwives and doctors at the hospital would back you up, wouldn't they?"

"You don't know what he's like – 'e won't listen. Specially people like that. And he's so jealous. And I didn't have any proof of how far on I was – missed my scans and all that, cause of movin' about so much. The really old members of our group believed the baby was stillborn as a curse, a punishment. That's what they all kept telling Joseph."

"Did anyone believe you?"

"No. No one did. 'Cause they'd already been suspicious, hadn't they? Seeing me with Tibor. I knew I should've gone straight home and told them about Tibor, well I did the first time, but Joseph was angry even then. He'd had a real go at me for that. But poor Tibor had no one and I wanted to help him so I saw him in secret – trouble was, someone was watching me."

"Ah, so the secrecy raised even more suspicion that there was something going on?" suggested Kay.

"It did, yes. Anyhow, I've brought great shame on his family. I ran off before he could hurt me but he'll be seekin' revenge. And he'll want Tom and Jason back, so I *mustn't* risk anyone finding me here ..."

"And the reported fighting and noise? Was that anything to do with this?"

"There was a lot of angry shoutin', mostly Joseph cursin' at me, and then his brothers joined in ... my cousins and Joseph's brothers were bashin' each other to bits. They're not usually violent, you know, but we have like rules, strict rules, about how girls and women should behave."

Kay held the silence for a few moments, then said, softly, "Oh Lena, and you had just been through a full labour and lost your baby." She felt close to tears. "You poor love. You can stay here, though, until we sort something out for you. I promise."

"I feel so *kinyo*," said Lena, sniffing. Just by looking at her Kay guessed this meant tired. "Thanks for listening. You're the only person I've told about all this since leavin'. If it wasn't for you, I don't know where we'd be ..."

"I'll make some hot chocolate and we must calm down a bit before going to sleep."

And, thought Kay, somehow I must stop Suzi coming tomorrow, but how?

10

Kay did not sleep well that night, snared in a trap with both ends closed. If Suzi came to stay, she would pose a real problem for Lena's safety, but no way could she tell her not to come. What could she say? She was too busy? Going away? The house was full? She was ill? None of these would be true and in any case, she was now worried about her young daughter and desperately wanted to help her. Part of her was pleased that at least she had asked for her help, turning to her mother rather than to a friend. It meant a lot, especially as they'd had their differences in the past. And family comes first – ironically, even Lena would agree with that. But if she were to come to the house for a few days, it was inevitable that she would meet Lena. She would just have to convey to her the importance of keeping Lena and her sons a secret from the local community ...

She sighed. Suzi wouldn't wear it, she just knew. And Lena had begged her, was prepared to take her chances on the road, in the woods, wherever fate took her away from people, with no food, no money, no shelter, nothing, rather than to take the risk of being exposed by Suzi. The children would be at risk.

She looked at her bedside clock. It was coming up to half-past two and she was no nearer dropping off than she had been three hours before. She tried deep, rhythmic breathing, tightening and relaxing muscles, but then Tibor crashed into her semi-conscious thoughts. He was key to this. Key witness. He must be found. But then, Joseph would probably go for this throat ....

It must have been somewhere around this point that she finally slipped into a restless sleep and when she awoke at about half-past seven, she could recall with great clarity a swarthy man with a knotted scarf round his neck plunging a knife into the throat of another young man, who was phantom-pale, thin, unshaven, and spoke in broken English. She felt shaky as she made her ritual morning tea and was glad that the recollection began to blur and finally fade into mental obscurity.

A brilliant thought then struck her with such force she spilled her tea – a possible solution to the immediate, impossible dilemma. She quickly reached for the bedroom phone to call Suzi, who took a long time to answer and sounded half-asleep, uttering little more than a grunt.

"Suzi, I've been thinking. It would be good to get away from here for a couple of days, you know. To tell you the truth, I'm weary of domestic chaos and so …"

"Oh … but …" Suzi sounded tearful even over the phone.

"What I mean is, how about we go and stay in a hotel close to where we lived. We could do some serious pampering things, cheer ourselves up, and check out parks, schools, other childhood landmarks, anything you like, around where you were brought up." Anything, she thought, except the house where we lived and where your father died. Not that.

Kay knew that Suzi would interpret this as more significant than a mere whim, rather a hint that, at last, she was ready to confront the past by returning to it. Suzi had always accused her mother of running away, trying to put her head in the sand, before laying to rest all those ghosts.

"Mm … OK … sounds good," mumbled Suzi, sounding nasal as if she had been crying.

"Oh, this'll be fun Suzi. And I'm a deal more sprightly than I was … I know not everything is hunky dory, but … I'd like to celebrate this, at least. Can you find somewhere that has rooms with a bit of class? Luxury? We can share, or have single rooms. Whichever you think best. I don't mind. You choose. Never mind the cost. Find somewhere that has all the works, you know, aromatherapy massage, mudpacks, gym, Jacuzzi ..."

"Yeah, yeah, OK, Mum, get the drift. For tonight is this? And tomorrow?"

"If you can ..." Kay's mind was racing. How booked up are London hotels? "Get on the phone now and start planning a programme of nostalgia ... are you feeling better than you were?"

Kay was so relieved to hear a little laugh. "Oh, Mum ... you're priceless. In two minutes flat you've somehow lifted me out of wallowing in the depths of despair into a place that's almost habitable."

"I should say so, considering what it'll cost!! I thought maybe I was being selfish. You know – it'll be good therapy for me too. Maybe a bit painful. But we can hold each other's hands."

"Definitely. I'll sort it and let you know asap."

"Fantastic."

Dunstan. She would have to instruct Dunstan, in no uncertain terms, that he should not come to the house for a couple of days, giving no reason.

She called him. "Could you leave the work for three days, Dunstan? In a rush, no time to explain."

"But ..."

"You remember our agreement ..."

"Yes, but ..."

"Dunstan."

"OK."

Lena. As soon as Kay had showered and dressed, she began writing a list of essential housekeeping tips such as locking up at night, including window locks downstairs; putting the milk bottles into the fridge in the morning; dangers of the gas hob; turning off lights and the TV to help save the planet; the fresh produce she could use in the fridge and how to defrost frozen food in the microwave … Then devices and other items they should not touch at all, such as central heating controls; a defunct burglar alarm; radiator knobs; various boxes in certain rooms … She ran through the list of do's and don'ts as Lena, Tom and Jason were dipping soldiers into boiled eggs, finally sticking it on the fridge door.

"But how will we manage here without *you*?" asked Lena, looking anxious.

"You'll be fine. I'll phone you from time to time and any problems, you can call my mobile. Use the house phone. Really, you'll be fine."

The plan seemed to fall into place neatly and quickly. A plumber who was coming to give an overall estimate for various projects around the house; the fitting of a burglar alarm; and the delivery of a greenhouse all had to be swiftly re-arranged. A small case was packed so that she would be ready for the off. Suzi called to say they were booked. "Health and beauty stuff not in hotel, but 'within a quarter of a kilometre' it says," she read aloud from her computer screen. "Excellent," said Kay, trying not to make it too obvious that she was almost ready to agree to share her bedroom with a horse, so long as it got her and Suzi away together. Once they'd agreed where to meet, Kay then debated if she was able-bodied and confident enough now to drive herself to the train station six miles away. Neither the MG, nor the BMW, had moved from the garage since her house move and she'd had to pay a garage to transport them here. Driving was an important milestone now, and had been an extra incentive for her body to mend since the hip replacement and the shattered leg coming out of plaster. But now, she worried that the car might not even start, or let her down on the way and spoil everything. No, she would keep things simple and get a taxi.

As she and Suzi walked along the banks of the Thames before finding somewhere to have lunch, just as Kay used to with friends, and sometimes with Marcus, she was torn by ambivalent feelings. Did she feel as if she had come home? Or, did the place seem rosy today because the sun shone and she could enjoy respite from what was becoming an albatross-round-the-neck-scenario in her new home? Suzi's emotional state was turbulent, which was bad, but she was happy to spend time with her to help ease things. She felt a strong need to be a close part of her daughters' lives, and with Claudia far away, she would be devastated if she and Suzi drifted apart, or worse still, could not see eye to eye. They would have to face the fact that Suzi's lifestyle was something that did not sit comfortably with Kay. They were going to have to acknowledge and overcome harsh issues.

With linked arms she was physically closer to her daughter than she had been for a while, silently bonded by memories, watching the swans, mallards, canoeists and motorised craft carefully avoiding each other as they sliced through the calm surface of the river. Suzi and Claudia used to come down to feed the birds, generally splash about at the water's edge; at weekends, Marcus would take them together with Cocoa, their chocolate Labrador. And Richmond Park was a spectacular beauty spot, with its herds of deer and renowned vista of St Paul's Cathedral and the London skyline. Why had she wanted to leave this pleasant neighbourhood, one of the most affluent in the country? Why did she feel it so necessary to seek refuge in the country when she had all this on her doorstep plus the city within easy reach?

As if reading her thoughts, Suzi said, "Are you glad you moved?"

Kay did not answer straight away. The move had involved things she had not anticipated, about which she had told Suzi nothing, that had muddied the pros and cons. In a way Lena's plight had given her focus, a distraction.

"It's early days to judge yet. Some things are tough. The upheaval, deserting the familiar, the good things about living here, but …" She swallowed. Her daughter seemed to understand so Kay did not feel under pressure to say more. She had a strong desire at that moment to tell her about Lena. In fact, it seemed ludicrous not to, but she held back. If Suzi reacted badly, it would spoil their time together, especially as the secrecy had initially prompted this jolly jaunt.

They ambled along for a mile or so before turning round to come back to the town for lunch, and talked about Claudia who had sent her sister more detailed e-mails about her travels, especially exploits involving new men in her life, presumably temporary men.

"For so many reasons, I just hope she's not behaving badly …" commented Kay, thinking aloud, thinking very much about her twenty-six year old daughter allowing herself to be bedded by all manner of strangers in foreign lands.

"Like me, you mean …"

Her head swung round as she realised how her words may have impacted on Suzi.

"Actually, I wasn't thinking of you at all, but of Claudia."

"Maybe … maybe, we're not quite so wayward as you imagine …"

"Mm …"

It felt strange having a massage, lying on her front, on a couch – or perhaps you would call it a table – alongside her daughter on an adjacent couch, the more so because this health spa was so close to where they used to live, yet Kay had never ventured into it.

Then, glowing and relaxed, sipping tea and spreading scones thickly with raspberry jam and clotted cream, they gave each other smug smiles. The lounge was softly carpeted, flowers on tables, modern art hanging on plain walls, muted lighting and, above all, it was peaceful.

"Mum, I know you think badly of me …"

"Suzi, not now. Let's not …"

"No, this is for the best. I don't like you to …"

"You're an adult. I'm not here to judge how …"

"Mum, please. Please listen a minute." Kay nodded, pouring more tea into both cups.

"It wasn't how I said. I do know who got me pregnant."

"Suzi. Don't mess with me. Tell me now straight. You know *I can't stand lies* ..." She felt the heat rise in her cheeks as she said this. Who was she to talk about concealing the truth? "I mean, why did you not tell me this in the first place, or, even tell me nothing at all? Why make up a story?"

"Mum, I was trying to keep it vague ... I don't know. It came out all wrong. I was trying to justify having an abortion I guess. I mean, having no father's name to put on a birth certificate ... it ... that would be pretty bad, wouldn't it?"

"It would."

"And I thought, with all the stuff you were trying to get over, I thought a big debate over it might set you back, and I knew you'd come off the happy pills and had moved house – big decision – and were being madly positive at every turn."

"You thought I'd rather believe you'd been having casual sex with so many men, that you couldn't name ...?"

"I didn't think it through. Stupid. Stupid me. Put like that it sounds worse than what actually happened."

"So? What did happen? Do you want to tell me?" Kay put down her cup, sat forward in the armchair.

Suzi closed her eyes and swallowed hard. "Yes. It was a guy who lives in my block of flats. Just knew him to say 'Hi'. I'd come home alone from a night out with a group of friends. A bit worse for wear. It was late and he was in the lift. Just the two of us. We got talking. He was drunk and so was I. Almost falling over, carrying my shoes. Giggly. Flirty. Anyway ... he came into my place for a coffee and I was too ... weak to resist. I mean, I can see now what a complete airhead I was, but ... these things happen, don't they?"

"You had unprotected sex and found yourself pregnant."

"I tried the morning-after pill, but it didn't work – I ... Oh God!" she groaned. "Probably because I was sick most of the following day. I'm sorry. This is awful."

"It's OK. Go on."

"Since the break up with Scott ..." Kay gave her a quizzical look. Who was Scott? "... I came off the pill. It didn't seem right to carry on taking it just in case ... yet now the idea seems quite a good one. I felt so guilty for allowing it to happen. And I knew you'd disapprove, so I just couldn't come clean."

"My darling, can you not see that what happened is not half as bad as your first version?" Kay reached over and squeezed her arm. She could feel a tear trickle from the corner of one eye and brushed it away with a finger.

"I thought you might think I should nail the guy, stick with it and have his baby! I was truly afraid you would persuade me."

Suzi was looking around, as more people had wandered in for afternoon tea. Suzi gave her mother a rueful smile and Kay felt a rush of love.

"At least you told me. You know, we all make mistakes." Kay could feel her eyes fill up now, hot, about to spill over and delved in her bag for some tissues. "Maybe everyone is entitled to a certain quota – it's how we learn."

Suzi raised her cup to her lips and Kay could see she was shaking. It had been hard for her to talk about what could have been interpreted as a rape, except that she had apparently consented, putting up no resistance, so was taking the blame. Suzi had been exploited by a man who saw an opportunity and took it, recklessly. Now it was clear from her body language – the folded arms, tightly closed mouth – that she was ashamed and wanted to end the conversation.

"Now, who is this Scott? I don't think I know about him."

Suzi sat up straight, looking startled. "Oh! A journalist – he was, is, my reason for living ... no, sorry that sounds over dramatic. I don't want to talk about him now. Not now. But it was that evening I got a text from him. It's no excuse but I was ..." Her voice was husky and her bottom lip wobbled, as it used to when she would come home from school and tell her she had been ignored by a boy she fancied.

Kay nodded. "... feeling fragile, hurt and vulnerable. I see. A man that can end a relationship by text is not worth having anyway. In my humble opinion."

Suzi looked away, apparently unable to meet Kay's gaze. For her, Scott was clearly not an alternative topic of conversation, so Kay decided to wait and see what would be comfortable for her

After a pause, Suzi turned and looked Kay straight in the eye. "You know, I never really knew what happened with Daddy. The night. You know. Not completely. I know he was attacked and died and you ended up with a broken hip and leg, but ..."

Kay felt the pressure now to open up and tell her the whole story, but what would she think of her mother if she knew the complete truth? A shiver of nerves went through her. She had, with great difficulty and some deviousness, shielded her daughters because ... it was too upsetting ... would not help, would change nothing. Or was it because of her own guilty conscience? All the counselling in the world would never rid her of the guilt.

"Darling, shall we move on – let's go up to my room, freshen up a bit."

"You're avoiding the subject, aren't you?"

"Oh, actually, no I wasn't. I just feel a bit conspicuous sitting here with mascara streaking down my face. It's frightening for the other guests!"

"I really want to know."

Kay could sense the implied reciprocal agreement. Suzi had faced and shared a shameful truth and now it was her turn to open up and tell Suzi the unexpurgated version of what had happened to Marcus. She nodded.

In her hotel bathroom, she splashed her face and quickly reapplied some light make-up ready for Suzi to come round and join her. There was a seating area with a small sofa, armchair and desk. How will it feel to tell Suzi? A bit like a priest confessional, possibly. Would she feel better afterwards? Purged? Or, would it drive a wedge between them?

Suzi gave a light knock on the door and Kay let her in. Together, they admired the view from the window.

"You've got the river …," commented Suzi, enviously.

"Well I didn't ask for it. You booked, if you remember. It's lovely though isn't it?"

"I just took what they had."

Suzi sat down in an armchair, with purpose. Kay knew there was no escape.

"You know about the letters, the threats, from the animal rights activists? Because of your father's work …"

"Course I do. It was a pretty major part of our life. I'd be a very thick kid not to notice! I even took one of the scary phone calls once. And they broke in and murdered Daddy? Extremists, uh?"

"Well, someone did. Just one man."

"But, we – Claudia and me – we always felt you somehow blamed yourself and we couldn't understand why but didn't like to ask. Never seemed the right time. Couldn't find the right words. I mean, what on earth *could* you have done?"

"You see, actually the man who killed you father *wasn't* an animal rights activist. The reports in the local paper erroneously made links with other news items and I … at the time I mean, I too jumped to conclusions … There had been so many of these death-threats – we all misconstrued."

"So who did it then? I know his name was Gary somebody, but …"

"That's right and he was mentally ill, psychotic, on drugs … just looking for money."

"OK. So he broke in. What happened?"

Kay closed her eyes and took a deep breath as if she were about to plunge into a pool of icy water.

"As we sat there, the two of us, in our own kitchen, listening to someone breaking through a back window, I was terrified! Just thinking of all those death-threats, I was fearful for our lives, my heart beating so hard I thought it would

105

burst. The smashing of glass, it was obvious what was happening. This Gary wasn't subtle, just desperate for cash. 'Off his head', as they say. Hadn't troubled to check the house was empty ... but I thought he was after *us*, not our money. Oh Suzi ..." She stopped and put a hand to her mouth, feeling engulfed by guilt. She gazed directly at Suzi who sat forward in her chair waiting, with a quite expressionless face, until she could go on. Suzi, completely ignorant of what this might be, must be anxiously anticipating something new, something she had not heard before. "Your father – I shall always remember him for this, as one of the last things he did – he put a restraining hand on my arm, gentle but firm, you know. 'Easy,' he whispered, and put a finger to his lips, telling me to keep quiet and indicating that we should head the other way, towards the front of the house. He did not want to ... to die a hero! But I didn't listen. Impulsively, I opened a drawer, and grabbed for a sharp knife. What was I thinking of? I suppose some survival instinct drove me to think it might defend us, frighten the intruder away if he saw us."

Suzi was now looking at her wide-eyed and Kay knew there was no going back. She'd never been exposed to the full facts of the court case before, was invited to stay with Kay's sister and family during the trial and had accepted the version of events that had been doctored for her benefit. Kay insisted she did not want any family members present and, over such a sensitive issue, they were compliant. It had surprised Kay that her daughters were not more curious, but on reflection she could see that at the time both Claudia and Suzi had had no reason to suspect there was more to it.

"Anyway, I kept hold of the knife – it was the long, sharp carver ..."

"The one Daddy used to sharpen each time before he used it on the Sunday roast – so worn down it was like small spear?"

"Oh God, Suzi. Yes. Yes, that one," Kay blanched at the apt description and swallowed hard. She must get through this. "I … I crept out of the kitchen on tip-toe, following Marcus upstairs. Then, we couldn't believe it, the man, Gary – he came upstairs too – we would realise later, looking for jewellery, aiming for the bedroom where, unbeknown to him, we were hiding. We could hear his footsteps and couldn't even make a phone call now. No phone in the bedroom and, would you believe it, neither of us had our mobile on us. Mine was in my bag downstairs and your father's was in his jacket pocket in his study. Gary blundered into where we sat quaking on the bed, and grabbed me round the throat with a tie, threatening to squeeze the life out of me if Marcus didn't give him valuables right there and then. He was threatening us, but probably would never have actually strangled me … we'll never know … Marcus snatched the knife off me, which I'd kept hidden behind me, before Gary had a chance, and turned it on him, but Gary was so quick and fired up with adrenalin, he somehow knocked it out of his hand, seized it and just stabbed him … straight in the heart." Kay felt breathless and had to stop for a moment. Suzi said nothing but sat very still.

"It was all so pointless! And it happened so quickly. Faster than the time it's taking me to tell you! He'd already got hold of my jewellery box, and wasn't to know there was a safe locked away in another place with the quality stuff … then he ran and left your father so obviously dead, lying on the bed, and me, choking." She paused. "I tried to speak to him, but he had gone, blood soaking through the duvet … oh Suzi, I'm sorry, you don't need to know all this, but the details, the vivid colour, the whole thing, I had so many recurring nightmares it's still alive in my head and I can't tell it any other way now. It's all or nothing." Kay broke down, head bent and wept quietly while still Suzi did not speak. She hates me now, thought Kay, wiping her eyes as she looked at her daughter face to face once more.

Then Suzi asked. "You fell down the stairs. Rushing? To get away from … what?"

"To get to a phone. To call an ambulance and the police … there was nothing I could do for your father, my darling, the gentlest of men. I mean, do you ever remember him raising his voice, let alone a hand to you, to anyone? I never got to the phone – as you know, it was poor Claudia who found us when she came back from a night out with friends. What a scene to come home to!"

Suzi came over to the sofa and put both arms round her Mum. "You must have been in agony …"

"Me? Oh, I passed out with the pain."

"Why do you blame yourself?"

"Why? Isn't it as clear as day? If I'd listened to him and done as he said. If I had not grabbed the knife. If I had not pre-judged. If I had stopped to *think* …"

"Rubbish. You can't take on all that. No way. It happened."

11

Once she and Suzi had split, Suzi returning to her flat in Hampstead, Kay put her head back on the train seat, thinking how good it was to be able to do that these days without wondering how many greasy heads had been there before. Smart new trains seemed to be the norm now, replacing their draughty, dirty, noisy, smelly predecessors. It glided along almost silently, save for messages to reassure passengers of their whereabouts, and offered carriages free from both cigarettes and mobiles. Despite her amenable surroundings, however, Kay could not help feeling some unease as she conjectured what might have happened on the home front in her absence. An accident? Injured children? Someone could have come to the house and found them, questioned them. Or perhaps Lena had decided to do a runner with as much as she could carry …

How can I keep Lena a secret from Suzi now, she thought, after all the painful sharing of secrets, the emotional outpouring they had been through? So long as I feel soundly justified in helping Lena, then it logically follows that I should be able to convince Suzi, she reasoned with herself. But Suzi's view of people was so very different from her own. Moreover, Kay had already confessed her poor sense of judgement in a crisis that could detract from her defence. Also she had promised Lena not to betray her confidence; so to share their secret with Suzi she must first get Lena's agreement. That would now be her top priority, the next would be to find Tibor.

When she arrived home on Sunday evening, she was firstly surprised by a homely smell of baking that swept her back to her childhood. These days, she was usually the one doing the cooking and to find the role reversed felt strange but good.

Tom and Jason came to greet her, wrapping their arms round her legs, which brought a lump to her throat. They seemed almost like family and she realised the emotional dangers that lay there.

"Mm ... what's your Mummy up to?" she cried, ruffling their heads.

"It's *pobbles* with crumbly bits on top. We helped her," explained Tom.

"S'prise ..." chipped in Jason, jumping up and down.

As Kay set down her bag and hung up her jacket, Lena came through to the hall from the kitchen, wearing one of Kay's aprons and wiping her hands on it, for all the world just as her mother would have done.

Lena smiled the widest smile Kay had seen yet. "We made apple crumble. If you've already had something, though, you could always have it tomorrow."

Kay put an arm round her shoulders and gave her a hug. "Lena that's lovely ... has everything been all right while I've been away?"

"Yes. It's all been good. The boys are more settled here than I am, to be honest ..." There was still a look of despair in her eyes.

"Children are very adaptable ..." and, thought Kay, why would they not enjoy the comforts of a house, despite missing their familiar things, especially the people? At least they had their mother, the single most important person in their lives.

Lena had been busy. Random objects had been sorted and tidied, organised into piles. Books were lined up on shelves in order of size. Kay commented on the gleaming windowsills, the polished wood panels in the dining room, the shiny ornaments.

"I wanted to do somethin' to help – *Kair posh*. You've been so kind to us."

"What a wonderful homecoming. Thanks Lena."

More than anything she was relieved that nothing disastrous had happened. No fires, floods, or gas explosions, no broken glass or injured children, no unexpected arrival of Dunstan or other people that could have caused her problems.

The next morning, the sight that greeted her in the garden filled her with more serious concerns. There was evidence that Lena had been collecting sticks, moss, Leylandii branches.

"What's going on here then?" she asked.

"Hope you don't mind," said Lena. "I remember my great-grandmother used to make stuff to hawk – *kipsies* – baskets out of hazel twigs. And wreaths for Christmas, using moss and *saffern* – these," she said, pointing to the conifer sprays, "and holly. You've got a big holly tree down in the far corner. I cut up my skirt too into squares to make lavender bags, if I could buy some lavender from you. Then, I thought you could take them to the craft shop in the next village, there is one there I know and …"

"Oh Lena …" sighed Kay, not wishing to dampen her spirits in any way, but knowing that to scrape a living in this way would be an impossible dream. It offered no real solutions and she could not see it as a realistic way forward. "I'm glad you've found things for you and the boys to do while you're here …"

The bond growing between them filled Kay with conflicting emotions. When the boys had gone to bed and Lena brought her a cup of peppermint tea, made just the way she liked it, it struck her that the set up was in some ways working well, too well. She was becoming very fond of all three of them and she felt loved and valued by them, which, in the absence of friends, relations and immediate family, was a comfort. But she knew that this was not good for them and would make the eventual break doubly hard, the longer and the more firmly they cemented their relationships.

She stayed up late that night to search the Internet for information about immigrants and asylum seekers from the Czech republic and Slovakia. After breakfast on Monday, she closed her study door to call the local council offices about the homeless register, but was given short shrift, more or less instructed to get off the line. "We are extremely busy taking priority emergency calls," a housing officer said, barely listening to her enquiry. She suspected there would be some issue with Data Protection confidentiality and, anyway, as Lena later reminded her emphatically, "He would *never* have been looking for council housing." Just as for Lena, this would be anathema to him, but maybe hostels, some temporary roof over his head as he roved around looking for his relatives, were more likely.

When she told Lena what she had done over breakfast, she agreed. "It did slip out in our chattin' that he was stayin' in some hostel for the homeless – they didn't ask too many questions, he said – but took him in for a few days at a time. He had no bad problems, like mental nor drugs, so no need of any help or stuff like they do. Just moving on, always moving on. *Jalling the drom*."

"But he wouldn't be straying too far from this part of the country, would he?"

"No, he was just lookin' more or less round 'ere and counties close by."

"Right!" said Kay, decisively. "Then I can at least *try* to find him."

Lena gave her one of her wide-eyed looks, mouth open. "What? You'd do that for us?"

Kay did not like to say that she could see no other solution to the problem, other than turfing her out to fend for herself, or informing the local authorities – police, social services, borough council. Lena would hate her for that and she would despise herself. The only way forward was to effect some kind of reconciliation between her, Joseph and her travelling group. To prove her innocence, Tibor must be found, although how could he *prove* that he had not fathered the baby Abigail? Not even DNA tests could help in this case. It would need more than simple words and denials to convince a madly jealous husband that Tibor had not had a relationship with his wife. Hopefully, hospital records would support the truth.

"Well now, Lena, I take it you don't have a photo handy of this Tibor?"

"Course not," she replied scornfully.

"Then I don't have much to go on. A surname?" Lena shook her head.

"The family names he gave me to search were, I think Kaleja – I remember that 'cause he said it means *Hey, black one*! Another was Balkin or Bulking, and Liknova, I think. But I don't know which was his name."

Kay noted down these names. "I'll need a detailed description then."

"I could probably draw a picture too," suggested Lena.

"Excellent …" Kay scurried off to find sheets of plain paper and pencils and Lena immediately got to work, alongside Tom and Jason who were eager to join in. They set about drawing pictures of trailers, foxes, cars and people they remembered, including their father.

"He is not tall, just about my height, and quite thin, so really a smallish *mush*. He looked hungry, like he needed feeding up which is one reason why I felt sorry for him. He smoked roll-ups, which annoyed me, 'cos he had no money. Bad skin, stubbly beard – 'cos he sometimes had nowhere to shave, I think. His *yoks* … er, eyes were …" Lena paused, looking up from her sketching, having to think quite hard. It was clear to Kay that she had not spent much time staring into them. "Bluish-grey, I think. Dark eyebrows and lashes though."

"Age?"

"Not quite thirty probably."

"What about his clothes?"

"Didn't really notice – just normal jeans, anorak, tee shirt … He carried a large black rucksack with all his things."

"Any other really distinguishing feature?" asked Kay hopefully. "Mole? Piercings?"

Lena bit her lip and quietly thought. "Not really. He was just ordinary looking. A bit scruffy, bit *hindity*, obviously …"

Kay guessed what she meant. "But he could've cleaned up and be looking different by now, clean-shaven, well-fed … How's the sketch coming on?"

Lena passed the paper across and Kay drew a gasp as she stared. The drawing was brilliant, very detailed considering how quickly she had done it, showing a characterful, potentially charismatic face with heavy brows, a long, rather sharp nose and high cheekbones. His curly, dishevelled hair, which Lena had marked as 'wet mud colour' was beginning to recede already.

"Lena. This is amazing. You're very talented. Did you know that?"

She turned down the corners of her mouth, embarrassed by the praise.

"Dunno about that! Like drawing though …"

"You can sing! And draw like this. You could have such a future, you know …"

Lena just sighed. It was of no apparent interest to her.

"I really think this will help. I can photocopy this and give it to people. I'm going on a hunt for this man. In a few days' time. Just need to square things with my gardener."

How would she possibly forbid Dunstan to come to the house or garden *again*? What reason could she give? The pressure was on to tell both Dunstan and Suzi for different reasons. Lena would resist. For her to agree to one person would be impossible, two would be a miracle.

She decided that, for the benefit of Lena and the future of her children, *if necessary*, she would confide in Dunstan. She would have to take the risk that he could keep his mouth closed. If he blabbed, she would take the rap.

He turned up that afternoon, as agreed. "I have to go away again for a few days – not sure how long and would

114

prefer it if you didn't come round here until I get back," she gently broached, testing the water, watching his face.

His tense jaw and knotted brow was intimidating. There was real anger in his eyes.

"What is happening? OK you need to be away. That's your business. But this is the busiest time of the season! I need to be planting, hoeing, weeding, watering … lots to do. I can surely do some hours in the garden while you're away?"

"I'd prefer it if you didn't. I …" she paused, the words petering out as she struggled to think of a plausible excuse.

"You don't trust me, do you?" he said, quietly.

His face had now relaxed into a sorrowful expression that pierced her heart. He looked genuinely hurt. Maybe he was indeed a Gypsy and this was a reminder of past prejudices he had suffered but somehow she couldn't ask him outright now. The timing was wrong and could only make matters worse.

"I trust you implicitly Dunstan, absolutely …"

"Then …?" They stood in the kitchen, a Mexican standoff.

Kay could still think of nothing to justify what must seem an increasingly bizarre attitude.

"If you can't *trust* me, then I'm not sure I want to do this at all …"

She had pushed it as far as she dare.

"Dunstan. Please sit down. I shall now tell you something, but you must promise that it will go no further … Do I have your word?"

"Unless you've committed a crime, or are a danger to yourself or others …" he replied, rather surprisingly. What a mystery of a man.

"Nothing illegal, just a bit crazy, but all done with the best intentions. This is to *test* your trust. It's strictly confidential."

She made them both a cup of coffee and told him the full story. He listened intently.

"There's no reason for me to tell anyone about this," he reassured her.

"Thank you, Dunstan," she said, touching his arm lightly. "You see the difficult situation I've got myself into …"

"I have a camper van, which might be good for touring round and stopping off here and there and would be happy to help. These hostels for the homeless are no place for a woman to go on her own, and you may still need some help with walking …"

Kay was thinking about the law on parking caravans. Did that not apply to camper vans too? Surely you can't just stop 'here and there' …

"No …" she said.

"I think you could put yourself in danger. You'll find drug addicts, angry people, mentally ill people … all sorts."

"I meant no I don't need help with walking. I feel my recovery is almost complete now … but … your offer of a camper van, and your … company …" and she could feel the heat rise in her cheeks as she spoke, not even daring to think what the sleeping arrangements might be, "I gratefully accept."

"Good."

"But don't you have other responsibilities you can't leave at such short notice?" she probed, hoping to unearth something more about this man.

"Hah! No, that's fine." As ever, he would reveal nothing whenever she questioned him about his private life.

"And what about the garden? The garden that needs your attention so much?"

Dunstan's face creased up. "All things are relative. This takes over, doesn't it?"

"Well, I think so. It'll be good to not face this alone …"

She just had to tell Lena that she would be leaving on her mission with Dunstan now on the case too.

12

Kay was up early, ticking off her long list of tasks around the house, making sure there was enough food in the fridge for Lena and the boys. Finally, she packed a small bag in case an overnight stay was necessary and a folder with twenty copies of Tibor's portrait she had run off on her fax copier machine, at which point the film cartridge had run out.

Lena and her children came into the kitchen as she was putting some muesli into a bowl. The sun was shining through the window already, the sky a glorious clear blue.

"Ah good morning. Hello Jason, hello Tom," she said brightly. "How are you today? Now, Lena, something's happened and I think it's good, really good. Sit down, my love, I'll make you a cup of tea …" She was hoping she could sell the fact that she had broken her word with the best of intentions without triggering too much of an emotional reaction.

Lena poured some milk for the children as she did routinely every morning now, without asking if it was all right for her to do so.

"I'm going on a Tibor hunt. Well, we talked about it didn't we?" Lena nodded. "OK, well, the good news is that we have an ally! Someone who can help us."

Lena sprang up. "What? What d'you mean …?"

"Dunstan. I could *never* have got away if I had not given sound reasons for me going off again so soon, well not really *that* so much as forbidding him from coming to the garden which he just would *not* accept and I *knew* he wouldn't. But Lena, he's fine about it and has promised to keep your existence a secret, and straight away offered to help me, so

117

we're going in his camper van to search out hostels ..." Kay spilled out the words almost without taking breath to make sure that Lena did not have a chance to interrupt and start an argument. "Isn't that fantastic?"

Lena's mouth had fallen open and she shook her head in disbelief. "You promised you wouldn't tell. How well do you know Dunstan? How d'you know he'll keep his promises?" There were tears in her eyes. She added huskily, "People often don't do what they say ..."

Kay instinctively put her arms round her and gave her shoulders a squeeze. It was the first time she had been quite so tactile. As she pulled away and looked into Lena's eyes, she said, "We have to do something. We can't keep up this charade forever, Lena. This is the best course of action I can come up with. Yes?"

Lena bit her lip and looked sulky, her eyes still swimming. She turned away to hide her face from Jason and Tom. Kay sensed she was more hurt by the fact that she had gone behind her back, than she was worried about the possible consequences of word getting out in the village.

"Unless you can think of something better ..."

Lena shook her head.

"I travelled around a good bit when I was a kid – different then back in the fifties," said Dunstan, conversation coming easily as he drove them out of the village.

"Were you from ...?" Kay's question tailed off. Why could she not just ask him directly if he came from the Travelling community? If he had no connection, he might be offended. That was the problem. But why should he be? Questions were rolling around in her head.

He turned his head slightly waiting for her to finish her question and she felt foolish. "...sorry, I mean are you from around this area? Do you know it well? You live in Appley Green now, but ..."

"Well enough – in parts. Suggest we head for here first of all ..." he pointed to a town on the map she had brought with her and had lying open on her lap. "I know the people who run a hostel there."

"How come?"

"Ah, well, long story. Did some counselling – with the young men there, y'know. Tried to help. Tough call, though."

"Really? What kind of problems did they have?"

"Oh, you name it! Money, drugs, crime, depression, psychosis, relationships breaking down," he reeled off, "Yeah, broken homes mostly at the root ... the chances of finding your Tibor, y'know, are pretty slim, I'd say," he added.

Kay nodded. "But worth a try. I really don't know what else I can do to resolve the situation, apart from getting her on some housing waiting list ..."

"Mm. She'd probably stay at the bottom of the list awhile anyhow, not belonging permanently to the borough council's area ... and she'd hate that, anyway, wouldn't she? Isn't that what she's told you?"

"She certainly has," laughed Kay, recalling the venomous expression on Lena's face each time the issue of housing was mentioned. "She calls my house a *kennel*."

Dunstan's face creased up. "Ah, *kenner*. Sounds much same I suppose. Their word for house ... Anyhow, need to get her back with her family." He spoke emphatically, as if there were no alternative even worth considering.

"I agree. But where are they? And will they want her back?"

The hostel was a rambling Victorian building, close to the train station. A slim, young woman, with cropped blond hair and studs in her nose and eyebrows, opened the door after they had announced their arrival via the security system in the porch.

"Dunstan!" she cried, in a strong Irish accent. "Bloody hell, what the fuck brings you 'ere?"

Kay watched Dunstan's face for signs of embarrassment, but he just smiled, then gave her a hug and a light kiss on a cheek.

"Siobhan – I'm after some help and straight away thought of you …"

"Well why wouldn't ya? Come on in," she urged them, giving Kay a curious look.

"This is Kay – she's a friend of mine, looking for someone, don't ask why, it's complicated," said Dunstan, as the two of them crossed the threshold, following the small figure wearing tight jeans and a faded grey T-shirt.

"Sure, isn't life always complicated?" she said over her shoulder, with a chuckle. They passed through a quite Spartan lobby with an office coming off it, down a busy corridor filled with many youngish people, some in a hurry, others talking in small groups. She took them into a side room furnished with tattered armchairs and a sixties style glass-topped coffee table, with office paraphernalia in one corner. Posters and photographs on the wall displayed activities of the hostel – and Kay was fascinated to see that as well as ICT classes and workshops, there were poetry and music groups.

As soon as they sat down, Kay produced Lena's sketch of Tibor's face and passed it to Siobhan. She sat at her desk, with a leg folded up under her, and stared at the portrait.

"How'd you get hold of this?" she asked, and for a moment Kay thought she must've instantly recognised him and she felt a little fizz of pleasure inside her.

Dustan chipped in smartly. "Don't worry about that, it would waste your time to go into the whole story, trust me, Siobhan." Siobhan just nodded, continuing to stare at the picture.

"It's good, that's all," she said, looking up at them. "I was just wondering who the artist was …"

"No idea," replied Kay, smartly.

"How do you know this young dude at all? He has a quite distinctive face and his name is …?" She looked at Kay.

"Tibor. And there are three possible surnames – I've written them down as they're foreign – Czech. Not sure of the spelling either."

Siobhan looked at the names and muttered them to herself, thinking hard.

"I'll get them checked against our records – though I'm not sure I should be doing this without knowing why," she said, giving Dunstan a cheeky grin. "But I guess I owe you a favour or two …"

Dunstan looked smug. "I guess you do," he replied laconically, as she sped off towards the administrative hub. There was a wild disregard for rules about him that Kay found both endearing and exciting.

She was back almost instantly. "Anyway, he's not residing here just now – is that right?" asked Dunstan.

"Correct. I'd recognise him if he was here now – and I have to say I don't recall either his face or his name."

"OK. Siobhan, d'you have a list of other hostels hereabouts and in adjacent counties?"

"Sure I do," she said at once, jumping up and reaching for a large Lever-Arch file on a shelf above her desk. After a few minutes leafing through its contents, she opened it up and pulled out exactly what Dunstan had asked for. Kay began to wonder how far she would have got in her mission without him.

"It might be worth having a wander round, asking a few guys here if they know him? Yeah?" she said, looking at her watch. "I've got twenty minutes before I need to do some admissions."

"Thanks so much," said Kay, "we can but try."

They first went into a large, high-ceilinged kitchen, fitted with old cabinets, formica topped tables and an original butler sink – now strangely fashionable, thought Kay – where five young men and a girl were being supervised in chopping carrots, opening tins of baked beans, scrubbing potatoes.

"They're cooking lunch for all clients living here who don't have a choice. If they achieve set goals, they're given more freedoms, like buying and cooking their own meals, but we have to be careful they don't spend food money on cigarettes, booze and drugs," explained Siobhan, as if she were giving a guided tour. "Anyway, you don't need to know all that. I'm so used to people coming here and answering their questions, I don't stop to wait for the questions any more ..." She laughed.

"Siobhan has won awards for the schemes they run here," Dunstan said, turning to Kay. "Since she's taken over as manager this place has gone from strength to strength." Kay had to stop herself from gasping, surprised that this slip of a girl, looking down-at-heel and over-pierced, held such status. There she was jumping to conclusions, pre-judging again, she reflected.

Pulling herself together quickly, she commented, "Incentives must be so important ..."

"Key," agreed Siobhan, nodding seriously.

"What kind of people .... How do they come to be homeless?"

"Ex-cons. Or parents kick them out, or they leave violent domestic situations, some have been abused as kids, or break-ups with partners ... mostly that kind of thing ..."

"Failed relationships then – not so much jobless?" asked Kay, interested.

She shrugged. "Sometimes – well-educated types hit a slippery slope, you know? But, plenty of people without work live in social housing with benefits. Usually this lot, they have a package of problems, often including unemployment, eviction, lack of skills, and depression which leads to drugs, which leads to theft, prison ... and so it goes round in circles. Very unstable, need help to get back on track ..."

The portrait was passed round and all the young men and the girl shook their heads and turned down the corners of their mouths. A grey-haired woman bustled into the kitchen and Kay overheard her tell Siobhan that she had not been able to trace the names on the piece of paper.

Siobhan led them on to other haunts within the building, where they stopped and quizzed young men and women. "Most people will be out and about at this time of the day," she explained.

122

"Thanks Siobhan — we'd better be heading off. See you again," said Dunstan.

"Sure now, don't be a stranger, you old devil … Kay, I'll put this picture up with a message on the notice-board in the common room."

"Thanks for all your efforts, — here's my mobile number if you hear anything …"

A similar experience followed at the next hostel about thirty miles away. Dunstan was greeted warmly by the manager or whoever was on duty, but no one knew of Tibor.

Kay enjoyed the day spent with Dunstan. At lunchtime he had pulled the van off a quiet road into a lay-by, made bacon sandwiches and heated up some tomato soup, having turned down Kay's offer of buying a pub lunch somewhere. She sensed he did not like being interrogated about personal things so they chatted comfortably about issues in the news — global warming, the Olympics, Tony Blair and George W Bush, farmers' markets …

"More people should be doing what you're doing," he said. "Cutting down on food miles and so on. It's the way forward for the world."

Kay was with him in principle, but recalling her enjoyment of many holidays abroad and gas guzzling cars, felt slightly cut down to size. "Of course. You're right. But some would say a revival of self-sufficiency would be like turning the clock back …"

"Some people are not looking at the absurdities we live with …"

He vented his strong opinions on the soulless, over-packaged, throwaway, materialistic society and Kay found herself agreeing with everything he said. She began to realise that he was fast becoming a kindred spirit, the more so because she was sharing with him a secret mission. And he was a willing collaborator.

By late evening they had covered three hostels and, poring over maps together, had prepared a route for the day ahead. After a meal of smoked wild salmon, followed by barbecued fillet steak and salad, Kay could see that Dunstan knew how to live. Thrifty in many ways, but not afraid to spend money on quality food, why did he choose to labour for her as a gardener? Although he had offered some reasons and she thought it rude to push for more explanations, she still did not understand the man. He never spoke of family or his home. She had tried, but her probing always drew a blank. They sat outside on grass he had covered with a rug, between gorse bushes and slender birches, Kay with a glass of wine and he with a bottle of beer, the air, thought Kay, tasting more like champagne. He had found a wonderful high spot in the heart of the countryside with a breathtaking view of the south coast, which faded from sight as they watched the orange sun gradually sink through a marbled pink sky into the dark horizon to their right.

Had he invited her into his bed that night, she feared she would not have had the strength of will to decline the offer, but as it turned out he magically transformed the vehicle into two separate sleeping areas where before long they were both sleeping soundly. She had to remind herself that she was not of her daughters' generation, even if, that night, she felt as if she was.

13

The following morning they carefully avoided each other in the rather cramped conditions of the van as the mechanical procedures of getting washed and dressed took place. Kay had learned the previous evening that toilet facilities were 'anywhere out there'. She assumed this saved the unpleasant chore of emptying the van's chemical loo.

Now Dunstan was rummaging in the small fridge for some breakfast options. "I know you like muesli …" he began.

"That's really thoughtful, but …"

"I have none," he teased.

"And herbal tea or good Italian coffee?"

"Ye-es?" she said warily.

"Uh-uh. There's eggs, sausages, mushrooms, bread, marmalade and tea or instant coffee."

Kay hesitated, not sure she could do justice to a plate of fried food before eight o'clock.

"Why don't we go for a walk to work up an appetite first?" she suggested.

"Why not?"

He locked the camper van, looking around furtively, possibly suspecting that a traffic warden might emerge from behind a blackthorn bush. There were no marked footpaths, just tracks perhaps made by rabbits and deer, and the heath was rough ground, requiring concentration to avoid stumbling.

The morning was hazy but promised a fine day, the slightly damp air feeling fresh on Kay's cheeks. The van, Kay realised, was perfectly sheltered at a point where forest met the smoother turf of herbs and coarse grasses that undulated between them and the sea. Apart from birdsong in the scrubby trees, it was so peaceful she could hear the blood rushing in her head.

"I wonder what today will bring," said Kay. Dunstan reached out a hand, lightly touching her elbow to steady her, and she slipped her arm companionably through his. "If nothing comes of anything, we'll have to call it a day. I can't expect you to give up any more time. I'll make enquiries about Travellers stopping at other unauthorised sites." And, she thought, I must try and get Lena to contact the hospital for back-up testimony, as soon as I get back.

"You'll have trouble getting near them ..." Dunstan warned. Kay noticed he had binoculars hanging around his neck.

"What makes you say that?"

"Travellers are wary of outsiders. That's all." He stopped briefly and held the binoculars to his eyes, fixing his gaze on the branches of an old oak tree. "I thought I heard both nightingale and nightjar during the night, one so melodious, the other so raucous!"

Kay admired his knowledge. "You've no idea what a treat it is for me to be able to do this ..." she said, linking her arm again through his for support, soon feeling masculine warmth through his jacket. "Since my accident, you know, I've missed long country rambles. My husband and I used to go on walking holidays – Langdale Pikes, Peak District, the Amalfi coast ..."

He did not pick up on this and ask about her accident, her late husband or, indeed, their travels. It was perhaps his way of not entering into those private realms lest he should be expected to reciprocate. He pointed out early gentian, purple and green-winged orchid, seemingly quite absorbed by his surroundings.

"You can see a dazzling display of butterflies here ... clouded yellow, and little blues – or you could once. They're attracted by the vetches you see ... Ah look, look Kay," he touched her shoulder and pointed up into the sky. "A kestrel hovering there right above us. Well, isn't that a sight to behold before breakfast? Did you hear the old owl last night? You must've …?"

Suddenly, Kay's mobile phone rang and she snatched it from her jeans pocket, angry at the intrusion, wishing she had thought to turn it off. She could see it was neither Lena nor Suzi calling.

"Hello? Kay here."

"Siobhan. Someone here remembers seeing him in town."

"Tibor? Really? That's amazing …"

"It was a few weeks ago. He was trying to find some relatives but, meanwhile, he'd found some work in a quarry in Hertfordshire. He was bragging a bit, well excited y'know, desperate to earn money."

Kay was pleased beyond measure and surprised to have such positive news so soon, simultaneously realising this would require travelling in the opposite direction, a few hours' driving.

"Anything more specific – name of the quarry or whereabouts in Hertfordshire?"

"Sorry – we think it was sand and gravel, but no idea where."

"Please don't apologise. That's really useful," said Kay. "I can make enquiries."

"Could I have a quick word with Dunstan?" asked Siobhan and rather reluctantly Kay passed the phone to him, suddenly feeling excluded. The magic of a few moments before had been spoiled.

She watched Dunstan nodding and listening. "No, no of course not. Don't worry. I understand," he was saying. "Thanks a billion Siobhan."

He passed the phone back to her, saying, "She's worried she'll get into trouble for breaching confidentiality. We must be careful not to let anyone know the source of our information. OK?"

Kay nodded, feeling further attracted to him in this conspiracy they were sharing.

They drove through Hampshire and Surrey, finally joining the M25 and crossing into Hertfordshire. They had discussed ways of identifying quarries – planning offices, local newspapers for job ads, Ordnance Survey maps and by a combination of all three methodologies, drew up a short-list of names. They stopped off at a public library to look up their telephone numbers in a directory and then spent a while making calls. On the third call they struck lucky and found themselves cheering loudly at their extraordinary success. It was all going so well.

"Dunstan! This is amazing – how exciting. I feel like that lady detective in Africa – have you ever read any of those books? Mma Ramotswe – do you know who I am talking about?"

He shook his head. "Can't say I do a lot of reading ..." he muttered.

"Oh, you'd enjoy them ..." insisted Kay, not really listening.

"Can you look at the map now and give me some directions," said Dunstan, rather abruptly. Kay was already planning a SatNav system for Dunstan's Christmas present.

Kay cooked up a bit of a story for the man running day-to-day operations at the quarry, who introduced himself as Bob Gibson. They said they had some news for his employee, whom Bob confirmed to be Tibor Likanova.

"Could we have a quick word with him? Perhaps in his lunch break?" asked Kay. It was around half-past twelve as they spoke.

"Does he know you?" asked Bob, narrowing his eyes suspiciously. "I mean he's a good worker, but he's jumpy about officials an' all that. Watches his back. Know what I mean? Like someone's after him. The old paperwork seems to be in order but he's had a very scary time, so he told me, anyhow …"

"Tell him we're from Appley Green," suggested Kay. "He won't know our names. Tell him … tell him we want to help him …"

They met Tibor very soon in the mess-room where dusty men in working clothes came in bearing large quantities of sandwiches, pies, cakes and flasks of hot drinks. Bob introduced them to Tibor at one of the tables and left.

"What is all this about? Do you have news for me of my family?" said Tibor, opening up his packed lunch and drinking thirstily from a bottle of water.

Kay knew he would be hanging on this hope and felt guilty for giving this impression, via Bob, but she knew this was probably the only way she could gain access to Tibor, the only reason he would want to speak to strangers.

"I'm afraid not. We're here to ask for your help …"

The expression on his face was a mixture of disappointment and suspicion.

"But perhaps we can help you too!" added Kay brightly. "Help you track down your Roma relatives?" Well, why not, she thought? Dunstan's eyebrows shot up, but she discerned a suppressed smile.

Tibor's blue eyes opened wide, thick eyebrows raised and he sat forward, clearly shocked and surprised that Kay knew this much about him. Now she really had his attention, but she knew this bonding was important in building up the trust needed to enlist his co-operation.

"Tell us how you came to be here," she said gently.

"Here? At this quarry?"

"Well, yes …" It wasn't quite what she had meant, but she would try and steer him back in a moment or two.

"It was an advertisement in the Job Centre, a driver needed for earth-mover in Hertfordshire! I could not believe it! Really lucky. It is what I trained for – what I do before in Czech Republic, you know. Until they found out I am Roma and then I was bullied so I ..." he stopped, frowning, evidently finding it painful. "There is no time to tell you all the things I have been through, you know. I have to be back in fifteen minutes or so ..."

"Perhaps we could meet again when you finish ... but what we need from you is ... Well, Tibor, do you remember speaking to a young woman, a Romany Gypsy, a few times in Appley Green?"

"You mean Lena?"

Dunstan and Kay exchanged glances. It was a special moment.

"Yes. Lena."

"Oh yes. She listened to me, she gave me food and money and said she would try to find my aunt and uncle and cousins who came to UK in 2001. She said her husband did not like her talking to me, so we had to meet secretly, but she could see I was desperate. Living like a wild animal, to be honest with you!"

This tied perfectly with Lena's version of events. Kay explained how she had been accused of flirting with Tibor and that he was under suspicion of having fathered the baby girl that Lena had lost. As she spoke she was afraid that he would be terrified away.

"She's been cast out of her group, or at least she's left, feeling so threatened that she dare not go back, even if she could find them. They have, of course, moved on now. She's living with me for the moment, but is very unhappy ..."

"This is terrible for Roma. Terrible! To be alone! The worst possible nightmare." And, of course, thought Kay, he would know. "Of course it is all a lie. I did not touch her. Never."

"If we support you, and if we can find her husband, would you be willing to tell him this to vouch for her? To clear her name?"

"I think I would have my throat cut!" he said, slicing his hand across his Adam's apple. Kay's instincts somehow told her that this would not happen.

"We will be there too. You will never be alone with him and I will get Lena to obtain evidence from the hospital too, that the baby was miscarried two months early …"

"I don't know. I could get into trouble with this, if they do not believe me. They will say 'of course he will deny it', won't they?"

"If you could do this, I will do everything I can to find your missing family. Is that a deal?" Kay knew she had played her last winning card. If this did not work, then nothing would persuade him.

"I'll think about it. Meet me … in the café down the road, I don't remember its name, next to the roundabout as you go east from here. It's where lorry-drivers go. Say at half-past five."

Kay looked at Dunstan, wondering if this would be a problem for him, but he nodded agreement.

"Thank you Tibor. We'll be there."

They came away feeling torn between satisfaction at talking to him and frustration at the uncertain outcome. Would he help or not? If she could get Lena to make contact with the hospital now, this would provide the hard evidence needed to support his story.

"I'll call Lena. She'll be thrilled we've found Tibor, and I'll try and get her to see the importance of calling the hospital now, without delay," said Kay, as she and Dunstan walked back to the camper van.

"I can't see her doing that, from what you've said …"

"Well she'll have to eventually. They won't give *me* the details, I know that. If she phones so the telephone number can't be tracked, she could call, identify herself somehow verbally and …" she pressed her home number on her mobile and the phone promptly died on her.

"Oh damn it, the battery's gone. How am I going to get that re-charged?"

"Here – borrow mine," said Dunstan, pulling his mobile from his jacket pocket.

"Thanks. What would I do without you?"

Lena put up all kinds of resistance just as Kay had imagined she would.

"Tell them that, for your own personal records, you need them to provide some paperwork that will show clearly the date of your premature delivery and how far you were in your pregnancy ..."

"But they don't know that, because I never knew. Not exactly."

"Well, in their medical opinion. An estimate. They will have had some idea from the development of the ... of your little Abigail, and probably other ways. They'll have something, I'm sure, that could help you. You have a right to your own records. Look, Lena, it's great news we've found Tibor, but to get him to back up your story ..."

"It's not a story," cried Lena down the phone. "It's the *truth*!"

"I know ... it's a true story, I know that ..."

Eventually, Lena seemed to be agreeing, but short of leaning over her shoulder, Kay could not be sure that she would make the call to the hospital.

"Now, what shall we do for the afternoon?" asked Kay. "Well, first of all I can buy lunch ... and, maybe the restaurant will be kind enough to charge my phone for me while we take our time ..."

She insisted on finding somewhere quite special ...

Later, Tibor told them, "I have memories of our family when I was about four years old. I can't remember before that. Always on the run. Now I know it was the time of the Velvet Revolution. Always travelling – from one country to another, then we were finally returned to our homeland as we had nowhere else to go."

Kay and Dunstan listened, genuinely interested. "But some of your family made another attempt a few years ago and were successful? Have you had any contact with them since they came to the UK?"

"At first there were letters. And we tried to write back to them, but their address was just a site, and we could tell from the last letter we had from them, they were not receiving ours. So they probably thought we had not bothered. They stopped writing to us."

"So Lena tried to find them for you, through members of her group?"

"She was going to try, but it was complicated. I did not want my name to be spread far and wide because I was, well, you have the saying 'on the run'. I had committed a theft."

"Ah," said Kay, averting her gaze for a moment. "So were the police looking for you?"

He shrugged. "Possibly. I had been working for a gangmaster for around eight months … terrible life. It gets you into debt just to survive. They demand money for the lodgings and make you work long, long hours. It was bad, very bad and I was hoping to be able to send money home to my mother. You know, she understood my wish to leave home for a better life, but it broke her heart for me to go. I told her I would send her money home. You know all her life she has been chased from … you say … pillar to post, from one country to another across Europe. We are not even recognised as citizens in our so-called homeland. Nobody wanted the Roma. "

He stopped as a waitress came along to clear their table and Dunstan ordered another round of coffees with some pastries. He went on, "I met this strange young woman. She was … anxious … It was Lena, of course, looking over her shoulder all the time, shy but excited to hear about my mission. She told me about her group but did not think I would have much success to join them, in hope of tracking down my relatives – 'we are very distrustful of outsiders, even other Gypsy families sometimes,' she said to me, but I could see she felt badly about this. So then she offered to try and help me find my family herself."

He paused briefly and Kay commented, "Your English is so good."

He smiled. "My mother made sure we all learned English from an early age to increase the family's chances of getting here. We could not trust to hope alone, she would say! I decided to save up some money – maybe this would help, I thought, if I had something to offer the Roma people here. And there was my mother, who has so little. I keep trying to find them. All my life my family and I have been chased, now I am doing the chasing!"

Kay looked at Dunstan. "We would like to help you. What could we do?"

He handed her a scrap of paper. "These are the names of my people – perhaps you could contact someone from the settled community who has dealings with the Romany people?"

Immediately, Kay thought of Max Leatherson. He could certainly start the ball rolling, discreetly.

"Sure thing," said Kay. "You've tried telephone directories, I take it? Electoral registers?"

He nodded. "Nothing – which makes me think all the more they're with a Romany group. Or, they could just use mobile phones. I don't know."

"OK. Now, we had a deal, didn't we?"

Tibor nodded. "Yes, if you do this for me, I will help your Lena. Of course. This is my mobile number. You can call me on this, or text me, to let me know when she has the other information you mentioned and then I will travel down – one weekend, it will have to be."

"Ah well, one step forward, three back! Now all we have to do is find Lena's husband, get corroboration from the hospital and locate Tibor's lost family!" said Kay to Dunstan as they left Tibor to make the journey back to Appley Green.

"Oh – is that all?"

As Dunstan drove home, Kay quietly reflected on the challenges that lay ahead, wondering anew at how her life had changed in the past few weeks. True enough, she had wanted a change! She had been actively seeking a new direction, but little did she know back in March that Natalie's arrival on her doorstep could have set off such a chain of events that she could have neither anticipated nor engineered. With the benefit of hindsight, would she have invited Natalie to revisit her? Would she have gone to the meeting in the Village Hall? Had she done neither of these things, would she have welcomed a stray Gypsy and her two children into her home?

They had covered about twenty miles when her phone interrupted her thoughts.

"Mum," came Suzi's voice. She sounded frantic. "Where have you been? I tried and tried to call you earlier this afternoon …"

Kay could feel her own heart beat fast, hearing the agitation in Suzi's voice. "Sorry love, my phone ran out of juice …"

"Where are you?"

"On my way home now," said Kay, vaguely.

"Well you may be interested to know that I popped in to see you as a surprise on my way back from a friend's wedding in Devon – which was yesterday and I stayed over - and good job I did …" Kay held her breath. Oh no! "You'll never *believe* what I found! Just some girl – honestly younger than me, I'd say, with two kids *squatting* in your house. You wouldn't believe how she'd made herself at home – I mean how long have you been away? I had to threaten her with the police before she'd budge and then you should've seen her *move*! Obviously guilty of something. And do you know what? She even had the bloody nerve to insist she had your permission!"

14

The house was empty and quiet. Kay felt as if she was rattling around from one room to another, devoid of purpose. She stepped cautiously into the bedroom that had been home to Lena, Jason and Tom for so many weeks, where they had left traces of their existence – some toys, unmade beds, a few smears on the window-panes where the boys had gazed out, probably noses pressed to the glass. She felt an ache in her throat.

The thought of now explaining Lena's presence to Suzi was giving her a sick feeling deep in the pit of her stomach, tension spreading through her body like a physical pain, so sure was she that her daughter would be unforgiving on the secrecy, and accusatory for being 'soft'. Already she could imagine Suzi's open-mouthed consternation at her reckless behaviour, the dressing down she would get for being naïve, inviting trouble, setting herself up to be used and abused. With castigations already ringing in her head, she even flirted with the idea of extending the deception a little further. Why tell Suzi at all? Lena had, after all, gone. Why should she feel responsible?

She could just wash her hands of the whole situation and draw a line under it. Lena was no longer in her house. Her destiny was her own.

As soon as Dunstan was apprised of the situation, his split-second response was unequivocal. "We must find her. Lena. Before all else. She'll be vulnerable." There was no question, doubt or debate.

The guilt grinding away would never let up if she did not come clean with Suzi, she decided. Like Raskolnikov in *Crime*

136

and Punishment, it would haunt her forever ... She took deep breaths, with sharp reprimands for being over dramatic. No one had committed a crime! This was getting out of proportion, but a guilty conscience moved in mysterious ways.

No, Lena could not be allowed to just disappear. Dunstan was right. This would be an on-going project she must follow through, and Suzi would have to be told, but not just at that moment. She was too shaky.

She ambled round the vegetable plot, nursing a mug of coffee. It had been raining hard during the night and dripping foliage glistened in the pale sunshine. The well-tilled loam, sectioned into raised beds or defined rectangles, was a rich, dark brown and Kay breathed in its earthy smell. She noticed the divide where Dunstan's hoeing had stopped last time and nature had retaliated, a carpet of healthy groundsel, bindweed and other anonymous impostors turning the ground green. She began to understand why the possibility of just leaving the garden to its own devices for days at a time would have been a problem.

In future she would listen to him. Even if she did not seek out Lena herself, she knew that he would set things in motion to do all he could to retrieve her. Her heart was, in any case, telling her that she would not sleep at night if she did not find her. And how would she ever forgive herself, if she simply did not bother and then woke up one morning to a newspaper headline: *BODIES OF YOUNG WOMAN AND TWO CHILDREN FOUND*... Now she was being over dramatic again, but she knew from bitter experience that sometimes real life was more horrendous than you could believe possible. It could spring disasters on you and that was one she must prevent at all costs. She drained her mug of coffee and made her way back to the house, now as clear as the fresh morning air on what must be done.

She flicked through her papers to find Max Leatherson's number.

"Good morning Max, you may not remember me – we spoke a while ago, and you e-mailed me, about the group of Travellers in Appley Green ..."

"Yes, of course," he broke in, reassuringly. "Kay Brackenbridge."

A good start, she felt. "I was wondering if you could help me with a couple of things?"

"Well, fire away. Can but try ..."

"Too convoluted to explain, Max, but I'm trying to track down some Czech immigrants. Romany. I have some names and I just wondered if you had come across them ..."

He chuckled. "I think I may have to ask why. How come you're getting involved, Kay?"

"I just want to help a young man. That's all you need to know," she insisted, not wishing to be drawn in. "I wouldn't want to take up your valuable time with unnecessary detail. He's been desperately trying to find family members who came over to UK a few years back."

"I don't think I can help you on that. Not sure ... but I'll certainly bear it in mind on my travels around the groups and pass this on to anyone else who may have contacts. Immigration authorities, mm ... Leave it with me."

Kay thanked him and gave him the names. "Any news of the whereabouts of the group that was here?"

"No – they're an elusive bunch! One thing I can tell you, though, is that they are highly unlikely to ever return to Appley Green! Your residents have won the battle I guess."

Kay's heart sank. Untraceable, and unlikely to return. How would they begin to look for Lena or her husband? She could feel the distance between her and the Travellers stretching out as he spoke.

He went on, "Normally I can't predict, but in this case, before they upped sticks, they were overheard saying they'd never be coming back. Couldn't stand the residents' hostility any longer. Unknown for them to take it that hard, to be honest, they're that tough ... Anyhow, trouble is, they'll go to somewhere else new and receive the same reception and so it'll go on ..."

"They've been coming here for years, haven't they?"

"Regulars. Year in, year out, for ... oh probably, centuries. Real tradition gone wrong. Sign of the times. There you go."

"You sound resigned."

"Well, maybe they're somebody else's problem now ..."

Kay found their conversation unsettling, unsatisfactory. It was brushing crumbs under carpet, head in sand stuff, really skirting around the issues. It struck her as frankly rather spineless and had the effect of making her more determined to do all within her power to set things right. Another task to add to her growing list of objectives; 'to win the hearts and minds of local *Gorgios*'.

"Suzi, can you come over this weekend?"

"What's up? Are you worried about more break-ins?"

"Break-ins? How d'you mean?"

"Is your memory OK, Mum?"

Kay realised she just had not made the connection, their perceptions were so different.

"No, no, not at all," she assured her, "just a few ideas I want to chat over with you ..."

"I was going to a friend's birthday do on Saturday in Hampstead, but ... is it important? Can it wait till next weekend, or could you do it over the phone?"

Kay thought for a few seconds. "It is important ... to me. Go to the party, but come over one day soon if you can." It was a bit of trek to come down in a day, but Kay had to be firm on this without ruffling her feathers too much, or raising alarm bells.

"Oh and Suzi, did you actually involve the police when you ...?"

"Well, of course I did! You can't have people just *intruding* ..." Kay's stomach flipped. The press reporter after Marcus's murder had used the word 'intruder' and it would forever have painful associations. "…into folks' houses. Did she take anything? The girl?"

"No … no I don't think so. Did you give the police a description?"

"*Doh!* Mother, bless you, do you think I'm a complete airhead? They *obviously* asked me and I even *more obviously* told them. Her looks, her accent, her children, clothes – the lot. Blinking pikeys." Kay flinched. It sounded crass, felt like a personal insult.

She would call the police and explain that there had been a misunderstanding, that she did not wish to press charges, but most probably this was a kind of communication she could not entirely undo. If Lena got into any kind of trouble, however petty, someone might remember her description.

Kay checked her post, e-mails and diary late that evening. She had carpet fitters coming tomorrow and a greenhouse being delivered, and she could picture how the latter would bring a huge smile to Dunstan's face, even if it was a bit late in the growing season. He … no, together they could get some peppers, chillies, aubergines and tomatoes going, all of which had fared badly in the garden due to lack of sunshine and heavy downpours of rain. Where was global warming when you needed it?

She then summarised her position, feeling a need for clarity before she could enjoy a sound night's sleep. Max was on the case for Tibor and tomorrow she would call him again for a list of other sites he knew of within a radius of fifty … no, a hundred miles and any contact details he may have. The reason for this request could be tied in with the Tibor issue. She still felt it right not to betray Lena to anyone official, even though she was out there – somewhere. She would not want to be instrumental in her being discovered by people she was still trying to avoid. She racked her brain for smart ways to seek out Lena, without raising alarms. Then there was the hospital … If she attempted to get confidential patient information of this sensitive nature, they would ask questions and decline to give it anyway, so it would not be worth even trying. There was no point contacting Tibor until she had some news. He was unlikely to play his part without the medical record and who could blame him? And they had a deal, so she needed to make some progress on the hunt for his relatives before all else.

It was all so frustrating. She felt ineffective, just playing a waiting game. She could simply drive around the area trying to spot Lena. Without much money, she could not have gone far away, but she would be keeping herself hidden, even now. She had sent her text messages: "Lena, worried about you. Are you OK? Please come back. Kay," but felt it unlikely that Lena's mobile would be charged and able to receive.

Searching on the Internet and in books to enrich her knowledge of Romany culture, she came across a wealth of information on Gypsy society – folklore, fairs and festivals at Appleby and Stow on the Wold; crafts that still helped provide income. She delved into history that both fascinated and horrified her. Six hundred years ago, she read, the spread of Islam in a westerly direction caused the Romany people to flee across Europe and they were nothing more than slaves. She winced as she read that some males were castrated so they did not pose a threat to women they served. Female house slaves were given to visitors for amusement. As for children, the going rate for purchase in the sixteenth century was the equivalent of thirty-two pence. Some of their work was predictable: charcoal-burner, knife-grinder, maker of bowls and troughs … there was a long list. They would not have had the freedom to be horse-dealers in those days, she assumed. The variety of occupations made her smile and wonder: torturer, bear-trainer, violin-player, goldwasher and executioner … Coppersmiths were the largest Romany group – the Kalderash – and she reflected how even today even after wars, plagues, industrial, technical, medical and educational revolutions, their focus had endured, with copper still highly prized by scrap metal merchants. Moving away from the past she found details of support groups, local authority initiatives in education, the difficulties of day-to-day life, of which the general public she felt were unaware. Discrimination seemed ubiquitous.

She began to make a list of all the positives about Gypsies and their way of life. For the moment, she was putting to one side the negative views held by non-Gypsy people, many of which were sustained by isolated bad experiences, rumours and prejudice. She recalled the press articles she had seen at the library. All bad, every single one of them. No section of society is perfect, (look at some of the people in those hostels, she thought) but to never have anything good said about you, as a job lot, must be so demoralising. Perhaps if the settled community could at least meet them half way, offer them more decent jobs, give them a chance, welcome them into their shops, pubs and restaurants. Buoyed up by a strong sense of purpose, by the opportunity to do something big, something that might make a difference, not just for Lena and her family, her group, but for other travelling groups around the country, around the world ... she reined herself in, scarcely noticing that it was past one o'clock in the morning.

The local newspaper would be her launch pad. She was used to dealing with the press – admittedly the IT trade and consumer publications – but there was a time when she had written pieces on anything from *Pet Allergies* to *Sailing in the Aegean*, when building up her portfolio of published articles. Know your audience, your market. Be topical. Do your research, write to engage the reader – and the editor. She had the expertise.

Although her head was buzzing, she fell into a deep sleep by about three o'clock and woke around seven, full of energy and raring to go. By half-past eight her new carpets and a team of men to lay them had arrived and, she felt euphoric at seeing all the old floor coverings being wrenched from their moorings and disappearing into their van for long overdue disposal.

As she was looking through the morning's post, mostly junk mail she quickly binned, she heard the slight metallic

142

sound of her new letterbox in the front porch. Her heart jumped. Lena? She could easily come back. But surely, she would knock on the door, ring the bell, or come round the back? Was she so afraid? Lena must know that she was her friend and would support her against Suzi. But then, she had not even told Suzi yet. And why? *Why?* The truth was, she had to confess, that even she, her own mother, dreaded her reaction, ridiculous and cowardly though that was. It was so much easier for Suzi to be kept blissfully ignorant – apart from the massive misunderstanding that had completely upset the applecart. Suzi would have been intimidating, she knew that, and not a person that Lena would want to risk coming across again.

By the time she reached the front door, no one was there. She hurried down the path that cut through the front lawn to the pavement and looked up and down the road. A woman with two golden Labradors was walking away, towards the village. A man with a stick was posting a letter about fifty yards away in the other direction, and a young Mum with a toddler and a baby in a buggy was crossing the road probably, thought Kay, heading for another road that led to a council estate. She thought of Lena, without a pushchair, carrying little Jason on her hip, with no place to go, in the rain. Tears welled up in her eyes as she imagined the night the three of them might have had …

Perhaps they were hiding in her shed! Feelings of hope rippled through her.

In the letterbox was a note inviting her to a local Neighbourhood Watch meeting. She wondered why the person delivering it had not wanted to speak to her. Weren't these schemes all about being neighbourly? Never mind, it was timely, very timely. What better opportunity to gather more local material for her articles, to find out more about people's prejudices and grouses? She then headed off for the shed at speed.

15

Dunstan was more than happy to set up the greenhouse ready for action, while Kay scoured the countryside. She chose to use the black BMW, which used to belong to Marcus, rather than her more conspicuous bright red sportscar. Three years ago opulent cars were part and parcel of the normal lifestyle where they lived and now they had immense sentimental value. Just the sight of the BMW conjured a picture of Marcus driving off, perhaps to a conference or some laboratories. Touching the steering wheel with her fingertips would remind her of happy family journeys. It felt wonderful to be driving again, although she knew she would have to seriously consider her position regarding carbon emissions.

She notched up over fifty miles, careening through quiet lanes, venturing into woody areas, train stations, calling at libraries and peering under bridges, anywhere that might provide shelter from what was proving to be an extraordinarily wet summer.

But by lunchtime she surrendered. It all seemed entirely hopeless, not a smart strategy at all, the words 'needle' and 'haystack' coming to mind. She felt hot with embarrassment now for even imagining that Lena and the boys would have bolted for the shed. Suzi would have seen them go there and, even if they had run off and come back to it, how would they have possibly existed alongside the rusty tools and variety of creepy wildlife that probably inhabited its damp and mildewed crevices? She shuddered at the very idea.

Dunstan repeatedly expressed his concern for Lena. He had prepared lunch for Kay's return and they sat at the kitchen table eating cold beef salad and warm granary baguettes. "Gypsies are great survivors, but very rarely on their own. I've put out feelers with some people I know …," he said, stuffing meat with slices of tomato and onion into his bread.

She was about to protest. Would Lena want that? But commonsense was kicking in. What else could they do? Her name and appearance would *have* to be passed on by word of mouth if they had any hope of finding her, especially amongst the right people. And Dunstan seemed to know what he was doing, just as he had in the search for Tibor. Had Lena been from the settled community, then the police would be involved, but she sensed that they would simply shrug their shoulders. She could imagine their reaction. *She's a Traveller, you say? They move on. That's what they do.* No point in deploying scarce resources to hit a moving target and she had committed no real crime.

The conversation had moved away from Lena to greenhouse matters, when Claudia called. She was in Rome, but making her way back home.

"Enjoying your quiet country life, then Mum? Not getting bored are you?" she asked, in all seriousness and Kay was unable to speak for a moment. "Mu-um? Hey, you OK? How's the hip and stuff?"

"I am healed. It's just fantastic and … no, I'm far from bored. I'll fill you in when I see you. Can't wait to hear all about your travels. How long then, my love?"

"Hard to say. Maybe a week." Not that long, thought Kay, filled with both pleasure and panic, sure she could feel a heady mix of serotonin and adrenalin being released simultaneously into her bloodstream like incompatible drugs. "Could be three weeks, even longer." Analgesic relief then washed through her, despite her best maternal intentions. "Depends if I can get some casual work – fast running out of cash." Was this the reason for the call? No, thought Kay, she wouldn't offer more funding. It was time her firstborn came home, took up her career again and faced adult responsibilities. Wasn't it? Always moving on … what kind of a nomadic way of life was that for a young woman? The irony struck her as the questions chased around her head.

"Darling, you make the most of your time away. Your … freedom. Once you get committed to career, mortgage, children, the chance will be gone!" Allowances had been made for Claudia to physically distance herself from the trauma of her father's death scene, its emotional impact likely to stay with her for the rest of her life.

"Tell me about it! But, actually, I'm looking forward to a bit of calm, homesy stability, to be quite honest with you. Friends, you, Suzi – my own place, find a job." Kay hoped she actually meant, 'find a job and get a place of my own,' in that more financially viable order. "It'll be so cool!"

As the morning sun climbed higher in an unexpectedly cloudless sky, some were complaining of the heat and lack of shade in the garden that a local retired solicitor's wife, called Maggie, had opened up for the Neighbourhood Watch meeting. A mixed race (possibly British Afro-Caribbean) plumber called Tony, and a painter and decorator who looked Italian or possibly middle-eastern (even Arab or Asian) but spoke with an East European accent (Polish, maybe, even Turkish) who worked together inasmuch as they promoted each other's trades to their customers, were in charge of the barbecue. They had moved south from the Midlands and Tony spoke cheerfully with a strong Birmingham accent. Kay discovered this, whilst dipping *crudités* into a bowl of mayonnaise on a table close by. She felt as if she were back in the metropolis.

Maggie's husband, Norris, then appeared with glass jugs of Pimm's, which somebody promptly took from him as he gave instructions to add fruit and cucumber. He soon busied himself with retrieving sunshade umbrellas and awnings from a capacious shed just visible at the end of the garden. There was plenty of time to chat and nobody seemed too keen to move things on to the business side of the meeting, namely, thefts, burglaries, muggings, anti-social behaviour and 'means

146

to deter and combat such crimes by bonding as a community and looking out for each other', as the leaflet suggested.

There was just one scheme for the whole village, with a population of some three thousand, so the attendance today represented just a fraction of the total village membership. Although it was a Saturday, some people would be working, shopping, out with their families, or just happy to leave it to others. Kay spotted Mrs Patel, not often sighted away from her glass-fronted Post Office counter and she went up to her.

"Beautiful day! Welcome respite from all the rain. Lovely garden, too," commented Kay, accepting a glass of fully garnished Pimm's that suddenly appeared on a tray between them. "How's things at the Post Office?" She had to start somewhere …

"My assistant and Mr Patel coping on their own for an hour or two … Difficult these days as you can imagine …" Mrs Patel did not smile.

"Oh, no. You haven't been closed down …?"

Mrs Patel frowned. "No. Still waiting to hear about that. Nothing is certain. We go on. Do our best. Work hard. Bring up our children. Encourage them in their education. What more can we do?"

Kay sensed there was more. Mrs Patel looked close to tears. "Is there … some other problem …?"

"Just well, with my father passing away, you know."

"Oh – I'm sorry. I didn't know. I do remember your husband telling me you were visiting family a while back …"

"I thought everyone in the village must know. I had so many cards – most of them bought from our shop!" She forced a smile. "The problem now, you see, is what to do with my mother. All the family have emigrated from India, you know, and she is left alone with just one daughter who is blind – the diabetes – and cannot support her. It is such a worry, I do not sleep at night."

Kay felt humbled and ashamed for not having picked up on this before. She must be the last one in Appley Green to know about this and offer her sympathy.

147

She struggled to find the right words. "So … will you be going out there again …? From time to time? Are there friends who can help your mother and sister?"

She shook her head and then nodded. "Flights are expensive, and, anyway, I'm needed here. Better to save and send them the money instead, I say. All their money went on my father's medical care, you see. There are friends, yes, but they are poor, you know. Still hard to make your way up the ladder in India, unless you are young and educated – and happy to work in a call centre or in computers!" Again the shy smile. Kay began to warm to Mrs Patel. How could she help without seeming too charitable? We hear about India's booming economy, but its successes were not necessarily accessible to an elderly widow and a middle-aged, disabled woman. Kay silently vowed to listen more carefully to people and their problems. She was getting too caught up, too focused in her own world. Blinkered.

Kay mingled, tuning into groups, listening carefully to what people were saying, opening her mind. Most people knew each other and she realised she was still an outsider, having been so preoccupied over the months since moving into the village. She took a seat, a smart garden chair, as her legs were beginning to feel the strain of standing. The villagers must have dismissed her as a loner, that recluse she did not want to be. She doubted her PR plan for Gypsies could even get off the ground if she did not forge some strong links with the very people she wanted to 'convert'.

"Hello!" came a bright female voice. "You look lost."

Kay realised she had been sitting alone in pensive mode for a few minutes. "Oh, just resting my legs …," she replied. Did she need to explain her recent medical history? No. She offered the young woman an appreciative smile.

"I remember seeing you bombing about the village in your scooter. They're great, aren't they?"

Kay nodded. "They are. Prefer legs, though! And driving my car."

"I work at the hospital – think I saw you there too on one occasion."

"Oh very possibly … What do you do, then?" Kay was glad to grasp the opportunity to steer the conversation away from herself.

"Midwife …" Kay felt herself start, as sparks flew across her brain, making connections.

"At the hospital, the local one?" The woman nodded. "What an amazing job that must be! Bringing new life into the world. Can't think of anything more rewarding. But, like most occupations, it must have its share of problems …" she added, cautiously probing.

"Oh just the usual – stress, overworked, understaffed, underpaid!" she said, laughing. "I'm Sonia, by the way …"

Kay nodded. "Kay Brackenbridge. Thank goodness my parents blessed me with a short first name! But what kind of age are mothers these days? I can't see my daughters producing offspring until they're in their thirties – they can barely look after themselves! It seems to be the trend these days, freezing eggs and so forth …"

"True, although I see teenage mums too. Not always the best age, but they happen, possibly more so in rural areas."

"Something to do if you get bored?" suggested Kay flippantly.

Sonia did not laugh and Kay regretted saying this. "Some young girls, with difficult backgrounds, they … lack aspiration. They copy what their mums did and that's about it … then when they get pregnant at fifteen, they don't always get the family support they need. Sadly …"

They ambled over to the barbecue where people were forming a British queue for chicken kebabs, sausages and other charred, almost burnt, offerings. They carried on talking as they picked up some salad and bread.

"What about the Travellers?" asked Kay, seeing no reason not to.

149

"Ah, now, the Travellers. They do use the hospital, same as any other pregnant woman. Often they're young, if it's their first baby."

"But families stick together?"

"Oh definitely, they do. Sometimes they're due to come in and deliver and don't turn up – gone away, moved on, we don't know. But, yes, they like to have their family around and discharge themselves to get back to their husbands asap. Even the youngest of mothers will have a husband or stable partner, as well as mother and siblings. Rarely get single mums in the Traveller community."

"Do you remember a young Gypsy woman, with long blond curly hair, who gave birth to a stillborn baby – in March this year?" Surely, thought Kay, her fingers crossed, this was an event that might stick in the mind for a few months.

A look of recognition flitted across Sonia's face, as if this did mean something to her. "I ... er ... I can't discuss individual patients. Confidentiality and all that," she said, swiping her fingers across her throat. "Why are you asking, though?"

This was a big moment. She had got into the firm habit of not telling anyone about Lena, so much so, that she had to remind herself that Lena was out there! So, word might get to Joseph that she had been at her house and he might come looking for her, but she was no longer there. So what harm?

"I came across a young Gypsy mother, who ..." A potted version of the story spilled out in the hope that the humanity in Sonia might overcome her dedication to rules. Dunstan was good at this sort of thing.

"I do remember this case. I wasn't on duty, but I heard about her, because she left – well, escaped without trace. Discharged herself. Not all that unusual but we do worry that youngsters like that go before they're properly checked for ... problems ... emotional as well as physical ... I don't think any staff were aware of these paternal disputes. I can't reveal her records, though. I'm sorry. I see your concerns, but she would need to do that for herself. You could try the hostel for teenage mums …" Sonia took a small leaflet from her shoulder bag. "This gives the contact number, but not the address, as they don't publicise that. Some women use it as a kind of refuge from abusive partners … but you could try phoning them to see if she's there. No idea if they'll tell you though!"

Kay thanked her but knew that would be the very last place she would find Lena. Not even worth a phone call.

Over coffee, as time passed easily and pleasantly into afternoon, she came across Nancy, who had petitioned on her doorstep against the Gypsies. If Kay had hackles, they would have risen.

Nancy approached her, clearly remembering her from their brief encounter.

"Mrs Brackenbridge? Kay, isn't it? Enjoying our village, I hope?"

"Everyone's very friendly. I'm sorry I've been so busy with sorting out the house and garden I haven't mixed in with local activities as much as ought to have done. How are you?"

Nancy shook her head slowly from side to side, with a faint smile. "Well, still alive! I suppose that's something."

Kay wasn't sure if this invited a chuckle. Or was a carefully worded, follow-up question expected? "And what a beautiful day to *be* alive!" she responded, playing safe.

"You count every day as a blessing - oh, you don't know, how could you? Been battling with leukaemia you know for … mm, well, years would you believe? Managed to hang on so far …"

Kay felt she needed somebody to help her out, to give her a script. "I'm so sorry, I had no idea. You seem so well, so strong …"

"Ho-ho! Oh my dear girl, if you could see me first thing in the morning without my war-paint you might revise that a little!" Kay withered as she spoke, recalling her previous damning observations.

"How did you come to be involved in the Gypsy – the anti-Gypsy movement? This must take a lot of time and energy ..."

"I was a GP, here in Appley Green, the surgery here," she explained, as the shifting perception of this lady now re-arranged itself like a kaleidoscope inside Kay's head. Not the middle England wealthy wife with time on her hands. "Never married, always a bit vulnerable living alone. A few years ago, home was broken into ... oh, do you mind if we sit down?"

"Glad to ..." They walked over to a garden seat and squashed up against a couple of men who politely got up. "Well, we frightened them away, didn't we?" said Nancy, mischief in her eyes.

"Now then, where were we? Yes, the Travellers were pitched close to my home. Very close, you understand. My house on the end of a row, next to their rough site on the common. They had tried to get some treatment, an entire family knocking on my door, demanding to be seen. I told them that I was not A&E and they should come to the surgery, or go to the hospital if it was urgent. I did worry terribly in case it was something life-threatening, or a young child, a baby or something like that. But you know it's like when you give to beggars in India. It can break your heart, but you do it once and then have half the population following you ..."

Kay nodded. Fair enough. Nancy continued, "That night, my house was broken into, not vandalised, but a few things taken. I woke up to find ... well, it was the thought of them being in my house while I was asleep. It was really very frightening."

An icy shiver went down Kay's spine. She could empathise all too easily. "Did the police catch the ones who did this?"

"That morning, they'd all gone. Nothing ever came of it. They took fingerprints I believe, but it was probably too much trouble to pursue them."

"So there was no proof it was the Travellers?"

"No. No proof. But I knew. Make sure you have a good security system in your house, my dear. Do you have a burglar alarm or something set up?"

The gathering was called to order and the scheme leader stood to address everyone. A discussion began on local crime in general, leading to a specific item on the agenda, that of unwanted traders who knock on your door.

"Reports of this type of harassment have reduced considerably since the Gypsies left town. No surprise there." There were laughs all round and Kay wondered why this was amusing, despite Nancy's story. Kay thought of the homeless people – *Gorgios*, after all – in the hostels, who were encouraged to go round and sell household items from door to door, as an alternative to begging.

"Also, pleased to say that we've had an almost 100% take-up on the stickers for porches and front doors to discourage this kind of activity …"

"That would account for the reduction in traders knocking on doors then, wouldn't it?" Kay wanted to shriek.

"We've heard that the battle we have waged for so many years has finally been won! The Gypsy Liaison Officer has reliably informed me that the Travellers have said that they will be giving Appley Green a miss in future."

Cheers resounded around the English country garden. All was well with their world.

"Hi, Kay, it's Natalie."

"Natalie! How're things going? Enjoying the course?"

"Amazing, just amazing. Really good. Look, I heard about the Group, about them saying they're not coming back. I mean, I realise Appley Green must be … jubilant! But I call it a dismal victory, don't you? Are you still with me on this?"

Since Kay had just settled down to her computer to begin drafting some ideas for press articles, she could hardly deny that she was focused on the matter.

"Yes, I feel they should be given a chance, but it all hinges on turning round the people here and getting a transit site provided by the council."

"Yeah. I tried calling you but as you didn't answer either your phone at home or your mobile, I guessed you were busy – or just didn't want to speak to me!"

Kay just laughed. "Of course not – been away here and there ..." She paused, feeling short of the energy required to relay recent events, but she did tell her of her plans for getting coverage in the local paper.

"Great stuff, Kay! But I must warn you they'll try and twist things to make a story the locals want to read. It helps sell newspapers. They use them as the old scapegoats ... Oh and try and get them to spell Gypsy with a capital G, for a start!"

"I'll do my best."

"If you don't make it controversial enough they'll insert something contentious in their own version. Most probably they'll call my father for the opposite view to give a so-called balanced article." Natalie gave her the names of some further web sites and books that she urged her to read.

"I'll take legal advice if they do and possibly sue them for libel." There was a nagging voice in the back of her mind, urging her to tell Natalie about Lena, and she was about to launch into a synopsis when Natalie said she must fly as her boyfriend was hooting his horn outside. They were off to a Summer Ball.

"Have a wonderful time. Oh, to be young," she said, enviously.

Half an hour later, Kay paused in her internet browsing, thinking it might be worth making a visit to meet Natalie's father to find out if he could be persuaded to support her – somehow. If what Natalie said was true she needed to get him on her side. Was there a name for people who compulsively inflict themselves with unattainable challenges, she wondered?

16

Kay awoke that morning fired up and ready to murder the world. Suzi called to say she had started a cold, so would not be able to make it over to see her for a few days. The more time passed, the less important it seemed for Kay to tell Suzi about Lena, so she told her not to worry and wished her better soon.

Prior to going out, she was closing up the back of the house, checking the window locks, bolting the door, when she noticed a couple of young men helping Dunstan in the garden. She had not seen them before. They were doing heavy work together, lopping trees. Tree surgeons, she supposed, although she did not remember discussing this subcontracting with Dunstan. Presumably she would be informed, once presented with a bill. He still had this habit of going ahead with things without consultation, stretching the parameters within which he was supposed to work. It was irritating, but she did not want to be held up now by an argument.

She decided to give the MG a spin. It was a warm day, inclined to showers but she would take the risk and have the top down. She had achieved a lot during the course of the morning, calling Natalie straight after breakfast. It was a few days since they had spoken and she decided to tell her about Lena. Natalie was quite horrified by pretty much every aspect of the story.

"I used to play with Lena when we were kids. Well, you know," she explained, "like once a year, whenever the group passed through the village, but since she got married we drifted a bit. Had less in common, you know. Not seen her for years, actually. So *she* was the one who had a baby and caused all the rows and stuff. Wow! She kept that a bit of a secret. I hope she's telling the *truth* ..." Kay's stomach seemed to turn a complete revolution as Natalie carried on; she quietly determined to try and discreetly locate the group.

Kay had then contacted Natalie's father and arranged to meet him, which was now her intention. Whilst simply waiting on outcomes from various people – Max, Lena, Dunstan, Tibor, Joseph, it was satisfying to at least try and make something happen.

The 'farmhouse' was a vast Tudor mansion within a walled garden. Kay had to stop at the wrought iron gates to speak into the security system. Edward Devonish, was generally known as Ted, he told her as they shook hands. Close up, she could see the likeness between father and daughter, something about the eyes and jawline.

The interior of the house was a delight, with dark beams, oak panelling except where the walls were plain white, adorned with landscapes and portraits, and a large galleried hall. Vases of fresh flowers looked as if they were replaced on a daily basis. There was a smell of good coffee and lavender polish.

"Let's go through to the drawing-room, where we can talk in peace," he said, as if the house were teaming with boisterous children and pets, which was far from the case. A grandfather clock ticked loudly but otherwise it was awesomely quiet. She thought they were alone, until a slim woman appeared, well turned out in cream linen trousers and a duck egg blue tunic top. Her hair was a blondish bob and she looked younger than Ted. Was this Natalie's mother? Not your typical farmer's wife, thought Kay, but actually unsure as to what one might look like these days.

"This is my housekeeper, Gaynor." Not your typical housekeeper either! "Natalie's friend from the village, Kay Brackenbridge. Could you rustle up some ... well, what? Coffee, tea, herbal? Something cold perhaps? What's your poison, Kay?"

"Thank you. Coffee would be lovely …"

Kay was burning to know how this daughter-father relationship worked, with Natalie so fiercely pro Gypsies and him so clearly antagonistic. He had spoken against her at the public meeting – and on the radio, in the press, at every opportunity so it seemed.

"I've really come to see if you can help me – although," she said, with a smile, "I don't hold out a lot of hope …"

He threw back his head, laughing loudly. Kay noticed his Adam's apple sticking out like an egg. "Oh, right! Well, thank you for the vote of confidence. Do I sense this could have something to do with our Travelling friends? Thieves and vagabonds eh? The lot of 'em. Hah!"

Kay stifled a gasp until she saw the irony, in that he was deliberately saying the opposite of what he believed to be true. She could tell this by the way his grey eyes were crinkled up and he was watching her face mischievously.

"I understand that you and Natalie are diametrically opposed on this, but …"

"Natalie, I am afraid, lives in a romantic world. She would be off in a gaily-painted wagon, selling clothes pegs, married to some swarthy violin-playing horse-dealer if she could see it through."

"Well, forgive me, but I think you're wrong. She cuts through all the stereotypes, the old images, and just sees them as human beings of the 21st century, people who are not being treated kindly by non Gypsies."

"They do get up to mischief, you know," he said, tapping his nose.

"But, surely … Ted, there are good and bad right through society. Crime and poverty often go hand in hand, in general, wouldn't you say? And discrimination and discord between groups of people increase the likelihood of crime occurring. I can't employ these people, and they don't want charity. Most of them have no wish to settle in houses, but I would like to help give them a chance to be accepted. For their chosen way of life to be accepted."

157

"OK. Gotcha so far. What's your plan, Kay?"

A *cafetière* of coffee, with willow pattern crockery neatly set out, arrived on a tray with some small Danish pastries in a little basket lined with a doily. It reminded her of a certain nineteen-fifties genteel way of life.

"Natalie never told me she lived in such a splendid place!" commented Kay, just making conversation, as Gaynor was leaving the room.

"Oh, no, no. She's not lived here for – ah, now let me see, must be fifteen years. Her mother and I separated. Well, divorced now, long since. Left me for another man. Can you believe *that*? Hah!"

"I'm so sorry, it's none of my business. I had no idea. So you and Natalie are not that close then?"

"We try. But clearly not as close as if I had brought her up. Provide for her, of course, see her quite often, but not the same, not the same." She saw his eyes fill with tears as he cleared his throat. He struck her as a lonely man but it was early days, she realised, to make assumptions. He could lead a hedonistic, riotous lifestyle for all she knew. He might spend weeks at a time soaking up the sun in his gin palace on the French Riviera, be top man at a local golf club or be a bit of a gambler … But whatever kind of a man he was, he clearly would have liked to contribute more to his daughter's upbringing. Yet Natalie, with her spirit and independent mind, was a lovely girl, so … I must remember to be tactful on that one, thought Kay.

Kay decided to quickly get back to the matter in hand.

"Two things. First, they need a transit site. Second, and part of that anyway, they need the locals to be more tolerant, accepting. Welcoming, even! Less of the NIMBY."

"Mm," he said, sitting back in his armchair, stroking his chin. "Well, this is all very well, but they do make a mess and noise. It's not just rumour. It happens y'see!"

"Maybe. Sometimes. But then this is magnified. Always the negative side of their lifestyle is blown up, out of proportion. Exaggerated. People seem to enjoy it. My feeling is they get blamed a little too readily, sometimes without hard evidence."

"How long have you lived here, Kay? May I ask?"

"About three months."

The way he looked at her was a little unnerving, but she was determined not to feel intimidated. He did not know the close involvement she had had, and the research she had done.

She carried on undaunted. "I understand *you* won't provide land for them. Is that correct?"

He nodded. "Mm. I cannot legally do so. Unless they work on the land. I have no work for them. Sorry."

"Then we need to put pressure on the council. The main problem is the local people putting up resistance to the idea but I intend to turn them round. It's a question of hearts and minds!"

She enthusiastically outlined to him her proposed press campaign.

"It's time we redressed the balance. The media have done the Gypsies no favours over the years. Not quite so biased now, but the harm caused still lives on. Can I count on you not to feed the press any counter arguments? This is my main request."

"I'll keep out of it, if that's what you want," he agreed, looking at her directly. She trusted this man.

They shook hands on it. She knew she would not get him to convert and actively support her in her campaign, but she had the agreement she needed and left feeling moderately triumphant. She could not help but notice too that he had squeezed her hand very tightly, with both hands.

There were gaps in her hedge of trees and bushes. It made the garden seem bigger, lighter, and she had always said she did not want it to completely block off the outside world, but it still irked her that Dunstan had not mentioned his intentions. She took digital photographs to help monitor the skyline in the coming weeks and as she checked the shots she had taken on her camera, she took a look at some old photos she had not yet transferred to her computer. Jason and Tom smiled back at her and her stomach went into a knot. How were they surviving? How was Lena managing to keep them clean, warm and fed? She kept checking her mobile for messages. If only she would contact her, reply to her texts, just to let her know she was all right.

When her phone rang the next day it made her jump, as, once again she had been thinking about Lena and willing it to ring.

"Is that Mrs Kay Brackenbridge?"

"Yes. Speaking."

"Tibor. How are you?"

"I'm well. Tibor, I'm sorry but our plans are pretty much on hold, until I can find Lena, so we can get the medical record. She's disappeared. I passed your family names on to Max Leatherson, the Gypsy Liaison Officer who will enquire at the right sources."

"How long will he take?" he asked, anxiety in his voice.

"I have no idea. But I'll await a response before considering any other kind of enquiry. He's our best hope, I feel."

"OK. If you say. Thank you, Kay. Please call as soon as you have news." She could hear the disappointment in his voice, but there was no point in giving him false hope.

A few weeks went by and a new set of tasks was lining up ready for Kay. Tasks of a culinary nature. The summer garden was starting to produce a supply of peas, broad beans, potatoes, all kinds of salads, herbs, tayberries, gooseberries, blackcurrants, – and rhubarb, well, enough to start up a jam factory! Soon there would be a crop of French and runner beans, spinach, carrots, onions, courgettes, squashes, raspberries ... Fruit and vegetables in bags and boxes of every description were left at her back door most days and she knew she must get to work.

She chose a suitable knife from the drawer, pausing for a moment, still unable to look at kitchen knives without feeling agitated. She ran a finger slowly along the blade, pushing herself, testing her own reaction. It was a just a knife. A kitchen tool. Life goes on.

The distressing associations faded as she began trimming and chopping rhubarb, tossing it in bags with sugar, ready for the freezer. Empty glass jars would need to be saved for making rhubarb and ginger jam. Potatoes could be just stored away for a while. Broad beans and peas needed podding. As she sat at the kitchen table, topping and tailing blackcurrants with nail scissors, the most brain numbing job on earth, she decided, but worth it as they were her favourite fruit of all time, she reflected that her 'kitchen garden' was way out of proportion to her needs. Of course Dunstan was happy with it. She was paying him very little so he was good value for money and the deal was that he could pass on the excess to people who needed it. But next year she would get Dunstan to downsize. There would be room to put in a small swimming pool, she decided.

The house was beginning to acquire a style and earthy colours she could call her own. She had done some things the wrong way round – carpets before decorating, for example, which would have caused Marcus to throw his hands up in horror – but everything was now light and airy, whilst retaining a rustic charm. Curtains and soft furnishings, lamps, pictures, mirrors and all those little accessories were turning her house into a modern, country home. She had a good friend and ally in Dunstan and was as close to happiness as she had felt since moving here, except for the constant worry over a girl who just a few months ago was a complete stranger to her. She would make more effort to join in with the village activities. There was far more going on than she had first thought – gardening clubs, the Summer Fête and Carnival, many voluntary organisations helping the disadvantaged.

Kay had begun to make a list of headlines and notes for articles she could write for the local newspaper to improve Gypsy public relations. The headline should encapsulate the essence of each piece.

Strong Families Stick Together (vs broken homes, dysfunctional families etc ...);

Fathers who do take Responsibility for their Children (vs failure of absent fathers to support mothers, mention old Child Support Agency ...);

Single Teenage Mothers (vs married teenage mothers – a bit contentious, that one – is it good to marry so young? Discuss ...);

Gypsies' Low Carbon Footprint, (Good one – topical – recycling, thrifty lifestyle, use less resources ...);

Cleanliness by Tradition (without being obsessive about it, OCD in the news a lot these days ...);

Evicted, On the Road with Nowhere to Go (get in all the legislation, the prejudice, stress, suicides, low life expectancy ...);

Taking Care of Elderly Parents (no Gypsy family would entertain the idea of a nursing home; respecting your elders in the extended family etc ...);

Apprentice to a Trade? (might reduce ASBOs ...);

Why such poor exam results for the Gypsy Roma? (Five GCSEs grades A – C achieved by less than 10%, compare Chinese 79.3%, White British 57.2% and Indian (the original Roma ethnic group) 71.4%);

Kay ended up with a list of about twenty nuggets and soon had two or three complete articles ready to submit to the local newspaper editor. She felt confident they would be seized upon as a fresh take on a common press theme in this neck of the woods.

Making the most of a sunny afternoon, Kay reclined on her new garden swing-seat, dozing after lunch. She was expecting Suzi to arrive and, having finished her household chores was feeling surprisingly relaxed, considering she was on the brink, at long last, of sharing the Lena story with her daughter. Shifting position slightly as her book had fallen off her lap, she looked up to see a young man at the foot of the garden. She had not seen him before.

17

On closer inspection, the youth had bad skin and strange eyes. He leaned on the end of his rake handle, staring at Kay as she approached him.

"Hello!" said Kay. "Helping Dunstan?"

He nodded, looking embarrassed, now unable to meet her gaze.

"On your own?"

"'E said 'e 'ad too much work to do, so asked me to finish off this bit o' tidyin' like. It ain't rocket science or nuffin'." He ventured an awkward smile, shifting from one foot to the other.

"My name is Kay. You are?"

"Alan." He fidgeted with a grey woollen hat that sat on his head like a neat tea-cosy.

"Right Alan. So … what's the arrangement exactly? I pay Dunstan as my gardener. Does Dunstan pay you?" This 'sub-contracting' was getting out of hand.

"Nah!"

So what's in it for him then, wondered Kay? Ah, payment in kind, perhaps. Vegetables, fruit and so on. "So do you take some of the veg?"

"No-oh," he boomed, defensive now, chin jutting, lifting his shoulders as if spoiling for a fight.

"No – sorry I didn't mean take, as in steal. No, no. I mean does Dunstan pay you with produce, instead of money?" Surely, this was the answer. He must be of the Travelling community and one of the recipients Dunstan mentioned right at the start. It was part of their deal.

"No!"

"Well … Alan, I don't quite understand. You just do this work … for nothing?"

The lad shrugged. "Yeah."

She would have to get this explained by Dunstan later. If Alan is a Gypsy, he might know something of the whereabouts of Lena's group.

At that point Suzi breezed into the garden, asking where the cream tea was that Kay had promised her earlier.

Then followed a lengthy update from Suzi on her social life and, specifically of a man she had met who might actually help her forget her lost love, the adored journalist. Barely pausing for breath, she launched into a detailed account of her week at work when Eugene had taken the unprecedented step of handing her one of his commissions for an upcoming fashion retailer, as he had more work than he could cope with.

"That's wonderful, darling? Does this mean big bucks?"

Suzi looked aghast. "Oh no," she said, "it's just editorial. Good publicity for my name. But the experience, Mum! I mean, this will lift my portfolio clean out of … of mediocrity. This will shine, stand out and help me get commissions of my own. Now, it's upwards all the way. *And* I get paid expenses!"

Her daughter looked as if she had won the lottery, or been awarded the equivalent of a BAFTA, so she tried to share her euphoria. "Well done, I'm so proud of you. I really am. What can I say? Have another scone!" Then she braced herself. "Suzi I have something to tell you …"

"No!! You're having an affair! A 'relationship'! That Gypsy gardener! I knew it. Ugh! At your age … Disgusting, but I suppose, if it makes you …" Suzi could become flippant when she was on a 'high'. Kay had had to cope with her mood swings many times before.

"Suzi, listen!" said Kay, sharply. "This is hard, because … I feel I kept something from you for a long time …"

Suzi was nearly falling off her seat. Suddenly her face crumpled and she gasped. "My God. I'm so sorry. Oh! My big mouth. Are you ill? Something serious ... like terminal?" She put her hand to her mouth.

"No, no, no *no*. You know the girl you found here that day a while back ..."

The whole story came out while Suzi's eyes grew wider and wider.

"But, this is so amazing ..." she interjected, as Kay described the children and how good a mother Lena was. "How on earth does she cope? At her age? I wouldn't have the slightest idea! And she lost a baby? I mean, a fully formed ..." Tears filled Suzi's eyes.

Finally Kay, in the final chapters of her story, explained that she was still looking for Lena, Joseph and Tibor's relatives.

"I do *so* wish I could help ... but with this new job ..." Suzi looked distraught. "I really can't give up this opportunity – and I'm off to Greece tomorrow for the shoot."

After Suzi had left that evening, exuberant, genuinely warm and sympathetic towards Lena and her plight, Kay reflected how, once again ... how wrong she had been. She had seriously underestimated her daughter's capacity for compassion. As she sat watching the news on TV, (about Tony Blair's new role in mediating between Israel and Palestine), she felt her faith in human nature restored. Suzi had lightly dismissed Lena as simply a 'dosser', with little empathy and perhaps she was right to do so at the time but, armed with more facts, she had done a U-turn. People hold within them a huge potential to change which can be realised if they have the right information, she concluded, which renewed her hope of succeeding in her press campaign.

Tomorrow she would call the local newspaper editor (even though she knew this was unprofessional behaviour) to check he had seen her submitted article - the first of many. Now she had another up her sleeve, which would be about something to do with first impressions sometimes falling dangerously short of the truth.

When Ted called her the following week, his timing was impeccable, so she told him.

"I really need someone to act as a sounding board. The local newspaper editor tells me my article is not 'news'," she explained to him over the phone. "Not enough of a 'local slant'. I thought it *was* - topical, community issue, the kind of thing people would want to read, but ..."

"Well, happy to help, but don't expect me to agree with everything you say, will you?" he replied light-heartedly. "Anyway, I was wondering if you would do me the honour of joining me to peruse a local art exhibition, followed by lunch at some nearby hostelry? Short notice. Tomorrow in fact. Any good?"

It was an awfully long time since a man had called her up for a date and this was really rather unexpected and ... well, gave her a pleasant feeling. It was flattering.

"That sounds wonderful!" she said, thinking of what she had planned – making more rhubarb jam, sorting out the airing cupboard ... "Just what I need ... and if you don't mind, I'll bring along some reading matter for you ..."

As Kay walked into the village early the following morning, armed with umbrella and wearing a waterproof jacket, her thoughts strayed to Lena, as they often did. She would give anything to know what she was doing, where she was, how little Jason and Tom were. Pewter coloured storm clouds gathered until by the time she was in the Post Office, a tropical downpour marooned her along with many others, people she did not know.

"You count your blessings not to be living near a river – eh?" said one woman, who had left home less well protected than Kay, her vest top clinging such that it was difficult to know where to look. "Those pics on telly!"

"Last year bloody hosepipe ban, this year folks flooded out their homes ..."

"And stuff growin', crops an' that, all ruined. Poor old Dunstan was saying all his gardens have suffered one way or the other …"

All his gardens? *All his gardens*, did they say? What?

"Certainly mine, my garden …" chipped in Kay, "Dunstan does gardening for me – is pretty waterlogged in places and some plants could use more sunshine … um? Did you say, he has other gardens?"

"What, Dunstan? He works in quite a few – people seem happy. Gets good results – plenty for him to sell on and make a good living, so I've heard."

Kay felt herself go hot and cold, as if she might pass out. She didn't want to make it too obvious that she was completely in the dark. How naive she was.

"He certainly produces more than I can use," she said, with an apparent calm, "er … not sure where it all ends up, though …"

Kay began to experience the joy of gossip. People were only too keen to show off their knowledge.

"Well, he sells stuff at the market in Colesby – but he gets his young lads to man the stall quite often." His *young lads*. What? He was beginning to sound like Fagin. She wished she had him here right now. She felt so angry she felt an urge to kick him in the shins, or worse.

"He supplies hotels and restaurants and even the supermarket just out of town, just the little one mind, that boasts 'local, organic vegetables' in the local paper …ooh, is it easing up a bit out there now, d'you think?" Quite a throng had assembled, Mr Patel trying to maximise the selling opportunity, by revealing a cache of umbrellas he had been saving for a rainy day.

Had Dunstan been profiteering at her expense? Without telling her? And using slave labour? What were these boys all about? She stormed out of the Post Office. He had gone too far. He should have told her. She felt hurt, angry, used and abused.

'Having it out with Dunstan' had been promoted to the top of her 'to do' list. But where was he? Days, weeks indeed, were passing by and he was nowhere to be seen. The garden needed him. Alan, who had come in to mow the lawns, so must be working somehow under Dunstan's direction, said he was busy sorting out some problems, but would not enlarge on this. It was mystifying. It was frustrating.

She started picking produce and then a weedy patch would distract her and thus she found herself being drawn into turning the soil over with a fork, pulling out pesky bindweed and thistles. Could she manage without him? The bleak thought plunged her into a kind of sadness she had not felt for many months.

The whole situation threw Kay into the doldrums, a mood swing that surprised her. Her health was excellent and she was learning to live with her emotional past. Marcus' death was now something she could refer to at will, but did not flash up uninvited, as had been the case until a few weeks ago. She had had a pleasant lunch with Ted (and was seeing him again at the weekend), confiding in him the whole Lena story. He seemed happy to listen and, though surprised, made all the right noises and she had found this cathartic. Her articles had gone off to the newspaper and she felt satisfied that they would be published now that she had made adjustments. And, after all, no one was breathing over her shoulder, urging her to do this. It was her own chosen project. Suzi was happy (delirious). Claudia was on her way home and Kay hoped her months of travelling had helped her come to terms with the harrowing sight of her father's corpse when she came home that fateful night … Lena was no longer her responsibility … or was she? She knew she would not rest easy until she had sorted out the Lena, Joseph, Tibor conundrum, but otherwise, she reasoned, she should be happy, content and pleased with life, but instead she felt anxious, wretched and permanently close to tears.

She would call Max. If he were unable to help she would set about contacting various authorities herself. She would think of other ways to find Lena ... Brimming with good intentions, yet verging towards a narcoleptic state, she had gone to bed early with a book, when her phone rang. She picked up the handset by the bed. It was Natalie.

"I hear you're *dating* my father," she teased. "He's said some very nice things about you. 'Plucky!' 'Caring!' A whole string of adjectives I've never heard him use before. It's not like him at all."

"Don't get too carried away, Natalie!" murmured Kay, stifling a yawn. "One lunch does not a relationship make."

"But how cool would that ... Anyway, you'll be pleased to know I've managed to locate the Travelling group that left Appley Green ..."

Suddenly Kay felt awake. "That *is* good news. Where are they?" She sat up straight. Maybe now she could set about finding Lena's husband.

"Oh, just about ten miles away."

Kay was dumbfounded. "So near! And yet ..."

"Exactly. They're well hidden away ... I'd never have come across them without my contacts there. You know, people I've known since I was a kid. I went to see them ..."

"You did?"

"Yep. And before you ask, no they've not seen Lena but have given me some ideas as to where she might be. Joseph's not there either – apparently he's on the road looking for her as well!"

"Oh no! She's quite terrified of him, you know. He could be violent towards her, or grab the boys. This is *bad* news, Natalie." She reached for pen and paper to jot down the whereabouts of the site and list the suggested places to look for Lena.

18

When Ted popped round unexpectedly one morning, Kay had just come off the phone to the editor.

"I need someone to shout at," she said, smiling at him over her shoulder as she led him through to the kitchen.

"Sounds painful, but as it's you ..." he responded, good-naturedly, leaving his hat on the hall table.

"*Preachy!!* The editor," she blurted, grabbing a sharp knife to slice up some carrot cake. "He said my articles were too preachy. Huh! Editors. Think they're so high and mighty. Omniscient, omnipotent. It amounts to censorship. He probably doesn't agree with what I'm saying. Honestly."

Ted sat down, leaning back in the kitchen chair, crossed his long legs and drummed the table with his fingers, looking pensive. Then he sat forward, clasping his bony hands together.

"He may be right," he said.

Kay hesitated with the knife in her hand mid-air, noting, so fleetingly that it was barely a conscious thought, that her relationship with knives was changing. A tool to cut cake, not a weapon to stab human flesh ...

She pursed her lips. "You're joking, aren't you?"

"No, I think they're too good for local news – you could send them to broadsheets or a country magazine. Even an academic journal that deals with social issues ..."

"No, no. Academic circles already publish sociological, anthropological papers. The point is, I need to reach the locals. I've no need to speak to the nation, not as the first priority." She felt a little exasperated with Ted, that he had not quite grasped this. "He's so damned clever – he got me

171

talking and I found myself telling him all kinds of things …about how I met your Natalie … and …" She stopped to pour coffee, but also to make sure she did not drift into telling Ted that same private, personal stuff that somehow the journalist in the editor had wormed out of her. *What got you into this whole Gypsy thing then?* the editor had asked. *Where did you move from? Why* … Then he exclaimed, *Ah-hah! I thought the name Brackenbridge rang a bell. I remember that story — not big enough for the nationals but made the Evening Standard I believe.* Judging the story on its newsworthiness, its media ranking — how dare he do this! *So you're the wife — sorry, forgive me, widow,* he said, with such damned courtesy, as if he would never have the temerity to be rude, or intrusive …

"He's really got to you, hasn't he?" commented Ted, as she sat there scowling into her coffee, her piece of cake untouched. "Maybe, maybe … you should just leave it for a while."

"No, I don't want to *just leave it*. What really does get to me is ignorance, that the people here are so unaware of what the Gypsies have to suffer. Yes, suffer!" As she glared at Ted, she cast her thoughts back to the harsh words he had uttered against them. How had they come to be friends? At least he was there, listening.

"I mean, take the children. You know, they're not getting the opportunities and skills they need in today's world. They could be happy in their closed family-orientated community, their culture has *much* to offer, but if they have nowhere to live, no means of earning a living other than sorting refuse, or processing scrap metal — I mean, it's a far cry from the so-called golden days … No wonder some of them give up and 'live off the state', as everyone thinks … and children need basic comforts, don't they and to be accepted by settled people?"

"Look I've read all your articles, and I know how strongly you feel. They read well. Powerful stuff. You don't need to …er … 'preach' at me. I think you've turned me round, anyway," he said, gently, reaching across to touch her arm. "If that helps."

Kay instinctively shrank away. You know nothing about me, she suddenly thought. She could not tell Ted that the editor had shown such … such professional interest in her story … *Ah, now. That we would publish! What caused you to leave London, how Appley Green has helped you heal … you know the sort of thing?* Oh sure, she thought, with reference to my husband's *gory demise* no doubt, or similar, sensational, attention-grabbing term - that would be the hook you'd need, wouldn't it? But, nobody in the village knew about all the baggage that came with her. They probably saw her as a slightly eccentric, initially frail, retired person, who had kept herself to herself. Hopefully they had also noticed her metamorphosis into a fully mobile socialite.

She reflected on Ted's visit later that day, as she picked the first of the runner beans, pulled up withered broad bean plants, pruned back the fruit bushes and spread some compost, hoping that Dunstan's slave, young Alan, might turn up so she could quiz him further about Dunstan's skulduggery. Whatever else he might be up to, she would like his advice on the places supplied by Natalie for possibly seeking out Lena. There were shops, markets, fairs – but nothing she could find on a map.

It was around four o'clock when she made her way back to the house, with her basket of beans, courgettes, onions and potatoes. Her whole body ached and she longed to sink into a warm, foamy bath.

As she began her ascent upstairs, the doorbell rang and she cursed mildly. Her heart-beat quickened as she thought it might be Dunstan, but he usually came straight round the back. Perhaps Ted? Hopefully, just a charity collector. All she really wanted was to get cleaned up and relax for the evening … Or, could it even be Claudia?

She opened the door and nearly fell back into the hallway. Tibor stood before her, smiling broadly, softening his rather lugubrious features.

"Mrs Brackenbridge. I found you!"

"Tibor – what a surprise! Well, come in." She led him through to the kitchen and put the kettle on. "I am very dirty – from gardening," she explained as she washed her hands in the sink. (Lena would never do that, she thought.)

"I asked people in the village and soon discovered your address. I had to see you – could not wait any more. I thought I could help in some way to … make things happen faster …"

"I don't want to raise your hopes. I've still heard nothing more from Max."

"You are the only person who has ever given me some hope," he said, earnestly, "or been prepared to help me. I am very, very grateful. I decided to take two days off work and come here to see you. Perhaps together, we …"

Kay felt something familiar shoot through her. Was it panic? "I'm sorry Tibor, but you can't stay here. I'm expecting family …" Claudia could, after all, be here any day …

"Today? Tonight? Well, as soon as they come I will hide away … or go out, but … er … is there a cheap hotel or somewhere I could go to near here?"

Oh my God, why is this happening to me? She couldn't think of anywhere suitable nearby and … she yearned for a bath, a quiet meal and early bed.

The phone rang and Kay inwardly groaned. What now?

It was Dunstan.

"Dunstan, where are you?" Torn between anger and relief, she said, "I've had no way of contacting you and …"

"Please, Kay, listen a minute, if you would," came his soft voice. "I do apologise. Honest, I'm sorry for not being in touch these past few weeks. My mother, in Ireland, had a massive stroke and she has now … God rest her, passed on."

Kay's hand flew to her mouth. "I'm so sorry …"

174

"The funeral and all. You know. Other problems here too … Some young people I know. Overdose situation, attempted suicide … " Kay gasped, the wind taken effectively out of all her sails. "I hope Alan has kept things ticking over."

"Of course, Dunstan. Of course, he has. But - when will you be back?"

Kay had no chance to ask him all the questions she'd planned, questions that demanded to be answered. The other gardens? Selling her produce? The 'young lads'?

"Soon."

Tibor suggested, as she soon as she came off the phone, "I could call the – how do you call him? Gypsy Liaising …?"

"Liaison Officer …" Kay was about to agree, to give him the number and usher him out. She was so tired, this seemed an attractive way forward – (Dunstan would soon be here, although what did 'soon' mean? This evening? A week's time?) – but the idea was that she would help Tibor so that he would help her to provide evidence to support Lena. She felt pressure to keep her side of the deal, or he would surely pull out.

"Let me call him while you're here …" she said, looking at her watch. "If we're lucky, he may still be in his office. Or, I have his mobile number …."

She tried both his office and mobile but there was no reply.

"We can try in the morning," she said, after leaving a message for Max. "Look, you go off and see if you can find somewhere to stay nearby and if you can't, come back here and I can put you up in a spare room …"

She just hoped that this was something she would not live to regret. After all, he was a virtual stranger. She could never claim that she knew him well or that he was entirely trustworthy.

175

19

Kay wandered around her garden after breakfast, assessing how much work she could do herself and how much called for extra manpower. She had to face up to the fact that, if Dunstan had been capitalising on her produce without telling her, this represented a serious breach of trust. Their friendship was definitely threatened and it weighed heavily on her. The idea of managing without him had the effect of distorting the dimensions of her land, as if it stretched out to infinity. The rampant weeds seemed that much stronger, the grass that much higher.

She decided to cast her mind upon other things, until she could talk it through with him and hear his side, but she couldn't see how he could possibly justify his actions. Making a 'good living' they had said, supplying shops, restaurants and hotels. He was a businessman! Using unpaid labour! No wonder he turned up for his so-called interview, when she felt as if he were vetting her instead of the other way round, dressed in a sharp suit. That is what he is – sharp!

She sat down in a comfortable chair in the conservatory to call the editor. During the night, during a restless spell, she had thought it through. What harm would it do to 'come out' in the local community? Her past was part of her true identity. It would be hard, at first. People might stare. They might whisper behind her back – but she had never been accused of any wrongdoing. It was just that grey, troublesome area that lay between her and her conscience, the 'if only' aspect to what happened when Marcus was murdered. People would see her in a new light, as she both confronted and revealed the truth. Her husband had suffered a violent death and she had come to live in the country for a fresh start. It would be a harmless enough little piece for his paper … and the locals would soon forget and re-focus on their own lives.

"If I do 'my story', will you publish my other articles?" she asked him, before this rush of confidence deserted her.

He laughed. "Oh, good try. Sorry, I don't do deals like that. It doesn't change my view on your Gypsy articles."

"Pompous prick," she muttered, as she hung up.

As soon as Tibor returned, as planned, from the Bed and Breakfast place he had found not far away, they settled down to call Max.

"Good morning Kay," was the greeting that met her as soon as she got through to his desk phone. "Uncanny coincidence – I was about to call you!"

Kay put her hand over the phone, "Sounds like he has news …" she whispered to Tibor, who raised both thumbs in anticipation.

"As you know the proper process for developing a transit site is long and tedious, starting with an assessment of Travellers' accommodation needs, but it *has* begun." Kay shook her head at Tibor to try and indicate that this was not what he was hoping for … "That's the good news – I think for you, anyway, and for the Travellers. The bad news is that it will take a while … involving the planning and housing departments of the local district council, identification of a piece of suitable land which meets the planning criteria, applications for grants from central government, securing planning permission …"

"Is there anything we can do to hurry things up?"

"The whole thing is fraught, because, as you very well know, no one wants a traveller site near their property, then there is putting the construction work out to tender. The whole process from start to finish could take five years at a conservative estimate."

"Would local opinion – if it were reversed, have some bearing on this?"

"It would certainly help in many ways to have the residents of Appley Green in support. But, that is, unfortunately an impossible dream! They will resist at every step. We know that. But if, by some miracle, they changed ... and actively leaned on the local council, of course, it would really move the planning permission forward ..."

Kay's brain was churning, then whizzing. *This* was the 'window of opportunity' she needed – now she must act. She *must* get this campaign going. It really could work, *could* make a difference ...

Tibor was jumping up and down and on the brink of snatching the phone off her.

"And Tibor?"

"Yes, I know. I have tried, but so far nothing. I will chase it. I promise. Good-bye for now, Kay." She could sense that with the other matter now in hand, Tibor's family, which for sure did not come under his job description, was not high on his list of priorities.

"He's going to chase it," she repeated back to Tibor, who was looking so dejected, her heart softened. "Look, please stay around here today and we'll call him later on to make sure he really is taking this seriously. Keep calling him to let him know we're on his back ..."

Tibor frowned, clearly not quite with the idiom. "If we keep reminding him, he is less likely to forget. Yes?" He smiled and nodded. "And if he can't help, we'll draw up another plan."

While Tibor was settled down reading a newspaper, Kay was planning her next call to the editor. *Now* she had some 'news' he would want. He would snatch it off her as fast as a rat up a drainpipe ...

But the editor beat her to it. "OK," he said, "been thinking about your ... mm ... proposal. I think we could a do a deal – *between ourselves*, you must understand. But you'll have to shorten them."

Kay gasped. This was a big breakthrough, to say the least. A result. "The assessment ..." she began, then stopped. No, she must get her PR venture established first, warm up her market before making people aware of the assessment that had, after all, only just begun and would not come to fruition for many a long month. She must, like a good marketeer, prepare the ground before 'closing'.

"Yes, I'll shorten them. No problem. And I'll add a few more local touches … I'll let you have the other piece by … when's your deadline for the next issue?"

"Tomorrow."

"By tomorrow first thing, then."

After lunch Kay withdrew to her computer. She shut the door. This would need concentration and care – in the composition, the wording and in the handling of her emotions. It would, after all, be opening up old scars.

She would never forget the sound of thumping on her front door after she had been at work for about an hour. Then the shouting which made her look up from the screen and stop typing the words: … *the sound of someone breaking into our home invoked terror, yet this was without any knowledge of the tragedy that was about to befall us. Yet I instinctively feared for our lives because …* She froze, wondering for a moment if her addled brain had confused past with present.

But no, she could distinctly hear the noise of people moving round the side of her house to the back door. Someone was in a hurry, making no efforts to be furtive or stealthy. More than one set of footfalls. Even closeted as she was in her study, she could sense the impatience, hear the raised, angry voices. A man was shouting something like, "When we *gell* in *a kai*, if 'e's there, just *pogger* 'im …" Then she heard Tibor yell out loudly, sounding desperate and terrified. Shaking, blood draining from her face, she slowly rose from her desk and fumbled for her mobile. She dialled 999. "Police," she said, deciding, in the light of experience, not to intervene. She answered their questions with as much composure as she could muster, all the while feeling as if she

179

might faint. "There's a fight in my house – please come. I'm on my own …" She realised, as she said this, it sounded odd, contradictory.

"Mrs Brackenbridge!" Tibor was shouting, "Please come help me."

Afraid for Tibor, she edged the study door open very slightly, just enough to be able to take a quick look. She could see no one. His disembodied voice seemed to be coming from the kitchen. Now it had gone quiet, ominously so. She shivered, cold from shock, sick with terror. Memories of Marcus' death came flooding in, and she could picture herself in vivid Technicolor reaching in that drawer for the knife … Had Tibor been attacked? Knocked out? Worse? She could hear the sound of her own heartbeat drumming in her ears.

"Tibor?" she called, in a hoarse whisper, clutching the door-frame.

Three men appeared in the hall and Kay's mouth went dry with fear. The police should be here soon, she thought. They would disappear then at least, or be apprehended.

The man with black hair tied back into a ponytail standing slightly in front of the other two was tall and muscular, the more imposing for the stance he adopted. Feet wide apart, head held high, he said, "Where is she? I know she's here."

Of course. Joseph. "Where's Tibor?" she gasped, feeling a somewhat irrational sense of relief, as if he were someone she knew, not an utter stranger.

"He's not talking for a while." What did he mean?   "So you keep my wife all *cushti* and 'er … 'er bit on the side hidden here as well? Even worse than I'd heard …"

Who told him that Lena had been here? How did he find out? She thought of the people she had told – the midwife, Ted, Dunstan? Was it Dunstan? Had he blabbed? Or perhaps Natalie had clumsily given them a clue on her travels …

"She's not here."

"She *is*."

"No. She … she was, but …" Kay stuttered, "she left a few weeks ago and I don't know where she is. I wish I did.

And Tibor is *not* her lover. Never was. You must understand this. I am trying to help him trace his Czech family who may have joined a Romany group in this country …" she kept talking, fast, to keep him off her, to let his anger abate until the police arrived. The police! This was the very last thing she needed. If this reached the press … police car racing through the village, zooming up her drive … the gossip would be spinning!

"I think they're still cooped up here like chickens. I want to see her."

"You're welcome to look. She's not here." While the three of them scattered around the house like children on a hide-and-seek, albeit they were heavy-footed and would scarcely catch anyone unawares, she crept warily into the kitchen as if she were breaking into her own house. Tibor had been gagged and tied to a chair.

"Oh Tibor," she cried, rushing to him. "I'm sorry. This is all my fault." She reached for some scissors to cut the string that bound him. "Are you all right?"

As soon as his mouth was freed, he assured her, "Yes, they scared me but I am not hurt …"

Suddenly Ted appeared at the back door and Kay almost flung her arms around him. Of course, she had told Ted about Lena. Was it him that had spread the word, she wondered?

He instantly pieced together what had happened, requiring little explanation.

Joseph and what looked like his brothers came thudding down the stairs, almost falling over each other, and when they saw Ted they stopped dead. Knowing, sidelong glances were exchanged. The short stocky man to Joseph's left muttered to Joseph, "Oh *dordi*, what's the *gearie* doin' here?"

It was clear they knew him … and Kay was uncertain as to how to read the expression on their various faces. Was it shock? Fear? The three of them seemed rooted to the spot and fell quiet. Kay noticed some colour had now returned to Tibor's pale face as he relaxed. Ted must have seemed to the poor man like a god, a knight in shining armour who had come to save and protect him.

"Joseph," said Ted, coming forward, courteously extending a hand as anyone might at a business meeting. "Ritchie. Kirk. Are your parents well?" Kay was lost for words, as she watched them all shake hands with Ted. Their attitude towards him denoted ... and now the word came to her quite plainly ... respect.

"Mr Devonish," Joseph replied. "Well, yes. Pretty OK. Me Dad's back never good, but ..."

"What's all this about, Joseph?" asked Ted, wisely, Kay observed, giving him the opportunity to explain their side of things.

"Lena, my wife, is ... well, maybe not now, but she was here with *him*," and with the old anger flashing in his eyes, he thrust a finger towards Tibor. "And my two sons as well ..."

"My dear chap, I can understand you might think all that. Perfectly reasonable mistake. Anyone might think the same, but ... it is just that. A mistake. Your lovely wife was staying here awhile. You're quite right about that ..."

Joseph's heavy browed eyes cast a withering glance at Kay, but he seemed relatively cowed so she ventured, "Perhaps we could all go and sit down in the sitting room?" leading the way so all would follow. "You too, Tibor," she added, as he hung back nervously.

The three men sat together on the sofa, which was just big enough to take their large frames.

Ted calmly sat back in his chair, legs crossed revealing a narrow strip of white skin above pale yellow socks and tooled leather brogues. Kay heard the crunch of gravel outside, followed by the doorbell. "That'll be the police ..."

Joseph and his brethren jumped up, scowling, unconsciously making fists.

"Tell them there's been a mistake Kay – it's all under control. In fact," he added, getting up, "I'll explain to them myself." Kay gladly left him to it and sat down, as did all others assembled in the room.

182

Kay decided to keep quiet now and observe. Everyone seemed edgy and there was an air of expectancy.

After a tense minute or two, as they waited for Ted, Joseph asked, "Where is she then?"

"We don't know," replied Kay and Ted in perfect unison as he returned to his chair. They exchanged smiles.

"I bet *he* knows!" cried Joseph, again jabbing a finger towards Tibor who sat on a footstool in the corner of the room, arms tightly folded across his chest, as far away from Joseph as he could be. He vehemently shook his head, a terrified look on his face.

"No, no, I have no idea where the devil she is."

Ted put his fingertips together in a steeple and raised his chin, which somehow brought the gathering to order again. He was about to speak and Joseph and his brothers sat forward as if joined at the hip, to listen.

"You were led to believe, I understand, that Lena and Tibor had a secret relationship and that she was expecting his child. Is that correct?"

Joseph pursed his lips and nodded abruptly.

"Your baby girl was born – stillborn, sadly – two months early. Did you realise that?"

Joseph shook his head. "It's what she said, but I knew she was seein' ..." and he cast a murderous look at Tibor, who raised his chin defiantly, saying nothing.

Ted cut him off. "Well – it's actually true. We can easily get confirmation of that from the hospital, once we find Lena."

Kay held her breath waiting for the retorts, the demands for proof, but they did not come. Ted's words counted for something with these men.

"Now then, that means the baby was *in fact* conceived when *you* were with Lena, my dear chap, not when you were away working somewhere else. You see? You will be wondering why Lena was spending time with Tibor?"

"They were up to no good, for sure," mumbled Joseph, uncertainly. "Making a right fool out of me ..."

"She was simply trying to help a Romany Gypsy who was desperately lonely, away from his homeland and family, trying to find relatives who came here some years ago. He had nothing. Nothing and nobody." Ted looked across at Tibor as if checking the facts with him and Tibor nodded. "And he was not treated kindly in this country. He believed some aunts, uncles and cousins had joined a Travelling group. His old mother had wept bitterly – you can imagine - at her only son going but wanted him to find a better life. But, ahah, he had to keep *incognito* ... Yes? Secretly, he had to move around, as in order to survive due to a run of bad luck he had *stolen* something ..."

Nods all round. Clearly understandable. No details needed. Kay could almost see feelings of sympathy switching in the direction of Tibor and she gazed on in awe at Ted's diplomacy.

"Tibor here is not a bad man – and, because Lena is not a bad person either, she wanted to help him. She was his only hope. You see? Yes? You see? And how easily you were led astray to think what you thought. A mistake *anyone* could have made. But lucky for you, lucky man that you are, Joseph, Lena will take you back – if we can find her."

Was that a tear in the corner of Joseph's eye? This angry, violent husband who had caused Lena to hide for months in fear and dread, so fearful that he would hurt her and take her children, was a blustering giant with a soft centre, Kay decided.

He was not yet quite ready to give Tibor a comradely hug, or offer apologies for his hasty judgement and threatening behaviour. She could see that he would lose face. But his fury was visibly melting.

"Now I think you owe this lady here, Mrs Kay Brackenbridge, a great debt of gratitude for keeping Lena and her boys safe when they, too had nowhere to go. Joseph, maybe she was lying but she said that you were so angry that you wanted her out of your sight. You threatened her. With your mad jealousy, your rage, she thought you might kill her. Is that right?"

Joseph was wringing his hands. "I may've said summat like that, but I'd not hurt her. Not *kill* her, any rate …"

"I trust you will make amends once she's back with you," said Ted. Kay began to feel slightly uncomfortable now with his tone. Maybe a little too patriarchal, like some lord of the manor lecturing his serfs. Enough, she decided.

Her thoughts reverted to the article in which she had been totally immersed before the rumpus had interrupted her. She looked at her watch.

"I suggest we reconvene tomorrow to draw up an action plan. We must find Lena."

"But I've searched all over for her," confessed Joseph.

"That's why we need to think afresh," said Kay, gently ushering the three men towards the front door. "Come back tomorrow morning around ten."

She leaned back on the door after closing it, raising her eyes to the ceiling. Ted laughed.

"How did you *do* that?" she asked.

20

"So – did you tell anyone else about Lena – the whole story – or mention it at all?" asked Kay, setting down a tray of tea and biscuits on a small table. Tibor had gone so it was just the two of them left to reflect on the afternoon's drama.

Ted shook his head. "No, no. I sensed that would be unwise and a breach of confidentiality. You told me because you needed to unload. I knew that …"

"I wonder how Joseph got to know …" mused Kay, as she sat back in an armchair, still trembling inside after the morning's disruption. She felt shivery and knew that it was delayed shock from the initial break-in, that felt like a recurring nightmare.

Ted shrugged, dragging fingers through his silver hair. "That is something you may never know – unless you ask him, of course, and he chooses to tell you. If anyone knows, he should!"

Kay smiled. "Mm. They knew you, didn't they?"

Ted was now gazing out of the window distractedly. "Oh yes, they know me all right. We've had many an altercation … but their parents, grandparents and many previous generations have been supported by our family. Given work, y'know. Word has passed down. It's sustained a kind of …"

"Respect …" supplied Kay.

He nodded but said nothing.

"Or was it fear?"

Ted turned to face Kay, then cast his eyes down, folding his arms. "Mm … maybe a little of both. I have had the police onto them … more than once. Kay, I feel badly about that now. Since I met you …"

He advanced towards her and Kay panicked. What was he doing?

"I hope the possible police involvement didn't reach too many eyes and ears," she said hastily. "I wouldn't want this getting into the local paper." Ted sat awkwardly on the arm of the Kay's chair and she wished he would move.

"Even though they trespassed on your property, threatened you, effectively assaulted your house guest ... Have you considered what might have happened had I not turned up?"

Kay felt suitably chided but defended herself. "I'd have told them the police were on their way. I think, though, instinctively ..." she hesitated, knowing that her first impressions of people were not famous for their accuracy, "... that Joseph is more bark than bite. He's a formidable figure and uses that to advantage, but somehow I can't imagine him actually causing GBH. Has he a record of violence?"

There was a pause as Ted stood up, then sat in an armchair next to her. "Over the years? Mm. Mischievous child. Bit of a teenage daredevil, tendency to injure himself rather than others, as I recall. Moderate physical damage, I'd say. Fists never weapons. Quick to defend. Scuffles, colourful language. Not ... malicious, or calculating in any way. But unpredictable, hot temper. No guarantee of what might have happened ..."

Kay suppressed a smile at Ted's executive summary. "OK, I accept that, and I really do value your help."

Ted looked at her a little too directly for comfort. "Glad to be of service, m'dear. What are your plans now, Kay?"

She looked at her watch. "Well, now I must finish something on my computer and, tomorrow morning I shall have this meeting with Joseph and take it from there. Find Lena at all costs."

"You could leave them to it, couldn't you?"

"No. I need to see this through." Or die wondering, she thought.

"I can be here too, for moral support ..."

How could she decline this offer without seeming ungrateful? Without Ted overseeing, would Joseph relax and open up more, be less defensive, or would he let go completely and overpower her with angry words and gestures?

"I've caused you enough trouble – and anyway Joseph may not want me interfering ..."

"That is very likely," cut in Ted.

"Well, let me see how it goes tomorrow and I'll let you know. Save wasting your time. How's that?"

It was half-past ten by the time Kay was satisfied with the third draft of her article and as she read through her own life experience she felt strangely detached. Surely she thought, this happened to someone else – in a film or a book, perhaps. Maybe she was through with the hair shirt, the repentence, maybe even the sharp pain of grief was beginning to turn to more of a dull ache.

Just pouring it out, marshalling thoughts, clarifying memories and crystallising sentences had all helped. Revelations to the local people may yet take her recovery to another level. She was hopeful.

But this whole mission had turned inward and it was not supposed to be about her. She e-mailed it to the editor and looked forward to tweaking the Gypsy articles, as promised.

Just before ten o'clock the following morning, as she sat at her kitchen table with the newspaper expecting Joseph to arrive with or without his brothers, Max called.

"Good news for your Tibor," he said.

"Excellent – do you have his mobile number?" she asked, cutting to the chase in a businesslike fashion. This was, she rationalised, not being unkind – just good time management. Tibor was, after all, no longer the key to her plan's success and, so long as he found his family he would be more than satisfied and she had certainly played a pivotal role in facilitating this. Her conscience was comfortable with this.

"He could be reunited within a matter of hours," added Max. Kay felt an unexpected lump in her throat.

"Oh? Oh Max. He'll be overjoyed …" She could picture the emotional reunion like a scene in a film.

Joseph arrived late.

"I thought you weren't coming," she said, looking over his shoulder as his figure filled the back doorway, to see if he had company. "Shall we sit outside?" she asked, thinking he might prefer to be out of the house.

"If you like," he said. Once they were seated at the garden table, he added, "I know all the likely places. I've done 'em all over and over."

"It could be that you've just missed her. Did you drive round?"

"Drove, walked, rode a horse 'cross the common."

"Well it could be that she would be deliberately avoiding the places where *you* would expect her to be. As she is at the moment, she doesn't *want* you to find her. Remember you scared the living daylights out of your wife! That's why she stayed here for so long – she was terrified of being found by you."

He looked sheepish. "I dunno where else to try."

Kay noticed he did not speak so much in the Romany tongue as Lena; maybe this was because she was raised by her grandparents – another generation.

"Well we could go in my car and just drive around different places from where you've looked already." Am I being trusting, brave or stupid, she wondered, briefly?

He shrugged. "Where?"

"I don't know! See where it takes us. See where we end up." She really wanted to do this.

"No harm, s'pose," he agreed reluctantly.

"Who told you Lena was staying with me?" Kay felt she had to ask this question, wondering which of her confidants had betrayed the secret, even if unintentionally.

He turned down the corners of his mouth and shrugged, avoiding her gaze. "A few people – word got round."

Ted was right. She would never know. "Look Joseph, do you want to find your wife – and Jason and Tom? Think how much your youngest has grown by now. Little ones change so fast …"

"Yeh, yeh. I know. Let's go."

As they drove along, Kay found herself rambling a bit, keeping the conversation going, the atmosphere comfortable. She told him about the bacon pudding and the *kipsies*, baskets that Lena was planning to make from hazel twigs.

He was listening, somehow both frowning and smiling. "She's mad," he said, fondly.

"But people do make them – and sell them, do they?"

"Not so much hawking like they used to. More at fairs and that. We used to go to more of 'em. Appley Green never did nothin' like that though. Miserable lot."

A flash of inspiration struck Kay. "Why don't we organise one? A fair, or event of some kind in the village to show people things about your culture? Crafts, traditions, history, jobs you do now – how you live, the problems you face …"

Joseph looked doubtful.

"What do *you* do? How do you earn a living?"

"Refuse sorting – on the tip. Use machinery an' all that," he added this proudly, thus elevating the status of his work.

"I bet villagers would be …" shocked, she thought, unaware, "interested to know about your work. I bet half of them never even give a thought as to who does that kind of thing, or what it's like …" She reflected on Lena's cleanliness standards.

"Bah. It's a load of rubbish though," he said, with a dark smile that made his eyes crinkle and Kay realised at once what Lena saw in him. "Reckon I could get some horses along. Wagons and other stuff. Might work. But gettin' folk to join in summat like that where *Gorgios* are … they don't mix." He shook his head and heaved a deep, doubtful sigh.

"Maybe building bridges could make a better future for your group. Maybe the villagers would see things more from your side … I could contact some people I know who would join in this for sure." She thought of Natalie, Max, museums she had found on the Internet, the Travellers' Education Service that she recently discovered was trying so desperately to get off the ground. They would all have an interest … We could collaborate. Oh, go on Joseph – I need your help in this. It'd get in the press. It might attract Lena!"

He sat up straight and opened his eyes wide. "It might."

After a day of otherwise fruitless driving around shopping centres, business parks and housing estates; calling in leisure centres, pubs and hotels; scouring parks and playing fields, Joseph and Kay returned. The 'event' idea had saved the day. They now had something to work towards with great purpose. Kay had even suggested that Joseph might be able to get some hidden message to Lena in a newspaper item, which proved to be dramatically motivating. The fact that his wife was unlikely to buy a local newspaper was a thought she kept to herself.

The local paper arrived at the end of the week and Kay flipped through its pages to find her article. The first time, in her haste, she missed it then suddenly her own words caught her eye in the body text on the front page! The headline was *TROUBLE STRIKES TWICE FOR NEWCOMER.*

The editor was unavailable when she called. Enraged and betrayed, she paced up and down the room with the phone, suppressing a powerful urge to shout and kick and scream. If the editor was in the room now, within striking distance, she wasn't sure what she would do to him, but it would not be something he would forget in a hurry …

She had given her all to that piece about herself. She read *… a reported fight … echoes of the past for Mrs Brackenbridge … a gang of three Gypsies were seen marching towards her house … inviting* *trouble* … They had used every word of her carefully crafted prose (too lazy to edit) but, as she read it she could see they had craftily fused it with her recent call for help … *A 999 call was made for protection against our friends the Travellers* … How much had Ted told the police when he went to the door to send them on their way? No, no she should not cast any blame in his direction …

Would she let this demi-god get her down? Would she hell! Put on hold and weary of waiting, she slammed the phone down, hearing herself wail pitifully, "Dunstan! Dunstan where the bloody Nora are you?"

Kay took herself into the garden to pick runner beans and hoe between the maize that had suddenly sprouted thick hairy cobs and would soon be ready to eat. Nothing like sweetcorn picked and cooked within a few minutes – a sweetness you could never get from shop-bought. She clutched desperately to positive thoughts.

The garden reminded her too much of Dunstan whom she suddenly feared she might never see again. He should have showed up by now, surely, if he truly intended to return. Had his double-life somehow caught up with him? Perhaps he was guilty of something more. Maybe he knew that he had been rumbled and could not face her. She was reluctant to call him, giving the impression that she was desperate to see him …

Her mobile rang and she checked to see who was calling. Ted. Feeling mean, she switched off her phone.

She had noticed in the paper a craft fair advertised, about thirty miles away and decided to go and see if she could pick up any ideas for the Appley Green 'Event with no name'. It would get her out of the house, away from the garden, and give her an aim for the day.

The car park was choreographed like Disneyland with stewards waving her in to a space. Good idea. Parking essential and must be thought through. There were tickets, but as there were no people-proof boundary fences, everyone entering through the gates had their hands stamped as a check they had been processed.

She entered a wonderland of baskets, jewellery, carvings, marquetry pictures, soft toys, silk scarves, greetings cards, antiques and bric-a-brac, home-made cakes, jams and chutneys … Many goods, she could tell, were imported from abroad, India or China. Their event would be different, but she picked up useful tips on what made an eye-catching stall.

In need of refreshment, she spied a tent serving everything from cream teas to burgers. Another good idea caught her attention. Someone had pitched close by and seemed to be drawing the crowds. There was a poster pinned to the side of the tent "Portraits while you wait - £2". Very cheap – no wonder there were queues of families, many mothers with babes in buggies, wanting to have something different by which to remember their day out.

She wondered whether to give it a go. Just that morning, feeling a bit down, she had looked at her reflection in the mirror. Should she have one of those chemical peels, she wondered, fleetingly? No. Botox? Definitely not. Laser treatment? Face lift? Nothing appealed. Photographs became less flattering as you get older, though, she had concluded from the last few she had seen of herself. Maybe a simple sketch would play down her signs of ageing. Portrait artists were more likely to have customers if they flattered their customers. As she peered over a shoulder to see some samples, she caught sight of the artist – a young girl with very short hair. The drawings on display were good, some done in pastels, others with charcoal. A simple style … catching a likeness well, she suspected … very much like … Lena's picture of Tibor …

Her gaze flashed to the girl's face and she squinted. Was it? Was it? Then the girl looked up and their eyes met.

21

The following morning Kay heard from Claudia to say she was on her way. Expected time of arrival was in about two days' time. Suddenly Kay's focus shifted, as if she had switched channels. She must get another bedroom ready as Suzi would be coming to stay as well for a family reunion. The bed was made up with new pale pink linen, silk fuschia cushions artlessly scattered, organic toiletries in a gingham-lined basket. Suzi was bringing a big Welcome Home banner to go across the front door, which was so typical of her, albeit Kay was a little doubtful. It would be good for Claudia to get herself a home in her own good time. But for a while, it would be just the three of them. Wonderful though it was to discover Lena, and satisfying as it was for Tibor to eventually find his relatives, this was a major piece of her own life that was finally coming together. Her own flesh and blood and nothing, arguably, is stronger than that.

Home baking became a priority, as Claudia was the biggest fan of her chocolate brownies and lemon meringue tart. She was not so figure conscious as Suzi, who might enthuse over a small square or a sliver, never as convincing as Claudia who would munch through a large wedge in a state of apparent bliss, already looking forward to a second helping. Moreover, Claudia knew next to nothing about her mother's new home and Kay wanted it to live up to, or possibly exceed, whatever expectations she might have brought with her from the other side of the globe.

She hoped Joseph and Lena were good together now. Seeing them reconnect was nerve-wracking, but not at all as she had imagined it might be months ago. When they had parted in the spring, he had been mad with jealousy, yes. His macho honour and reputation were at stake, but more than this, his possessiveness stemmed from his love for her. Now he did not seem to need convincing evidence, or concrete proof. Lena was young and had overreacted. She had, after all, seen others who had been struck by their husbands, so she erred on the side of caution, a good survival trait for anyone.

Kay hoped this was all true, desperately so. For if it were not, then Lena could still be at risk with a truly violent man who was biding his time before seeking his revenge by physically abusing her or taking away the boys.

After they caught sight of each other at the fair, Lena had looked away, the colour rising in her cheeks. Kay could see she was shocked and embarrassed, so Kay held back awhile. Lena was busy working on a sketch of a baby girl, whose mother anxiously monitored progress, commenting at regular intervals, as the face of her little one gradually appeared on the paper. The crowd watched too with fascination and Kay felt a tear trickle down one cheek. How amazing that this raw talent had blossomed. Lena paused only momentarily when she spotted Kay.

It was about an hour later, as the crowd regrouped for the announcement of raffle winners, when Kay went up to Lena. Lena had not come forward – perhaps she needed time to adjust.

"I said you were good," she said.

"People seem to like 'em," Lena replied, modestly.

"Where are Tom and Jason?" asked Kay, looking around.

"Me mate, Sue, she does face painting and they're off playin' with her kids somewhere. Not far. They're OK." She nodded proudly.

"Could we maybe sit down and have a cup of coffee – for old times' sake? Have a chat?"

Lena nodded and began walking towards the cafeteria tent, close to where they were standing. Every ounce of Kay's being – physical, spiritual, mental and emotional – was aching to know what Lena had been up to all this time. What had she done after Suzi had sent them on their way? How had they survived? But she did not want to push things. Maybe Lena did not want to tell her.

They sat down at a table with coffee and cakes. "I'm sorry my daughter chased you away."

"I could understand, could see it through her eyes. My fault." She turned down the corners of her mouth.

"*Your* ...?"

"I didn't want you to tell her, did I? I made you not tell her, didn't I? Remember?"

"Oh Lena, Lena, my dear. I never saw it that way around. No, no, I should have foreseen the possibility and made sure it never happened. Anyway, let's not fall out over it. We'll agree to differ!"

Lena laughed. Maybe she had not heard the expression before.

"Yeah. Agree to not agree! That's good. I'll remember that ... I've remembered lots of things you said and did ... thanks for all that. You know. I'd never have made it away from Joseph if you ..."

"I've met Joseph. He's a fine young man."

Lena's mouth fell open and her eyes opened until they were almost round. "You've *met* Joseph?"

Kay nodded, deriving mischievous pleasure from giving titbits of momentous news.

"Mm," she said nodding. "Would you like to split that apricot Danish with me?"

Lena deftly spliced the pastry in two with a knife. "How? Where is he? Did he say ...? What did he say? About me?" Lena gabbled, the questions spilling out pell-mell, as she leaned forward, unaware perhaps that she had grabbed Kay by the arm and was shaking it.

"Lena, I think you know, looking back now, he misunderstood and spoke in temper – which caused you to run off. It must have been frightening. I can understand that, but basically he's as desperate to have you back, as you are to have him …"

Lena sat back in her chair, raised her chin. Kay wanted to ask her about her hair, but knew instinctively that it must've been an emotional wrench to have her heavy mane of golden hair cut off. It was an effective way to disguise herself from a distance, so the reason for doing it was obvious. "Well. I don't know about that," said Lena. "Actually. But what about Tibor?"

"Yes – of course – there's so much you don't know …" Kay put her hand to her forehead. "It's hard to remember where we were up to when you disappeared, but we found Tibor … well, Joseph can fill you in … when you see him, can't he?"

Then the tears and a brief wail as Lena buried her face in her hands, to hide it from onlookers. It seemed to Kay she was holding her breath. She was alarmed.

"Do you not want to go back to him? Is that it? Have you found another … life? What, Lena? What? Talk to me. My dear girl. Lena." Kay rummaged in her bag for some tissues and thrust them at her. "Come on, let's go outside and walk around."

Lena took the clutch of tissues and wiped her cheeks and her eyes. "No, I'll have to fetch the boys in a minute."

It struck Kay how different Lena looked from a few weeks ago, the new hair style, so short. She seemed to have lost weight too. "OK, well … Just tell me what you want me to do."

"'s been so awful Kay. You think – 'cos you see me now makin' a few pounds and people lookin' on. All that. But you don't see the days we spent in the rain and the boys goin' to bed with nothin' to eat. And me, cryin' all the night long …"

Kay reached out to squeeze her hand. Now her story would unfold.

"Tell me – if you want to. The boys are safe with your friend for a bit, are they?"

197

Lena sniffed and nodded. "Oh yeah. I don't think Sue has a watch anyway, nor do I."

"I wanted to find you – to help you," said Kay. "I tried, I really did. Why did you not respond to my calls?"

"Lost my phone – well, Jason dropped it down a drain."

"So where have you been living? How have you managed?"

"Sold my necklace – to a shop that sells new and used jewellery, y'know... Didn't say I was Romany Gypsy or Traveller or he wouldn't have let me in, most probably."

"How long did the cash last you?"

"Didn't spend it on food. Bought a tent from a campin' shop. Second-hand. It's good," she said. "The boys like it. Fitted it up with sleeping-bags and stuff to make it right cosy, but I knew I must get more money ..."

"How did you feed the boys and yourself?"

Lena shook her head indifferently. "Oh, we survived." Kay suspected the worst – supermarket skips, milk off doorsteps, people's vegetable gardens, but they had to eat, so she didn't probe. Maybe her methods lay elsewhere ... it was clear she would never know.

"Where did you pitch your tent?"

Lena suddenly went into what looked like a trance and Kay thought she hadn't heard the question.

"Where is Joseph now? Is he with you?" Lena asked, suddenly, looking anxious.

"No, of course not. I would've said. I don't know where he is at the moment. We spent hours driving round looking for you and he went off, an unhappy man ..." without leaving his phone number, she suddenly realised. "Does he have a phone?"

Lena shook her head. The recent past, her present situation seemed to be morphing slowly and silently into what might present itself as her future ...

Lena gave herself a little shake, as if to bring her back to their conversation. "We ... we were in the woods, different spots well under trees so as not to attract attention, moving gradually further and further away."

Kay thought how risky this sounded, her imagination quick to conjure up everything from owls hooting, snakes slithering in the leaves, spiders running amongst their clothes – to rapists and paedophiles. "Were you comfortable? Warm?"

"It leaked a bit. Weather ain't been good, 'as it?" She screwed up her face. "We just got by from day to day, night by night. Couldn't think as far as the next week."

"What about washing …?"

"Public toilets … not the best, but had to manage somehow, and if we found a stream …"

"Would you like something to eat now?"

"Na. Better go soon. The boys."

"What about benefits. Could you not claim something?"

"Not much, 'cos I depended on Joseph who had work. Anyhow, didn't dare try for risk of being recognised. It'd be an obvious place for Joseph to be askin' after me. Anyway, the good bit …" and she broke off to smile. "One sunny, dry day, when the sky was a pretty blue – *boktalo*! my lucky day – I found some paper on a tip and began drawing to help keep Tom out o' mischief. Miles away, I risked going to a market one day and there was someone paintin' children's faces, like animals and clowns, and I was watching her. Sue. Tom wanted his face done so bad - as a *weshen jukkal*. A fox. Moanin' and groanin' 'e was. So I started sketching one of her little girls, and said could we do a swap. She said, "yes, definitely" and she thought I could do sketches for money and tag along with her."

"What a lovely story …"

"Well, '*s tatcho*. It's true. How it happened. I sold six first time I tried … so kept going places where we caught families looking for ways to stop their kids moanin' and groanin'. Spendin' good *lolli* to stop 'em in fact."

"And does this make you a living?"

"Brings in enough to buy food and stuff we need to cook, with a bit left over. I got me *chavies* some clothes from a 'Care for the Aged' shop. The people are nice in there. We do OK."

"So are you happy now?" Kay asked, thinking she can't go on living for ever in a tent, surely. Not long before she would have to think about Tom going to school ...

"Happy? What d'you fink? I'm so lonely I cry meself to sleep every night and the boys need new *chokkors* and still ask for their Daddy every day ... even had to sell me hair to buy food ..."

Kay was shocked. Somehow a more desperate measure than those she had imagined. "At least you can grow your hair again ... Do you want to see Joseph, then?"

Kay watched the trembling bottom lip. Lena looked up, meeting her gaze very directly. "You sure he knows the truth? Believes it?"

"As far as I can tell," replied Kay cautiously, feeling cowardly, but having to cover herself. "He has accepted that it was a mistake. Tibor denied all the accusations very honestly and openly and Ted Devonish supported him, which seemed to clinch things ..."

"Mr *Devonish*? You know him? I thought he'd turned sour on us. His family used to give my grandparents work in the old days, but he ..." Lena screwed up her nose.

"He may be softening a bit. I think he wants to help but just can't see how to. We're going to put on a special day for people in the village to come along and learn more about Gypsy culture. Joseph is keen to help and I have friends who will do their bit."

"You reckon you'll get my people to take part?" Lena looked incredulous.

"*You* could help with this ... maybe. Why don't you come to my house for a few days? Joseph will be in touch with me at some point because of this event thing. He's getting others who'll bring horses or show crafts, old and new ..."

"We could pitch our tent in the garden. That'd be good."

Kay nodded readily.

But when Kay got home Joseph was pacing up and down outside her house, like a tiger in a cage, or an expectant father in maternity hospital. He marched towards her as soon as she opened her car door.

"I was thinkin' about this newspaper thing you said," he said, skipping any form of greeting. Kay was reminded of the call she must make to the editor about what she considered to be a cruel misrepresentation of the facts. "To write something with a hidden message, y'see we're good at that an' ..." he carried on. The expression on his face was then something that Kay would always remember – as he saw and heard his children in the back seat of the car, then realising that the young woman next to them with short hair was his wife.

22

The next few days were strange, Kay feeling as if she were an actress who had stepped into the wrong play without a script. Suzi and Claudia were with her, the latter brimful of stories and photographs until Kay – much as she loved her daughter and much as she was both delighted and relieved to see her home safe and well – could have wept for mercy. One more temple, one more beach, or group of "people she met" and she would be forced to take to her bed with some unspecific ailment.

Claudia loved the house, the garden, the village. Everything was "fantastic" and "cool". The village green, the surrounding woodland and heath were an "absolute dream" and she "could stay here forever".

"You must tell me all about your new friends," Claudia urged, as she appeared at the foot of the stairs on her first morning, clutching a pile of unwashed denims. "I bet there are some weird rustic sorts here. And the village gossip, Mum," Kay had to give her credit for being as enthusiastic about others' lives as she was about her own. "Don't tell me there isn't any!"

Kay nodded, with a secret smile, wondering if she would ever be strong enough to summon up the energy needed to relate the whirlwind events of the past months. She felt it might be beyond the scope of her verbal skills. She mentioned about the upcoming event, hoping the rest would come out in snippets and nuggets of news in episodic fashion over a period of time.

"Oh, great! Like a 'Folksy Festival'. When is it?" asked Claudia, consulting her minute electronic organiser. "I *adore* festivals. We went to this amazing … in Thailand, oh and near Vienna, but … you should've heard … and seen …"

Of course, thought Kay, *Appley Green Festival.* That would be it. No mention of Gypsies or *Gorgios* in the publicity to deter either camp.

Over the ensuing days, Kay kept wondering how the family were, now reunited – Joseph, Lena, Tom and Jason. She had little romantic cameos in her head – where they would be sitting down together at dusk, with Joseph and Tom tending a crackling fire outside ready for cooking kebabs or chicken drumsticks. Lena sits drawing Jason as he plays happily with sticks and stones in the soil, making an imaginary miniature garden just as he often did in her garden with Jason, where a sprig of heather became hollyhocks, and tiny florets of cauliflower would be lined up as a row of full-sized ones. Lena would be cautiously telling her husband about all that had happened to her, her tragic time in the hospital and the nightmare it was for her when no one – especially him – believed her, how she had been terrified by Suzi, how she and the boys had managed to survive on the road, in the woods … She would be studying his face for signs that he believed her and be reassured by the look of regret in his dark eyes and pride in her courage.

But darker scenes would erupt in her head, where Lena has bruises on her face, where the boys are cowering in a neighbouring trailer to escape the shouting, the harsh words, the stamping of heavy boots and breaking crockery …

Just a couple of weeks since the idea of the 'Festival' had been hatched, plans were coming together well and as Kay strolled through the village arm in arm with both her daughters, they were counting how many posters they had seen. Claudia and Suzi broke away to take a look at a new shop that had opened up offering beauty treatments and Kay saw a trio of villagers she recognised walking their dogs on the green. She didn't know them by name.

"Kay!" they called, coming towards her, one reaching towards her and giving her arm a squeeze. "How are you? We saw your bit in the paper."

Of course, it was bound to happen. She had seen few local residents since her past had gone public in the village.

"You must've had a tough time. Such courage. My God! I said to my husband, I think I would've just screamed or fainted."

"What is the world coming to? Not safe in your own home ..." said her friend.

"I was very unsure if it was a good thing to tell people about what happened," replied Kay. "Part of me said 'what's the point? it's all in the past now', but ..."

"Sometimes it's good to share. A thing as big as that – probably not healthy to keep it bottled up. Not as if you're ever going to forget it entirely is it? And you're living here now, so ... anyway, at least they got the bugger who did it ... but what about those ruddy Travellers coming to your house? After all you'd been ..."

Kay cut in. "That was nothing. A misunderstanding. They meant no harm at all. Newspaper trying to make a connection – sensationalising. You know the sort of thing."

Kay then decided to grasp the nettle. "I was wondering," she began to divert their collective attention. "Have any of you heard about Dunstan? Seen him?"

They shook their heads, muttering, "No, no, haven't for a while. Went off a few weeks back ... he's a busy man, though. Maybe it's his charity work taken him away." They clearly knew less than she did as they made no mention of his mother's death.

"Charity? What's that then?" asked Kay, quickly.

"Well, you know all the work he does – like that bloke what's-his-name on the TV, but our Dunstan did it first – working with youngsters that've ... what d'you call them?"

"Young offenders," supplied her friend. "And the homeless."

"That's it. Reforms them, he does."

"Is this … counselling work?" asked Kay, thinking back to what Dunstan had told her on their jaunt around the homeless hostels a few weeks back.

"Mm … not sure. He gives them what he calls projects. Gets them to help with working on the land – like that other chap, oh what *is* his name …? Yes, it is, sort of guidance I'd call it. Tries to put them on the right track by teaching them a trade and they learn what it is to do a day's hard work …"

Kay thought of Alan, the young man seen at intervals in her garden, digging, mowing, standing around gazing at the sky … "But do they get paid? Does Dunstan pay them?"

"I think … he doesn't to begin with. They have to prove themselves. It's an incentive. Seems to work well, so they say. He's had all sorts – drug addicts, muggers …"

"And are any of these youngsters Gypsies?"

They looked at each other, shaking their heads. "Mm. Shouldn't think so … villagers don't mix with the Travellers when they're here. He set up a charity trust and his work raises funds for this …"

"Do you know where he lives?" Kay carried on quizzing, feeling brave, not caring if they thought her nosy.

Again, they looked at each other. "No idea. Do you? Not in Appley Green, I'd say … He works for you, doesn't he?" Kay nodded. "You must be missing him. He's badly missed by a lot of people round here, that's for sure. Good sort is Dunstan."

"Oh yes. The best. Deserves a medal. These your daughters?"

Claudia and Suzi were waving as they emerged, giggling, from the beauty shop armed with small carrier bags and leaflets.

"Yes. I'd better get back to them …"

"So nice to see you. What lovely girls …"

Kay was glad she had been on her own when she first read her personal story in the paper. She was angered by it and would not have wanted Suzi and Claudia to see her in an agitated state. Moreover, she had considered how her exposure to Appley Green would be, but she had not really thought about the implications for her daughters and she felt guilty for not bearing in mind their feelings. Would they want the tragic death of their father raked up again and in the public eye? Almost certainly not.

She had tried to call the editor but was told he was away. Trying to fob me off no doubt, she thought. He will realise that she might not be too happy about them merging her sensitive biographical piece with the story of Gypsies coming to her house, her call to the police. He must realise that this would be totally counter to the theme of articles she had proposed to him. It was a betrayal and he obviously did not want to be confronted about it, even over the phone.

It was some days later when she managed to get hold of him. Claudia and Suzi were out horse-riding. When she was eventually put through, she was ready to launch into a tirade of accusations that had had time to fester and grow inside her for days.

"Kay! Hi!" he said, brightly, before she had a chance to speak. "Heard you were trying to get hold of me. Your messages. E-mails. Been away – laid up with slipped disc. One of the worst pains known to man, I do believe! Now, it'll be about that article a while back now. You must've thought I'd gone off my head."

"I couldn't believe you would do that ..." intercepted Kay at last, as he briefly paused for breath, but not for long.

"My sub. My sub-editor. He did it – cock-a-hoop at the scoop he was, too. Ha-ha ... Sorry about that. Really am. He didn't know about our little agreement – in fact nobody does. Not the most professional ... Between you and me wasn't it? Look, Kay," he said, his voice taking on a wheedling tone. It dawned on Kay that he had probably broken some kind of journalistic code of conduct and did not want her contempt and scorn to turn into recriminations, or village tittle-tattle. "What can I do to make it up to you?" he added, possibly digging himself an even deeper hole, if she were the kind of person who might report him to some organisation monitoring reporters' ethical standards.

Seizing the moment, Kay said, "How are my other articles coming on …? You must know about the Festival? Strong publicity will help gain support so …"

"Sure, sure. I really think people will like them, actually," he agreed, justifying his obvious intent to publish whatever she asked of him. "Interesting, informative, local …"

Suzi returned to her London flat and Claudia had found herself a job more quickly than Kay could have dared to hope.

"Just temporary," she told Kay, calling from Suzi's flat where she was staying until she found somewhere of her own to rent. "But a start. Teaching assistant, working with nine to ten year olds. Inner city – bit of a challenge."

"Darling that's wonderful, it'll be good experience for you to get back into your career path, what you were doing before … well, you know … before your … our world was turned upside down." Kay felt proud at how Claudia had knuckled down to applying for permanent posts, scanning the Times Educational Supplement for anything that might suit – wherever it took her. Kay realised, with a sinking heart, that soon she really would be alone – but this was, after all, just as she had originally planned. Her girls were capable, independent adults standing on their own two feet. If only Marcus could be here to know them as the young women they were.

"I really feel I can move on now. I think of Daddy every day though," she said.

"So do I. Always will, I think."

"But as he was in happier times, not the last time I … well, you know."

Kay wanted to hug her. She thought of the article. "I had something published in the local newspaper here about … that night and how living in a close community has really helped me …"

"Oh, well done Mum," replied Claudia without a moment's hesitation and Kay felt a huge sense of relief. "How did people react to that then – the village?"

"All right. Interested, but not morbidly so. Warm and sympathetic I'd say. Could you mention it to Suzi? I'll show it to you next time you're down …"

"OK. Must go now – my mobile's going …"

Whilst she had plenty of things to occupy her day – the Festival (where she was so looking forward to seeing Joseph, Lena and the boys), and a somewhat belated house-warming party she was planning for villagers who were now fast becoming close friends, as well as her old social circle who must have thought she had emigrated, or quite possibly died – her thoughts kept turning to Dunstan. He was unfinished business. The thought that she may never see him again was unaccountably painful. After all, she thought reasonably, she was a bit old for a 'relationship', wasn't she? Yet there was no denying, she never felt more alive than when in his company since she had lost Marcus, and to envisage life without his friendship was almost unbearable.

It was late August. Having picked the last of the runner beans, she was pulling down the cane wigwams when she heard a slight cough and turned. There he was, looking smart in a charcoal grey suit much as he looked when she first met him. Her very first reaction was one of shame at how she must look, in her oldest, faded jeans that had split, with her hair tied back in a scarf, muddy gardening gloves … Then she felt aglow.

"Dunstan. Dunstan … what … where …?" She felt shaky as she took in the full impact of his being there, standing in her garden, watching her.

"Did you get a good harvest?" Always he was the one to ask the right questions. It brought her back on track. She pulled off her gloves and stepped towards him.

"Moderately – the wet weather and lack of sun put paid to peppers, aubergines – even courgettes have been eaten by slugs – I'd have kept many plants in the greenhouse if I'd known that the summer was going to be like this, but there you are, you can't win all the time, can you?" She paused and he was looking at her strangely, perhaps with some affection. A gentle smile, his head slightly to one side. "All types of bean have excelled themselves. Tomatoes not too bad, a bit of blight. Freezer full. Anyway, how are *you*?"

"Me? Oh, I'm well. It's other folk that are the problem." His eyes scanned the garden as if assessing the damage that almost certainly must have been done in his absence. If he saw the forest of weeds, he did not comment. "Kay, I had to come and see you … to explain …" he began, with a slightly forced smile that quickly faded.

They ambled together back towards the house. She wanted to be sitting comfortably to hear his story and to let him know that she knew rather more about him than she did last time they were together, thanks to village informants.

"You will be in need of some refreshment?" Kay asked, cheekily, hoping he would stay for dinner. What a fabulous evening lay ahead.

"A cup of tea would be good."

Soon they were sitting like old times at the oak table in the kitchen. Kay had produced some fruit cake and a packet of supermarket biscuits.

"Not as good as your own . .." he said, dunking a cookie into his tea.

Kay shrugged. "Not worth cooking. Just me. Not the same, but I'm having a party soon so I'll get back into my apron and oven gloves for that … so you make a note in your diary … There was a silence long enough for Kay to realise that something was wrong, very wrong. When she had approached him in the garden, she had expected at least a peck on the cheek, as friends do, especially after the lapse of time. She had actually wanted him to hug her. A big bear hug would have been very acceptable. Appropriate, she felt. But no, he kept his distance.

"Kay," he said. "I've come to say goodbye."

Kay's head gave a little jerk with the shock. "Oh." She swallowed hard. "Why goodbye? Where are …?"

To save her distress, which must have been obvious to him, he added, "I must return to my family." Their eyes met and she saw that his were glistening.

"But … but Dunstan," she said, frantically counting up the arguments against this course of action. "How can you turn your back on all these young people who rely on you so much? And the *gardens*?"

She watched his face. He did not look surprised by her questions. Perhaps he thought he had told her all along. Perhaps he guessed she had heard about his activities from the villagers, as indeed she had. He would have to expand on his reasons for … for leaving, but before he vanished out of her life, she must hear his story from his own lips. She wondered if he had seen her article in the paper, but sensed that would have no bearing on his reasons for leaving.

"Dunstan, why did you never tell me that you worked for other people, in their gardens?"

"Well, I think … you never asked!"

"But surely you must see I would've liked to know."

"Why?"

"Well …" *I thought I was the only one. I thought I was special!*

"The fact that I was working in many gardens for many people makes no difference to any of you. I did my work, as agreed. On the terms we both agreed."

"I didn't know you were selling the produce *for profit!*" Kay exclaimed, trying to sound angry but knowing she would forgive him anything.

"My reasons justified the means," he muttered.

"Perhaps you could have shared that with me …" she offered. "Your reasons, this life you live in the community …

I mean, Dunstan, I thought we were friends. Why did you have to be so secretive? I know now a little about the commendable work you do with … difficult youngsters. I know the money goes into a trust fund to support and help them. But I would never have found out from you. Would I?"

Dunstan stood up as if to go. "You may not have believed me …"

"Why? Why would I have not believed you?"

"If I'd said at the start that I would be selling your produce, you would have naturally assumed that I would be pocketing the money for myself. Which I don't. I live a modest lifestyle, on the combined several small wages I receive …" He was verging on the defensive now, quite out of character.

"Where do you live? That's something else you've never told me."

"I live just outside the village – in a mobile home park. It's well tucked away."

"So – are you a Gypsy then, Dunstan? Are you one of the Travellers?"

"Ah. So. You see. I rest my case."

"What? What do you mean?"

To Kay's relief, Dunstan sat down again. "OK," he said. "No more secrets. I'm leaving anyway, so what's the harm in telling you …"

Kay would have liked to have a bath, wash her hair, do her nails, change her clothes and put on some make up but did not dare leave him for a moment in case she lost him and his story for ever.

"Will you stay for dinner at least?" she asked, planning in her mind a nice fish dish involving lots of French beans and garlicky tomatoes.

He looked at his watch, struggling with a decision.

"You've tempted me. It would be hard to turn down one of your gastronomic adventures …"

Kay opened a bottle of Chablis.

"You see, as soon as I say I'm living in a mobile home – and it is called that on my 'respectable' park, not a caravan, or a trailer, you made a connection. You add two and two and come up with seven and a half ..."

"I'm sorry."

"Once upon a time ..." he began, teasingly, taking a sip of wine. "Yes, Dunstan was a Gypsy. I guess in my heart I am still, and always will be but ..."

"Why don't you want people to know? That's what I don't quite understand."

"Kay! You must *realise*. Surely ..."

"But you've proved yourself, you're so well thought of in the village. Do *you* realise *that*?"

Dunstan scarcely acknowledged her comments. "Small boy Dunstan did well at school. He enjoyed learning and would throw a tantrum each time his family was moving on and he had to leave the school he'd got used to."

"I've heard some Traveller kids get bullied at school ..."

"I split myself in half. Managed to avoid that."

"How do you mean?"

"I made myself like non-Gypsy children when I was at school. They forgot who I was. Never talked about home. Made things up sometimes. So I was accepted. But back home, my family didn't want me to even learn to read. It's a common enough thing and I kind of understand it. A fear that I'd learn ways that would take me away from them and distract me from learning more practical skills – which is exactly what happened. I had to hide books and so, even more so as I grew older, lived a double life, to please both teachers and parents – to say nothing of the other pupils."

"Where did you hide your books?"

"Ooh, various hidey-holes ... sorry, even now it's ingrained in me never to tell. Anyway, when I was a teenager – as rebellious as the best of them – I was accused by my own people of being 'gadgefied' – like *Gorgios*. It had started to show. I loved my family, but could see other things in the wider world that I wanted. At the age of sixteen I decided to leave my community to travel on my own and see the world, working my way. I needed to sort my head out. I was one very confused young man."

"Teenage years are difficult enough ..." said Kay, refilling his glass. "Are you driving?"

He shook his head. "Walked. I'll keep this short. Managed to save enough money to move into a small bed-sit, got a job, about the age of twenty, did some training as a welder ... then, while still an apprentice, my boss found out I was a Gypsy and made life difficult for me. Prejudiced, you know. Nothing I could do was right. I was sacked for a theft I didn't commit. The bastard pinned it on me."

"That's terrible. Did you have a chance to tell the police your side of the story?"

"Trouble was, I didn't have a side to my story – I knew nothing, literally nothing about it. All I could say in my defence was that I didn't do it. He'd hidden some cash in my jacket pocket and, with witnesses, suddenly 'found the money' that had 'gone missing'. And, anyhow, my boss didn't involve the police but everyone there assumed that because I was a Gypsy I was a thief. You know Kay, I felt I just didn't belong anywhere. I knew my family wouldn't then welcome me back, but I couldn't fit in with the *Gorgios*."

Kay's phone rang and she briefly went to stop its noise, not actually even finding out who was calling.

"Sorry – go on," she said.

"I guess even you may not believe this story. Maybe you, Kay, are thinking – well, he probably did take the money and is lying through his teeth ... but we might never see each other again, so there'd be no point in ..."

Kay cut in, "No. Go on. I do believe you. So you were never actually convicted?"

He gave her hand a squeeze and the warmth of his rough skin felt more than comforting, closer to exciting. Honest working hands but ...

"No, he never pressed charges – big of him, eh? However, he refused to give me a reference, which made it tough to move on. After a long while without any work I got a job in a dark, dingy warehouse for which no qualifications were needed and where only desperate people worked. It was hell. But ... well, I worked hard, worked my way up, supervisor, manager, got an office job, well-paid, didn't tell anyone of my origins."

"I can begin to see why ..."

"It felt cowardly, but couldn't risk losing this job too. I was thirty-five by now – and married." Kay jumped. So is he still married? Is this another of his big secrets? "Vowed I'd never tell anyone of my ethnicity. So I married, still telling nobody, then ... finally one evening, like I'm doing with you now, Kay, I told Margaret ..." Oh, my God she has a name. This somehow made it worse.

"Just two weeks later, Margaret left me."

"So she was a non-Gypsy? A *Gorgio*?"

"Oh yes. A solicitor! But then, you see, bear in mind I too was well-heeled! Operations manager earning a good salary, playing golf, having expensive holidays, driving a BMW ..."

"But if she loved you – why would it make a difference?"

"She claimed it was nothing to do with my roots. She'd met someone else, but ..."

Kay could scarcely imagine how any wife of Dunstan would be attracted away from him for another man.

"She must have been mad ..." muttered Kay, then blushing like a schoolgirl.

He must've heard her. She saw laughter in his eyes.

"Somehow her view of me changed and – she was afraid others would get to know – our 'friends'," he said. "That's what I think, anyway."

"So what happened then? You were living alone? Any children?"

"No. Sadly, no children. Although, since we split, perhaps for the best, who knows? My job, my work, my whole life then became a bit ... aimless. Most of our friends were *her* friends. I had that same feeling I had when I was a teenager – a social misfit, I was. So I thought, what shall I do? I noticed

214

young men in the warehouse who came and went, unstable … with stories to tell and decided to help. Began working with a charity for the homeless … engaging youngsters, drug addicts, and so on in gardening projects, which I'd got into from initially going back to what I'd learned as a young child – tree surgery, as my father and uncles did. Found I was growing too much food! I'm good you know," he added cheekily, winking at Kay, "so set up a fund to help them, by supplying local outlets … I was actually … and I don't like telling people this one bit, but guess you'll accuse me of not telling the whole story if you find out elsewhere. I was awarded an OBE for my efforts, but you know I never discuss my past with anyone. No one in Appley Green knows. It's easier that way …"

"But if you're estranged from your family, how come you need to go back to them?" Kay asked, feeling as upset as a three year-old for whom Christmas had been suddenly cancelled.

23

Dunstan went, leaving Kay bereft, 'empty as a drum' (as a song she kept hearing on the radio goes) as she tried to focus on her mission. The Festival. The press campaign. And then?

She had formed a festival committee of Natalie, Joseph, Max and Ted all of whom had their own group of helpers with clearly defined tasks. Invitations had been sent out and plans were coming together so well Kay felt an enormous glow of satisfaction and, above all, of hope that it would be successful in its ultimate goal. Would it be enough to influence the villagers who were so entrenched in their views? The village was buzzing and she smiled as she overheard encouraging comments, "Are you doing anything? Got a stall?" "What time are you planning to get there?" "Exciting ... something different. See you there ..." Not that long since she had first caught snatches of conversation about her personal story in the local newspaper. Then to her surprise, even villagers she did not know at all came up to her, took her by the hand and said how they admired her for facing up to tragedy and for trying to help others. "No better tonic for depression ...," said one woman.

Dunstan had told her his reasons for leaving and there was little she could say or do to stop him. It would be wrong and selfish for her to interfere or attempt to dissuade him.

"My family, Romany Gypsies, are thin on the ground now," he'd explained to her. "My old Dad, sister, a few cousins. Others, like me, have scattered. They've had an unsettling habit of moving back and forth between England and Ireland at irregular intervals when things go badly. Always, the grass is greener, you know?"

216

"Do they make a living?" Kay had asked, anxious to understand.

"No. Not really. That's the problem. They need help, in so many ways. They begged me to … having forgiven me for walking out on them all those years ago, how can I just abandon them? How could I sleep at night when I've seen for myself first hand how they're not coping? You see this is what happens when families split up. A son is important to elderly parents."

Kay could feel another article writing itself even as he spoke. "But why can't they just come over here? Join a group where you can be within easy reach, without you having to uproot yourself now?" suggested Kay, stating what she felt was blindingly obvious.

He gave her a dark look. It made her stomach flip. He stood up and paced around for a moment, then turned to face her again. "Have you been listening to me? Kay! I've told you what happens to me when people know I have Gypsy blood flowing through my veins. Nobody round here knows and I have to keep it that way. My life – on two counts – was *ruined* … I can't risk that happening again."

"I understand that, but … you know my campaign. I really think people's attitudes will change …" She brought him up to date on the Festival and her PR ventures.

"Kay, I hope people do change. What you're attempting to do is … new and extraordinary. *You* are extraordinary … I wish you the very best of luck, but …"

Dunstan did not have enough faith, she reflected, in either her mission or in her.

Kay had to take her mind off the pain that was now eating away inside her. His doubts caused her to lose confidence. She began digging in the garden to make her body exhausted so she would sink into a deep sleep. Lying alone hour after hour during the night was the worst, even small daytime problems looming large and ominous. One thing that was not going to happen was for her to slide into a state of depression, not after all that she had come through, not when she was so close to sublime happiness as she had been just a few days ago. Claudia had come home and grabbed life by the horns; Festival plans were zooming ahead and slotting into place like a jigsaw; she had a party arranged for new friends; visits from old friends booked in to her diary for months ahead; and to boost her morale she was being pursued by Ted who was, after all, a distinguished local landowner; and Dunstan had come back ... yes, her spirits had soared, briefly. She had felt at one with the world.

As she turned over the soil, burying weeds in the hope they would suffocate and die, the spade occasionally slicing a worm in half which almost made her cry, she thought of what had changed to make her feel so disconsolate. The answer was all too clear and there was nothing she could do about it. At her age she should be over these unnecessary emotional upheavals. Move on, old woman.

To use a slightly different set of muscles, she put her spade aside and took up a rake. It was pleasing to see an area of soil take on a neatly combed appearance. Would she need to employ another gardener? Tears now spilled down her cheeks which she brushed away with her sleeve.

Surely Appley Green would not turn against him. If it came out that he had nearby relatives who were of the Travelling community, would they suddenly cast him out or refuse to use his services? Would his work with the youngsters crumble? Would they see him any differently?

"Of course they wouldn't!" she cried out loud, for no one else to hear but herself. His self-esteem was warped by his sad experiences. He had not heard what village residents say about him. He was well respected. And he had an OBE! Did anyone in Appley Green know that? She suddenly realised what must be done – and quickly.

Before Dunstan had disappeared down the road into the night, she double-checked she had his mobile number. After struggling to strip off her gardening gloves that were sticking to her hands, and tossing aside her gardening boots, she strode into the house and grabbed her phone.

"Dunstan? Yes, it's me, Kay. Do you realise how well respected you are here? By the villagers of Appley Green, I mean?"

"Pah! I don't know about that …"

"People here love you."

"Come on …" he growled.

"No really, they speak of you with great affection. They do, they do. I've heard them say as much. Often. Nothing would shake the way they admire you and your work. Do you know what I think you could do?"

"Well, what now?" he asked with a sigh, but even without seeing his face, she could tell he was smiling.

"Bring your family over here. Could you not 'come out' and tell your story? In the local paper? It helped *me* …" She was gabbling, she knew it, but there was no time to choose words carefully. "I did the same thing and I've found people come up to me and chat and accept. I thought the opposite might happen, but sharing secrets can help to bond with people. It does. Really. I can understand your worries because of what happened in the past, but … Where are you now?" She had assumed he was back in Ireland in the bosom of his diminished clan and she held her breath for his answer.

"I'm in my mobile home. Just packing up …"

She closed her eyes and took in a lungful of air. "Please Dunstan, meet me somewhere. I'll show you *my* article. It went in the paper, while you were away. It was painful to write and risky to have it all out in the open, but …"

"OK. I can be with you in half an hour …"

This could be her last chance. Kay moved fast. Shower, wash hair, perfume, make-up, clean buffed nails, new dress, tights, shoes …

This time Dunstan was dressed casually in old jeans and a blue shirt she recognised. She had come to know his clothes. He was unshaven.

"I came straight over," he said, as if apologising for his relatively scruffy appearance.

"I appreciate that," she said, leaning forward to kiss his cheek, gently but firmly grabbing his arm to pull him in.

They sat down at the kitchen table where Kay had placed all her newspaper cuttings and draft articles yet to be published. He took out his reading glasses and silently scanned them. She could see they were a revelation to him. When he came to the column about her life, he went very still, clearly absorbing every word. Silence prevailed in the kitchen.

Finally he looked up. "Why did you never tell me all this? Your husband? What you must have gone through? Kay, *I thought we were friends.*"

"Well, you never asked …"

He gave a wry smile, remembering a previous conversation. "Well, don't you think I'd've liked to know? To know the real you?"

It was quiet again for a moment. Kay allowed him time to think. There was no point in putting him under pressure.

An early morning mist was clearing as Kay surveyed the scene: trees all around the village now dressed in fire, rust and gold, set against a Wedgwood blue sky; vehicles from outside circling around the Green, heading towards car parking areas on the rim of the village and, above all - people! A jostling, chattering stream of folk on foot, competing for space with the traffic, was making its way towards the grass field set aside by Ted for the day. Glastonbury, thought Kay, must've started on this scale! Pushchairs and a couple of wheelchairs told her that nobody was missing this family day out.

Then the throng looked over its collective shoulder and stood to one side, with some respect, at the sound of hooves approaching behind them. Children pointed excitedly to piebald horses pulling a traditional *vardo*, newly painted, flowery and bright – a bit of a museum piece. Before and after were families, each member carrying some kind of artefact or tool, different groups representing successive periods of Romany history.

As they stared out, Kay could see Natalie with a man who looked a little older than her. They were entwined, locked in conversation and clearly enthralled with each other. She grabbed Dunstan's binoculars, somehow managing to look through them while they were still strung around his neck. After some searching around, making her feel dizzy, she managed to pinpoint the couple. She gasped with pleasure.

"Max! Max Leatherson! With Natalie. I remember suspecting there was something going on there." She sighed contentedly. "By the look of them, they've sorted out their differences …"

"Maybe *you*'ve sorted out their differences … would Max have moved on the transit site process so quickly had it not been for you?"

Kay shrugged, unwilling to take credit for something she felt may have happened anyway. "I can sense a big change, you know, just by looking and listening. It's your life story that's done it. Everyone in the entire village knows about you now. And they're swept away by it! People go on talking about you. Dunstan this and Dunstan that. You're a real celebrity."

"Away with you woman," he retorted, sharply, giving her shoulders a squeeze. "It's all your stubbornness and hard work that's won the day. But, surely, I've never seen anything like this here before."

"The council will see or hear about it. They've had letters of support already. I have a *realistic* – not idealistic - hope that future Travellers will be treated better next time. They will have a fair chance and then … well, it's up to them to make the most of it and not let themselves down …"

"And they'll arrive at their newly authorised *achting tan*, the transit site that has now been promised you say?"

"Not before next year of course ... these things do not happen overnight ... although Max says that a piece of council land has definitely been allocated."

"Kay, my dear, they've waited decades. A few more months will seem like nothing."

"And your family are there, amongst that crowd somewhere ... are they with the villagers or the Travellers?"

"Even though they're living on the mobile home park, if they have to take sides at all, they'll be with the Travellers. You'll be meeting them soon, maybe today. I've told them all about you ..."

Kay felt excited by this. "And Suzi and Claudia will be here soon," she said, looking at her watch. "So tomorrow – we start writing your autobiography? If you like ..."

"You're always planning something! Can't you just bide your time a bit and relax?" he asked, laughing. "No, of course, silly question."

"I have a regular column in the local paper now you know," she boasted mildly. "I've already started the next one. It begins, *Following the Festival on Saturday, the people of Appley Green have cast aside NIMBYISM, actively encouraging the development of a new stopping-off site ... it will be interesting to see what happens in the coming years ...*

END

Glossary

Atching tan	stopping place, campsite
Boktalo	lucky
Bori	big (pregnant)
Chavies	children
Chewed	bored
Chokkors	boots, shoes
Coshties	firewood
Cushti	good
Dordi	Oh dear!
Geari	man
Gil / Gillies	to sing / songs
Gorgio (Gaujo)	non-Gypsy person
Hindity	dirty
Jal	to go, to journey
Jalling the drom	travelling
Jass	run away
Jawing diviou	going mad
Kai	where?
Kair posh	help – to 'do half'
Kek pukker nixies	don't say anything
Kenner	house
Kinyo	tired
Kipsies	baskets
Ladged	ashamed
Lolli	money
Mokadi	unclean
Mullad / mullo	dead
Mumper	tramp
Mush	man
Nicked	stole
Pobbles	apples
Pogger	break
Rawnie	lady
Rommed	married
Roshto	angry
Saffern	greenery from a conifer
Scran	food
Shuvvali	pregnant
Tatcho	true
Tikno / tikni	small child
Traished	frightened
Vardo	waggon
Weshen jukkal	fox
Yoks	eyes

Bibliography

Books used by the author for background information.

Romany culture and Gypsy identity
Edited by Thomas Acton and Gary Mundy
Published by University of Hertfordshire Press

We are the Romani people
by Ian Hancock
Published by University of Hertfordshire Press

Gypsy politics and Traveller identity
Edited by Thomas Acton
Published by University of Hertfordshire Press

Moving On – The Gypsies and Travellers of Britain
by Donald Kenrick and Colin Clark
Published by University of Hertfordshire Press

A false dawn
by Ilona Lackova
Published by University of Hertfordshire Press

Incidents in a Gipsy's Life
by George Smith
Printed by Parchment (Oxford) Ltd

Historical Survey of The Gypsies
by John Hoyland
Published by the Romany & Traveller Family History Society

Gypsies and Travellers in their own words
Compiled and edited by Peter Saunders, Jim Clarke,
Sally Kendall, Anna Lee, Sakie Lee and Freda Matthews
Published by Leeds Travellers Education Service

Gypsy Jib – A Romany Dictionary
by James Hayward
Published by Holm Oak Publishing

No Gypsies Served

by
Miriam Wakerly

Two years have passed since Kay successfully campaigned for the Appley Green Gypsy Site, and four years since her husband was murdered. Life in the village was going so well, until the phone call and letter. Then comes the disastrous site opening. Worst of all, Dunstan, whom she realises is her best friend and ally, is giving her the cold shoulder for some unknown reason.

Dunstan is taking an emotional trip down memory lane, into childhood as a Gypsy on the road, and his eventual break from his people. Why is he so angry with Kay that he keeps away from her?

Chances of a longed for reconciliation look slim …

A sequel and prequel to **Gypsies Stop tHere**.
Available from Waterstone's bookshops or Amazon.

Shades of Appley Green
by
Miriam Wakerly

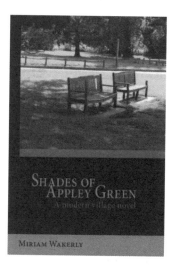

Steph is a special, but troubled young woman. Chosen by the most venerated man in Appley Green to fulfil his mission, she feels publicly admired rather than privately loved. She certainly does not trust men!

In helping a once famous, elderly architect with Parkinson's regain a social life, she finds herself taking personal risks, fending off objections, blind to danger. We wait for the moment when it dawns on Steph what is driving her deep-seated obsession; for only then can she find the happiness she deserves.

Appley Green is a charming English village. Everyone says so. But people are still people. With the emotional turmoil that comes with love, birth and death, a close-knit community can harbour betrayal and guilt, as well as joy and laughter.

First of a new series of Appley Green novels
Available from Waterstone's, Amazon and on Kindle.

About the Author

Miriam Wakerly has had short stories and articles published in magazines. Her first novel, **Gypsies Stop tHere** was launched the day after she retired in 2008; **No Gypsies Served** followed two years later. In 2012 she published **Shades of Appley Green**, the first of a new series of Appley Green village novels.

Her career history includes teaching, public relations and marketing in the IT industry; and community work. Now retired from work other than writing, she lives in Surrey with her husband. Their three adult children live and work in London. Before retiring she worked for two years with the Parkinson's Society, visiting people in their homes to offer information and support.

Miriam Wakerly has a BA Degree in Combined Studies (English, French, Sociology, Politics) from Leicester University. She is a member of the Society of Authors.

Find her on Twitter and her blog, Miriam's Ramblings: www.miriamwakerly.blogspot.com